PRIVATE INDIA

Also by James Patterson

PRIVATE NOVELS

Private (*with Maxine Paetro*)
Private London (*with Mark Pearson*)
Private Games (*with Mark Sullivan*)
Private: No. 1 Suspect (*with Maxine Paetro*)
Private Berlin (*with Mark Sullivan*)
Private Down Under (*with Michael White*)
Private L.A. (*with Mark Sullivan*)
Private Vegas (*with Maxine Paetro, to be published January 2015*)

A list of more titles by James Patterson is
printed at the back of this book

JAMES PATTERSON

& ASHWIN SANGHI

PRIVATE INDIA

CENTURY

Published by Century, 2014

2 4 6 8 10 9 7 5 3 1

First published in Great Britain in 2014 by
Century
Random House, 20 Vauxhall Bridge Road,
London SW1V 2SA

www.randomhouse.co.uk

Addresses for companies within The Random House Group Limited can be found at:
www.randomhouse.co.uk/offices.htm

The Random House Group Limited Reg. No. 954009

A CIP catalogue record for this book
is available from the British Library

Hardback ISBN 9781780891729
Trade paperback ISBN 9781780891736

The Random House Group Limited supports the Forest Stewardship Council®
(FSC®), the leading international forest-certification organisation.
Our books carrying the FSC label are printed on FSC®-certified paper.
FSC is the only forest-certification scheme supported by the leading
environmental organisations, including Greenpeace.
Our paper procurement policy can be found at:
www.randomhouse.co.uk/environment

Typeset by SX Composing DTP, Rayleigh, Essex
Printed and bound in Australia by Griffin Press

www.randomhouse.com.au
www.randomhouse.co.nz

PRIVATE INDIA

Prologue

2006

THEY EXPLODED DURING rush hour.

Pressure-cooker bombs hidden in the first-class carriages of commuter services running from Mumbai's financial district to its suburbs. Survivors would speak of bodies flung from trains, carriage floors awash with blood, screams and screams and screams . . .

The first bomb had gone off at exactly 6:24 p.m. All seven exploded in the space of eleven minutes. Over two hundred dead, over seven hundred injured.

And even Mumbai, no stranger to terrorist action, was shocked by the ferocity of the attacks. A city of thirteen million people, home to Bollywood, temporarily paralyzed, its airports on lockdown, its transport networks frozen.

And amid the hunt to find those responsible, fresh battle lines were drawn.

PART ONE

Chapter 1

FOURTEEN MINUTES PER room was all she had.

Whether it was tidy or left smeared with chocolate sauce, whipped cream, and telltale buttmarks on the recliner, fourteen minutes was what she had to clean each room. Start in the bathroom, change the towels, change the bed, clean the cups, dust and vacuum, and then on to the next room.

And though she would never have admitted it to her colleagues at the Marine Bay Plaza, Sunita Kadam took a pride in meeting (and especially beating) that fourteen-minute time limit. In fact, on her housekeeping cart was a stopwatch she carried for that very purpose. She picked it up as she arrived at room number 1121 and knocked smartly—maid's knock, loud but gentle—then began the stopwatch.

Twenty seconds. No answer. With a deliberate jangle of master keys she let herself in.

"Hello? Housekeeping."

Again no answer. Good. And what's more, the room was tidy.

Though an evening dress hung from a handle of the closet, the bed looked as if it hadn't been slept in. Nets at the window billowed beneath a blast of air conditioning, giving the room a clean, aired feel. *Six minutes to service this room*, thought Sunita. *Maybe seven.*

Unless, of course, there was a nasty surprise in the bathroom.

From her cart she collected towels and toiletries and went there now, clicking on the light at the same time as she reached for the door handle and pushed.

She came up short. The door would only budge an inch or so. Something on the other side—probably a wet towel that had slipped off a rail—was preventing it from opening.

Inside, the fluorescents struggled, flickering as she pushed the door. With an exasperated sigh she gave it one last shove and there was a splintering sound. Something heavy fell to the floor on the other side and, finally, the lights came on—and Sunita Kadam saw what was inside.

On the tiles lay a woman's corpse. She wore a white night-shirt and her face was colorless. In contrast, the yellow cotton scarf around her neck was a bright yellow. The marks it had made were a livid red.

Sunita stared at the body. A numbness crept over her. A sense of wanting to run but being rooted to the spot. Later she'd look back and stifle a guilty laugh about this, but her next thought was: *How the hell am I going to clean this up in fourteen minutes?*

Chapter 2

"YOU KILLED THEM, you drunk bastard."

With a gasp, Santosh Wagh pulled himself from the grip of his nightmare, fingers scrabbling for his spectacles on the nightstand. He pushed them on, squinted at the numbers on his bedside clock and groaned.

4:14 a.m. Drinker's dawn.

He pulled himself from bed, avoiding his own reflection in the mirror as he lolloped out of the bedroom. Who wanted to see a hungover man at 4:14 in the morning, a craggy, 51-year-old vision of guilt and shame? Not him. Right now what he wanted was a little something to guide him gently into the morning. Something to chase away the headache lurking behind his eyes. Something to banish the residual nightmare image seared into his brain.

His apartment was empty, stale-smelling. On a coffee table in the front room was a half-empty bottle of Johnnie Walker, a glass, and his Glock in its holster. Santosh dropped with a sigh to the couch, leaned forward, fingertipped his Glock out of reach, then drew the bottle and glass toward him.

He stared at the drink in his hand, remembering, casting his mind back to 2006 and the seven Mumbai train bombs. At the time he'd been an agent with RAW, India's intelligence agency, and the investigations into the bombings had brought him into contact with Jack Morgan.

Two years later, the car accident that plagued his dreams.

It was Jack who had asked him to head up Private India; Jack who had picked him up when he'd needed it most. And if he drank this drink then it would lead to another drink, and another, and with each subsequent drink he'd fall a little harder and fail Jack a little more.

He placed the glass back on the coffee table, pulled his knees up toward him. Decided to wait the morning out. He dozed, then woke, then dozed again, and each time he woke the drink was still there, waiting for him. He ignored its call. He chose Jack over Johnnie.

Even so, it was a relief when the phone rang and duty called.

Chapter 3

SANTOSH LEANED ON his cane and scrutinized the dead woman who lay on the bathroom floor of room number 1121.

"Name?" he said, without taking his eyes off the corpse.

Nisha Gandhe, mid forties, head-turningly attractive, even dressed down in cotton shirt, T-shirt, and jeans, marveled that her boss could be an investigative genius and still not know that breath mints were useless at disguising the smell of whisky.

"Dr. Kanya Jaiyen," she replied, reading from notes made on her phone. "Mean anything to you?"

"No," he said. He angled his head to study the face of the deceased. She was South-East Asian, middle-aged. Her sharp, attractive features looked incongruous pressed to the hard tiles of the bathroom.

"She's Thai—from Bangkok apparently," continued Nisha. "Her body was found by the maid. It had been hanging on a hook on the back of the door but when the door moved the hook gave way, and . . ."

Santosh glanced at the damaged door then back at the body. He scratched salt-and-pepper stubble on his cheek.

"No signs of sexual assault," he said, part question, part statement.

"Apparently not, but Mubeen is on his way. We should have a clearer idea once he's through," replied Nisha.

Mubeen was Private India's full-time medical examiner. Time of death, cause of death, manner of death—death was his specialty. He'd arrive with Hari, Private's technology geek, who'd be dusting for prints, scanning the cell phone that Santosh had spotted by the bed. Tech-wizard stuff.

Santosh shifted his weight on his cane. The car accident had left him with a limp.

"You do realize it's psychosomatic, don't you?" a doctor had told him.

"I'm keeping the cane," he'd replied.

"Have it your own way."

He did. One of the few advantages of being Santosh Wagh was that he had things his own way. Plus it was useful to have a cane sometimes. On a morning like this, for example, when he felt as though it was the only thing keeping him upright.

He palmed sweat from his forehead. "Okay, let's not touch anything until we get the go-ahead from the police. There's nothing to prevent us from observing though. And I'm especially interested in this . . ."

With the tip of his cane he indicated the victim's hands, both wrapped with string. A flower was bound to one, an ordinary fork to the other.

"And this," he said, motioning his cane at her foot. "What do you make of that?"

Tied to one of the dead doctor's toes was a small toy Viking helmet.

Nisha bent down to take a closer look. "Could the killer be a nut job with a Viking fetish?" she asked.

"Maybe. But if he was a genuine Viking enthusiast he'd know that real Viking helmets didn't have horns," said Santosh. "The bull horns are an artistic contrivance."

"Okay. So . . . ?" said Nisha. You could almost see the cogs of his encyclopedic mind turn, she thought.

"So—either our killer doesn't know about the horns. Or he doesn't care. Or the Viking bit isn't significant but the horn bit is."

"Right . . ." she said, uncertainly. "And what about the flower on her hand? A lotus. And the fork? Maybe she snatched it to defend herself?"

"No," said Santosh, lost in thought. "They were tied to her hands to look as if she's holding them."

Crouched down close to the body, Nisha noticed a black hair on the otherwise spotless tile floor. "There's a hair here I'd like to bag, when we can," she said. Santosh nodded.

"When do you think she was killed?" asked Nisha.

He glanced at her. "Look at the body. Consider the bed. The nightdress. When do *you* think she was killed?"

"Last night?"

"Exactly. Mubeen can tell us for sure, but yes—this happened last night. Did you check for signs of forced entry?"

"The windows are hermetically sealed. There's no sign the bedroom door was forced nor any indication of lock tampering," replied Nisha, glancing at her notes.

Santosh nodded. He looked from the body to Nisha with eyes that had seen too much pain. "This isn't the last, Nisha," he said. "Of that you can be certain."

Chapter 4

"WE HAD RATHER hoped to avoid involving the police," said the general manager, Mr. Singh—a nervous man who wanted nothing more than for the whole affair to go away. "After all, the hotel employs Private India for that very reason. Are you not the world's biggest detective agency . . . ?"

Santosh found his eyes drawn to a bottle of whisky tucked away in a corner of the office but Singh was pouring coffee instead. Probably just as well.

"We are indeed. But unfortunately we do not manage your internal CCTV system. Furthermore, this is a murder investigation, Mr. Singh," he said regretfully. "There is no avoiding the police, I'm afraid. However, as your advisor may I suggest the call is better coming from you than from me." He passed a card across the desk. "Ring this number, tell them there has been a suspected murder and that you have appointed the hotel's detective agency—that's us—to represent you in this matter."

Singh picked up the card. *"ACP Rupesh Desai,"* he read. "This is the policeman I should call?"

Santosh nodded. "Rupesh is the Assistant Commissioner at the Mumbai Crime Branch. I can promise you his cooperation and discretion. We're . . ."

He stopped himself saying "old friends"; even just "friends." Not since the accident that broke everything.

". . . we go back a long way. Now, tell me everything you can about Dr. Kanya Jaiyen."

"All we have is the information she gave us when she checked in," explained Singh. He passed a paper folder to Santosh, who scanned it quickly. A copy of her passport, a printout of online booking data.

"Excellent. You have a record of when the door was used?"

"Yes. It's on its way."

"And CCTV footage?"

"Also coming," said Singh.

"Good," said Santosh.

"So what now?" said Singh. "Can we assume the hotel will be kept out of any . . . unpleasantness?"

Santosh opened his mouth, then remembered that the Marine Bay Plaza Hotel was a client of Private India, and as the head of Private India he had to kiss ass every now and then.

"You can rest easy, Mr. Singh," he said with what he hoped would be an ingratiating smile. "Leave it to us."

Chapter 5

"WHAT'S PRIVATE INDIA'S interest in this case?" asked Rupesh bluntly, his hands pushed into his pockets.

He and Santosh stood in the corridor outside room 1121, now an official crime scene. For the moment Santosh had conveniently forgotten to mention the hair Nisha had recovered from the bathroom. And hopefully, if all went to plan, things would stay that way.

"The hotel chain employs Private globally," replied Santosh. "If it isn't a bother, Rupesh, we'd like to manage the investigation."

Rupesh looked him up and down with disdain, as though Santosh were wearing an expensive, tailored suit rather than the same shabby beige two-piece he'd worn for years. "Private India," he sneered. "You certainly landed on your feet there, didn't you, Jack Morgan's little favorite? Just think, without those train bombings you two might never have met. They were the best thing that ever happened to you, weren't they?"

Santosh tried to remember that he wanted Private India to handle this case. And for that, he needed Rupesh onside. So instead of sweeping the cop's feet from beneath him and ramming the point of his cane down his throat, he merely gave a thin smile. "To business, Rupesh, please."

Rupesh avoided his eye as he pondered the matter for a moment. "Wait here," he said. "I need to make a call. See what the Commissioner says."

He moved out of earshot, his back turned and his phone to his ear as he made the call. Moments later he returned with a smile that went nowhere near his eyes. "The Commissioner is fine with it."

"And you?"

Rupesh shrugged. "The Police Forensic Science Lab at Kalina has a six-month case backlog and half my men are on VIP duty. I'm happy to offload this case onto you."

He reached into his pocket and withdrew a pouch of chewing tobacco, placing a pinch of it in a corner of his mouth. Mumbai had long since banned the sale of all processed tobacco products. Not that the ban applied to Rupesh, apparently.

Just how deep are you getting, old friend? wondered Santosh.

"So that's settled," added Rupesh. "Private India can spearhead the investigation provided all information is shared with us in a timely manner. Oh, and as long as any credit for successfully solving the case comes to us." His grin was shark-like. "Mubeen will be doing the autopsy, I take it?"

"With your consent."

"Granted. Provided the corpse is first taken to the police morgue and that the state's medical examiner is present during the final examination. Fine?"

Santosh nodded and the two men parted. Rupesh back to the crime scene. Santosh headed to Private HQ. *What happened to us?* wondered Santosh as he waited for the elevator. *What happened, when we used to be so close?*

Had life come between them? Or was it death?

Chapter 6

THE COCKTAIL PARTY on the rooftop of the Oberoi Hotel was what's known as a "page-three event," where guests came to strut and pose like peacocks, hoping that the shutterbugs' lenses would alight upon them.

Events like this made Bhavna Choksi feel inadequate. Even the white-gloved waiters made her feel inadequate. Not for the first time she wondered how her dreams of great journalism had been reduced to this, eking out pathetic tidbits for the *Afternoon Mirror* gossip column.

She hated the fact that she was familiar with these people. Priyanka Talati, the "singing sensation." So what? Lara Omprakash, "Bollywood's hottest director." Sure, until next week, when there would be a new one. She hated the fact that she'd be reporting on what the politician Ragini Sharma was wearing, rather than her policies.

Keeping her eye on the door for new arrivals, Bhavna saw Devika Gulati—a yoga guru to the hip set—waft in through the doors at the rooftop, the cutouts of her gown emphasizing her body. Devika accepted a drink from a waiter, then stood, surveying the room.

Bhavna took her chance and moved over before any of the rooftop's single men made their move. "Hello," she said, extending her hand to shake. "It's Bhavna Choksi, from the *Afternoon Mirror*. May I say that's a beautiful gown."

Devika's gaze traveled over Bhavna's shoulder, still scanning the rooftop.

"Miss Gulati?" prompted Bhavna. "We spoke on the phone. I was wondering if you'd had second thoughts about an interview."

At last Devika focused on her. "I'm sorry. Yes, of course. I'm sure we can arrange that. Please, call the studio, speak to Fiona, and she'll fit you into the diary."

"Thank you." As Bhavna moved away, she was able to see what it was that had caught Devika's eye. Or, in this case, *who* it was: India's Attorney General, Nalin D'Souza.

Interesting, she thought as she heard the faint buzzing of her phone inside her tote. Pulling it out, she answered the call.

"Ah, it's you," she said. The voice at the other end spoke for twenty seconds before Bhavna replied. "Sure. Tomorrow morning is fine. I usually leave for work by nine thirty but I can wait for you. Do you need my address?"

Chapter 7

SEVERAL FLOORS BELOW the party that still raged on the rooftop of the Oberoi Hotel was a room, dark apart from the glow of a dim lamp, and silent but for low moans from the bed. Puddled on the carpet was Devika Gulati's metallic-blue gown. Beside it a pair of boxers belonging to the Attorney General, Nalin D'Souza.

In bed the couple moved to their own urgent rhythm. Naked, Devika was on top, skin bathed in a thin film of sweat. Beneath her Nalin arched upwards each time that she ground herself into him. He reached to cup her breasts as he felt his climax approaching. Some moments later they had switched positions and he rode her with double the passion.

Spent and tired, the couple remained intertwined under the bed sheets, breathing heavily. She switched positions again, clambering on top of him in order to gaze upon his handsome features, pushing a hand through his hair.

"You've had it cut," she said.

"The other day. Do you like it?"

"It makes you look younger. Where did you go?"

"The Shiva Spa Lounge. I'm told that Mumbai's trendy young things are flocking there. Talking of which, was that a newspaper reporter I saw you with earlier?"

"An irritating woman from the *Afternoon Mirror*."

"What did she want?"

Sensing a change in him, Devika moved off him and lay with her head propped on her hand, tracing his chest hairs with her fingertips. "She wants to speak to me."

Tickled and irritated, he brushed her hand away. "Why does she want to speak to you?"

"Wouldn't you like to know?" she teased.

But he had lost patience. "I've got to go," he said, shoving her to one side.

She pulled him back toward her and kissed him deeply, twining her tongue around his. "Sure you don't want to go again?" she asked playfully.

"I need to be back in New Delhi to prepare for a case tomorrow," he said, pulling away. "I'll give you a call sometime."

"That's crap and you know it," sneered Devika. "You will be too busy with your wife. The one who wants you to fuck her but can't inspire you to get it up."

"That's not true," said Nalin impatiently. "Her inability to produce a child has absolutely nothing to do with any failure on my part. You should know that by now."

"There are many stories about your other women," said Devika. "It's a bloody exhaustive list. How long before you tire of me—and what will happen to me when you do?"

The Attorney General smiled at her. She had one of the best bodies he had ever had the pleasure of pleasuring. Besides being beautiful, Devika was a seductress. There was an erotic charge to virtually everything she said or did. He still found it difficult to believe that she had once been in prison. What an amazing transformation.

He grasped the edge of the sheet and whipped it back, leaving Devika lying on the bed, resplendent in her nakedness. He felt the tumescence between his legs once more.

She laughed. "Don't you need to be back in the office?" she asked.

"Fuck the office," he snarled as he got back on top of her.

"I thought the fucking was reserved solely for me."

Chapter 8

SANTOSH STEPPED OUT into a scorching October morning for his walk to work. He never drove. Driving meant revisiting the screeching tires and the burned-rubber smell of his nightmares.

Mumbai—once known as Bombay—was a throbbing metropolis with the attitude of New York City, the chaos of Kathmandu, the vibe of Miami, and the infrastructure of Timbuktu. It was the fifth most populous city in the world, its population nudging a little over thirteen million.

It could be charming yet repulsive. Old British monuments jostled for space with corporate glass towers and filthy slums. At traffic signals, handcart pullers slowly made their way to warehouses, their bodies bathed in sweat, while chauffeur-driven Mercedes-Benzes transported their millionaire owners to luncheon meetings. Long queues of people waited patiently outside temples to catch a glimpse of their favorite deity while an equally long line of people waited to get inside the stadium for a celebration of India's alternative religion—cricket. Mumbai was a study in contrasts and people tended either to love it or to hate it. Santosh loved it when he was drunk—which was often—and hated it when he was sober.

It was a long walk but he made brisk progress on the way from Crawford Market to the Regal Cinema. Crossing the streets, he was greeted by beggars, bums, and vagabonds, as though he were a celebrity to them. A young boy wearing patched clothes smartly saluted him. Santosh nodded in reply.

"Tell your boss that I need to meet him. Chowpatty, usual day and time," he instructed.

At the Regal Santosh turned toward Colaba Causeway, a street notorious for its pubs, pimps, and pushers, not to mention hundreds of pavement stalls selling porn DVDs, vibrators, and electronic goods smuggled in from China, Taiwan, and Dubai.

He walked a couple of blocks down the main road until he reached an old and decrepit building. The ground floor was occupied by a well-known watering hole that sold the cheapest beer in town. Tables covered in pink checkered tablecloths were occupied by an odd mix of locals and hippies, while high above them ancient ceiling fans groaned and squeaked in an unsuccessful effort to keep cool air circulating in the stifling October mugginess. Above the heads of the patrons floated a thick haze of weed smoke.

Ignoring the pub, Santosh slipped inside a nondescript side entrance that led to a flight of creaking wooden stairs. Climbing to the top floor, he stood before a battered door, locked with an ancient padlock. On either side were cream-painted walls punctuated by peeling plaster. To the right of the door was a dented mailbox and above this a small ornate mirror with a cracked frame. To the casual observer it looked like the entrance to someone's home—and someone without much in the way of money.

However, an investigator looking closely would have found several inconsistencies. The old padlock could not be opened because there was no key slot. The apparently crumbling plaster could not be broken away. The door could not be rattled because it was entirely sealed. The mailbox was glued shut and the mirror stuck solidly to the wall, not hanging by a nail or hook.

Santosh stood in front of the mirror for a few seconds. Moments later the entire wall—with door, padlock, mailbox, and mirror intact—slid open with an efficient *whoosh*, like Aladdin's cave. Santosh entered and the wall closed equally efficiently behind him.

Unknown to the casual visitor was the fact that the dilapidated mirror held within it a sophisticated retina-scan unit. Only staff members of Private India identified by the biometric system could access the office. Established clients communicated with the firm via a dedicated helpline. New clients were only accepted via referrals from old ones. Investigators from Private India visited clients at their homes and offices rather than the other way round. The offices of Private India remained invisible to the world outside.

There was a specific reason for this secrecy. Private India had helped law-enforcement agencies solve a few key cases related to deadly attacks by Pakistani terror groups on Indian soil. The result was that Private India was on the radar of several Pakistan-based jihadi outfits. It was absolutely necessary for the safety of those who worked for the company to keep the office impregnable.

Inside, the office was the exact opposite of its shabby exterior. Light maple floors, recessed illumination, silent air conditioning, and white Corian wall panels ensured that the space was a haven of light, comfort, and tranquility. A middle-aged woman sat at the reception desk handling incoming calls. Santosh waved to her as he picked up an apple from a bowl that stood on the coffee table in the lounge.

Spread over the top two floors of the building, Private India's office was accessed via the higher floor containing the offices of Santosh, Nisha, Mubeen, and Hari. The lower floor contained the offices of support staff and junior investigators and could be accessed via a private elevator behind the reception desk.

All the window frames of the two floors had been preserved on the outside so that the exterior of the building retained its old and dilapidated character, but the frames had been supplemented by modern double-glazed windows on the inside.

Santosh's room straight ahead was connected to Nisha's smaller office and an oversized conference room equipped with videoconferencing and a 108-inch LCD screen. He took a bite out of his apple and headed right to Mubeen's lab.

Chapter 9

ALTHOUGH MUBEEN YUSUF was Private India's forensic expert, and thus blessed with the strongest constitution imaginable, he looked as though a gust of wind would be enough to blow him away. His shoulders were stooped, he wore his beard unfashionably straggly, and though he regularly smiled his eyes behind his spectacles were often sad.

Mubeen had been working as a forensic pathologist in Baltimore when his life had caved in.

Walking home one night with his wife and six-year-old son, a group of neo-Nazis had surrounded them, jabbing and taunting, breathing beer fumes and screaming obscenities. When the kicks and punches had begun, Mubeen had tried to protect his wife and son. Oh dear God, he'd tried. He'd fought like a tiger. And the last words he'd heard before he'd lost consciousness were: "Dirty Indian scum . . . go back home."

He had woken in hospital to the news that his son was dead, and after that no therapy in the world could keep him and his wife together. The guilt they had both felt at living while their son had died. It had been too much for them. Until finally they'd divorced and Mubeen had yearned to return home to India.

Thanks to Jack Morgan he'd gotten his wish. A murder case had brought Mubeen into contact with Jack, who had offered him a job at Private India's new office in Mumbai. On his first day at Private he'd met Santosh Wagh, and the eyes of his new boss were the same eyes he saw in the mirror each morning. They had never spoken about their losses, but the sense of a kindred spirit was shared.

He looked up now as Santosh approached.

"Anything for me?" asked Santosh and Mubeen pulled away from the microscope.

"Nisha recovered a strand of hair from the bathroom floor," he replied, and Santosh nodded. "I have compared it against a sample from the victim. It's different."

"So it should be possible to get DNA from the hair?"

Mubeen sighed. Forensic analysis of DNA was the most overhyped and misrepresented collection method. Santosh was making the same mistake most people made. They simply assumed that hair samples made ideal material for DNA testing.

"Unfortunately the successful extraction of DNA from a hair sample depends on the part of the hair that is discovered," replied Mubeen with a grim expression.

"Enlighten me," said Santosh, taking another bite of his apple.

"Hair is mainly composed of a fibrous protein known as keratin. This protein is also the primary constituent of skin, animal hooves, and nails. The hair root lies below the scalp and is enclosed in a follicle. This is connected to the bloodstream via the dermal papilla. The hair shaft does not contain DNA, which is only to be found in the root."

"So what exactly is the problem here?" asked Santosh.

"This strand of hair has been sliced through cleanly. There is no root available for analysis."

"So this was a *cut* strand of hair?" said Santosh.

Mubeen scratched at his unkempt beard. "It would appear so. Attached to someone's clothes, perhaps?"

"Yes, unless our killer stopped to give his hair a trim," said Santosh, thinking, then added, "Or perhaps it merely belongs to a former guest. I remember reading somewhere that in a small number of hair samples, forensic scientists are able to extract nuclear DNA from cut or shed hairs."

Mubeen nodded. His boss always managed to spring a surprise on him whenever his knowledge was called into question. "The presence of biologically dead cells or keratinocytes in their last stage of differentiation may make it possible to extract a profile derived from nuclear DNA," he replied. "It will take me some time to tell you whether that's possible or not in this case. It's highly probable that DNA will be absent."

"Absence of evidence is not evidence of absence," said Santosh. "Let me know if anything new emerges."

Chapter 10

SANTOSH LEFT MUBEEN'S lab and walked into Hari's office. At thirty-five the youngest member of the team, Hari Padhi was Private's technology geek. If you needed a cell tracing, you went to Hari. If you needed to know the precise speed and trajectory of a naked corpse falling from the twenty-first floor of a building, then you went to Hari.

He looked somewhat like a wrestler. His chest bulged out of his shirt and his arms were thick and muscular. It was evident that he spent a substantial amount of his free time working out at the gym. His gray matter was also in peak form.

He was seated at his desk, closely examining the video feed from the hotel's camera. His workspace was fitted out with high-capacity microprocessors, surveillance equipment, GPS trackers, signal jammers, bug-sweep equipment, password-decryption software, and wiretap-detection systems. Also available to Hari was a full suite of ballistics equipment including microscopes with digital imaging capability, sensitive measuring equipment, and instrumentation to check and record surface temperature, projectile velocity, internal gun pressures, trigger characteristics, and lock time.

He was using an ultra-high-resolution monitor and a high-density time-lapse deck with a built-in time base corrector to forensically examine the video feed from the hotel.

"Any news for me?" asked Santosh.

"We checked the room for fingerprints. Most of them were of the victim or assorted members of hotel staff. I've also been looking at the CCTV, and we have a guy going in and out of the room."

"Excellent," said Santosh. "Let's see him."

Hari scooted to the place on the tape and they watched as a man first entered and then, forwarding the tape, left.

He wore a baseball cap, jeans, his hands thrust in the pockets of a jacket. Conscious of the cameras, his head down.

"Not much help, is it?" said Hari with a pained face.

Santosh looked at him. "Everything's a help," he said. He looked back at the screen where the man was freeze-framed as he left room 1121, certain he was looking at the killer.

Hari looked up and wordlessly scanned the footage to the point at which the baseball-cap-wearing visitor had been recorded leaving the room. "See this? The time stamp shows two minutes past nine on Sunday evening."

"So?" asked Santosh.

"Now let's scan back further to see when he went in," said Hari and pressed the deck's rewind button to take the footage back by eleven minutes. "Ah, here we are. See this? Eight fifty-one p.m."

"Yes."

"Nisha spoke to receptionists and the doormen. Nobody remembers seeing anyone matching this description enter or leave, nor does he turn up on any of the reception CCTV."

"So he used a back entrance?" said Santosh.

"Sort of. There's a separate entrance from the bar at the rear of the hotel. There's no doorman, the reception area is set back, there's far less chance of being seen. But . . . they do have CCTV."

With a showman's flourish Hari clicked on his laptop's desktop and a new picture appeared. Once again it showed the same figure, baseball cap on, head down, hands in pockets. Once again there was no hint of any identifying features.

"He certainly knew what he was doing," hissed Santosh. "He must have known the location of every single camera in the place."

"It's frustrating, isn't it?" agreed Hari. "Except. The image from the rear entrance is a slightly higher resolution and something caught my eye. Here . . ." He clicked again. "Look at the shoes."

Santosh peered at the screen, in particular at the shoes. Expensive-looking, polished black shoes with a distinctive buckle at the sides, they were incongruous set against the baseball cap and jacket.

He straightened, nodding with satisfaction. His phone was ringing and he delved in his jacket pocket for it, gesturing from Hari to the image on the screen.

"Find those shoes," he said, his finger hovering over the call-accept button. It was Rupesh. "Find where they're sold and who's bought a pair."

Hari nodded and looked pleased with himself as Santosh answered the call. "Yes?"

"There's been another murder," said Rupesh. "And guess what? The victim has a yellow scarf around her neck."

Chapter 11

THANE, A NORTHEASTERN suburb of Mumbai, was home to several large housing cooperatives. The second body had been discovered in an apartment that was part of a gated community there.

Nisha drove past the security gate and down a long winding road surrounded by well-maintained lawns until the car reached the block that Rupesh had indicated. There were several police vehicles parked outside. Santosh, Nisha, and Mubeen got out of the car, picked up their equipment, and headed for the stairs. The police had already cordoned off the entrance to the third-floor apartment.

Rupesh was waiting for them at the doorway. "Her name is Bhavna Choksi, aged approximately thirty-seven. A journalist who worked for a tabloid—the *Afternoon Mirror*," he explained as he led them to the bedroom where her body had been discovered.

The apartment was a compact one-bedroom unit. It was

quite obvious that Bhavna Choksi was single but financially sound. The furnishings were simple yet elegant and the apartment was well organized and clean.

The body was suspended from a ceiling fan in the center of the bedroom. The room was completely still but for the barely noticeable pendulum-like movement of the corpse. Nisha shuddered.

Santosh sniffed, detecting the odor of urine. He looked down at the floor and noticed a puddle by the base of the bed. "She was strangled there," he said. "She peed involuntarily as she was being choked. Urination or defecation are known body reactions that can be triggered by strangulation. Yes, triggered by strangulation."

Unlike the first victim, who had been in her nightdress, the second was fully dressed in work clothes—cotton slacks and linen top—ideally suited to a journalist on the prowl in Mumbai's hot and humid weather. The slacks were damp with urine. Around her neck was an unmistakable yellow scarf to which a rope had been attached in order to suspend her from the fan. Both her hands had string tied around them. In one hand the victim had been made to hold rosary beads, and in the other a plastic toy bucket—the sort that kids use to build sandcastles on the beach—containing a couple of inches of water.

"Who found her?" asked Santosh as he looked up at the hanging corpse.

"The cleaning lady let herself in with her key at nine thirty," answered Rupesh. "She assumed that Bhavna Choksi had already left for work, which was the case most days."

Santosh took advantage of the police ladder that had been placed under the fan. Handing his cane to Nisha, he climbed up several rungs so that he could look at the ligature. It was the same sort of yellow scarf as they'd found on Kanya Jaiyen. He peered into the victim's wide-open eyes. Lifeless now, they must have been terrorized as a garrote choked the victim and deprived her lungs of air. *Eyes are the windows of the soul . . . reveal your soul to me, woman,* thought Santosh. *Tell me your story, Bhavna.*

"I need to swab her eyes," said Mubeen, pulling out two cotton buds from his satchel. Santosh snapped out of his trance and descended the ladder so that Mubeen could use it.

He climbed up carefully and gently swabbed each of her eyes, placing the buds into specimen tubes. "Why the eye swab?" asked Rupesh, who had never seen any of his own police medical examiners do it.

"Notice the room's temperature?" replied Mubeen as he came down the ladder and packed away the specimen buds. "The air conditioning has been left running and it's bloody freezing. I can't depend on the body's ambient temperature reading to estimate the time of death. A diagnostic machine in my lab can analyze potassium, urea, and hypoxanthine concentrations present in the vitreous humor of the eye. It provides a far more accurate estimate of time of death than basal body temperature."

"We saw the murderer on CCTV leaving Kanya Jaiyen's hotel room at two minutes past nine last night," said Santosh. "The cleaning lady discovered this victim at nine thirty this morning, leaving the murderer with a substantial window of around twelve and a half hours within which to kill a second time." He paced the room carefully. "A window of twelve and a half hours."

"Unless this second murder had actually happened before the hotel incident," argued Nisha.

Crouching down, Nisha noticed a strand of hair on the

floor exactly below the hanging corpse. She pointed it out to Mubeen, who immediately bent over to pick it up with forceps and bag it.

"Hopefully a comparison with the first sample should tell us whether it comes from the same person," he said to Santosh. But Santosh's mind was elsewhere.

"This murder scene is fresh," he said softly, almost to himself. "Fresh, because the urine on her slacks is still wet, not dry, in spite of the air conditioning. This killing happened after the hotel murder, not before. And forget about the goddamned hair. It's just another annoying prop!

"Crap!" he hissed suddenly under his breath, thumping his cane on the floor and giving everyone else around him a start. What did the objects mean? What was the killer trying to tell him? Why the single strand of hair at both murder sites? *Come out of your hiding place, bastard!*

"Unfortunately the CCTV system of the building was down owing to a technical glitch," said Rupesh. "So we cannot get a visual of the murderer. No signs of forced entry either."

"Any idea regarding the firm that handles security surveillance of the estate?" asked Santosh.

"Xilon Security Services," replied Rupesh. "They were in the process of sending over an engineer to rectify the fault, but obviously it wasn't soon enough."

"In all probability," said Nisha, "the victim knew her killer and allowed the murderer access, given that there are no signs of forced entry."

Santosh pointed to Bhavna Choksi's desk. "There's a cell phone and a laptop. Get Hari to examine both of them. Let's find out the last story that Bhavna Choksi worked on. Maybe she ruffled someone's feathers?"

Turning to Rupesh, Santosh asked, "Do I have your

permission to take over the case, assuming that the two crimes are related?"

"Why on earth would I have called you here if I didn't think they were connected?" replied Rupesh, placing a rather generous pinch of premium black-market chewing tobacco in the corner of his mouth.

Rupesh stared at the suspended body while chewing his tobacco. In his mind he saw a naked woman. Beaten black and blue, subsequently raped. Repeatedly humiliated and violated until she died. Death was a wonderful balm indeed . . . Rupesh snapped back into the present when he realized that Santosh was studying him curiously.

"Good. It's possible that someone may have seen the murderer enter or leave the premises. Let's question the cooperative's security guards, the neighbors as well as any nannies or children who may have been in the garden."

Chapter 12

I CAN FEEL the smooth fabric of the garrote around my neck. I grasp both ends and gently pull. Oh, yes . . . I can feel the compression. A little more pressure and I'm gasping for breath. I'm about to black out as I release the garrote and allow myself to breathe once again, allowing myself back from the brink of darkness.

How delicate is the fine line between life and death. At a given moment a person could be living, breathing, talking, and walking. At another moment she could be a cold, unmoving corpse. Of course, most people live like corpses in the humdrum grip of their prosaic and pathetic lives. Not much difference between life and death for the world's living cadavers.

I hold the yellow scarf in my hand and run it through my fingers lovingly. I bring it to my face and hold it under my nose. I breathe in the unique smell of death. There's an almost orgasmic quality to asphyxiation, isn't there? I could easily see myself getting addicted to the adrenalin rush.

Life has no meaning without the presence of death. Life is simply the absence of death. The fools of this world labor to prevent death, unmindful of the fact that it is death that will set them free.

I stand in front of the mirror and look at my naked body. I have shaved every inch of it. I run the scarf along my hairless arms. I feel the tingle of the fabric against my skin as I allow myself to lower the scarf to my thighs. The sensation is simply incredible.

I pull away the scarf and hold it before me at face level. I quickly tie a knot in it and pull the ends with all my might until I see the knot morph into a tiny lump.

Two down, but I have many more to go.

Chapter 13

THERE WAS A half-bottle of Scotch in his desk, but for the time being Santosh ignored its lure. He felt something. A sense that the tempo of the hunt was increasing. *Give me one murder to solve and I'll show you an enigma*, he thought. *Give me two, and I'll show you a puzzle to solve.* And he offered up a silent apology to the souls of the two women whose deaths made up the pieces in his puzzle, and promised to do his best to find the man responsible.

Two women killed within twenty-four hours of each other, both with a yellow scarf, both with trinkets attached to them, one an Indian journalist, the other a Thai doctor. Discovering what connected them, that was the key.

They had a call scheduled with Dr. Jaiyen's boss, a Dr. Uwwano. "Nisha," he called from his office.

Sitting at her desk, her head bobbed up. "Yes, boss?"

"What time is she expecting us?"

She glanced at her watch. "Five minutes."

"Join me. And bring what you have on Dr. Jaiyen."

As she came into the office he stood and moved to a magnet board, wrote down the two names on record cards: *Bhavna Choksi* and *Dr. Kanya Jaiyen*, placed them beside each other. Added a question mark.

"Bhavna we know," he said. "A journalist working for the *Afternoon Mirror*. But what about Dr. Kanya Jaiyen? What do we know about her?"

Nisha pulled a face. "That she lived in Bangkok. That she was a reconstructive surgeon. More than that I can't say."

Santosh nodded. "Plastic surgeon covers a multitude of sins. Plenty of people might have reason to silence a plastic surgeon."

"Half of Bollywood," tried Nisha, and was rewarded for her attempt at a joke with pursed lips from Santosh. She cleared her throat. "But it wasn't really a 'silencing' sort of crime, was it? What we've seen is more considered and ritualistic. The work of a serial killer."

Santosh's eyes sparkled behind his glasses. He was pleased with his protégée. "Exactly. And yet, on the other hand, perhaps these trinkets are red herrings, designed to throw us off the scent. Either way, these women were chosen, and finding out what connects them will help us understand how and why they were chosen. We need to speak to Bhavna Choksi's editor, find out who she'd spoken to recently. And as for Dr. Jaiyen . . ." He gestured to Nisha. "Do you have the number?"

She passed a slip of paper across and Santosh dialed the Bangkok Hospital and Medical Center, and then was treated to a recording of the Thailand Philharmonic Orchestra before a female voice at last came on the line.

"Uwwano," she said.

"Good evening, Dr. Uwwano. This is Santosh Wagh. I believe you're expecting me."

42

She sounded tired. "I am, Mr. Wagh."

"I apologize for the circumstances of my call. My condolences on your loss."

She sighed. Santosh had the sense that she had sat down. It was late there in Bangkok. "That's very kind of you, Mr. Wagh. This is very, very sad. We're all in a state of shock. How may I be of help?"

"Dr. Jaiyen was a reconstructive surgeon?"

"She was. A very good one. And if you're thinking that that's the usual kind of disingenuous rubbish I'd trot out in the circumstances then you'd be wrong. She really was a good surgeon. One of the best."

"I'm sorry, Dr. Uwwano. Please be reassured that myself and my colleagues are doing everything we can to try and catch her killer. If you'll allow me to ask some questions. I'm given to understand that Dr. Jaiyen reported to you, is that right?"

"Yes. I was her senior in the hospital's Reconstructive Surgery team."

"And what does that involve exactly—reconstructive surgery?"

"It's as broad as it sounds, Mr. Wagh. Whether it be for cosmetic or psychological reasons, in the aftermath of a car crash . . ."

Santosh froze, feeling as though he'd been slapped. On the other side of the desk, Nisha watched him carefully, concern on her face, then leaned forward, whispering, "Boss?"

"Mr. Wagh?" the doctor was saying.

He composed himself. "Sorry, Dr. Uwwano. Do go on."

"Well, I think I'd finished, really," said Dr. Uwwano.

Nisha relaxed back into her seat, dragging a hand through her hair and watching him warily.

"Of course, of course," said Santosh. He waved "everything's okay" to Nisha. "Well, you could tell me, what was the purpose of Dr. Jaiyen's visit to Mumbai?"

"It was a personal visit," said Uwwano. "She told me it was to meet an old friend. She applied for a week's leave of absence in order to take the trip."

"Did she tell you the name of the friend she planned to meet?" asked Santosh.

"No," replied Uwwano. "She was rather reserved about her personal life and I did not feel like prying."

"Was anything troubling Dr. Jaiyen? Did she have any problems in her professional life? And what about her family life? Was it normal?"

"She was happily married," replied Uwwano. "She did not have any kids, though. No, as far as I can tell, she had no worries. The only surviving family member other than her husband is her mother who lives in Chiang Mai."

"Had Dr. Jaiyen performed any surgeries that went wrong?" asked Santosh. "Any instances of lawsuits or complaints by patients?"

"No. As I said, Dr. Jaiyen was one of our best surgeons," explained Uwwano. "I'm having a hard time trying to find a suitable person to fill her shoes."

Later, of course, Santosh would realize the mistake he had made when he spoke to Dr. Uwwano, but for now he wished her good day and ended the call. And then, when Nisha had left his office, he reached for the bottle.

Chapter 14

IT WAS PAST eight that night when Mubeen reached Mumbai's infamous police morgue at Cooper Hospital. Strong stomach or not, he'd been dreading his visit to this most dilapidated of the city's facilities. What's more, the man he was meeting, Dr. Zafar, had a certain reputation for eccentricity.

He got out of his van and crept past the muddy porch with a handkerchief held to his nose. The smell was overpowering, almost the equivalent of a few dozen dead rats decaying in a corner of the filthy building. Mubeen knew better, though. The overwhelming stench was not from dead rats but from rotting human bodies. It was the stench of death.

Mubeen could hear his own footsteps echo as he reached the dark entrance, a single light bulb casting an eerie glow. He began walking through the long, dimly lit passage. On both sides were gurneys bearing human forms covered in sheets. Despite his training, Mubeen felt a hollow in the pit of his stomach. He swallowed hard as he forced himself to cross the passage lined with cadavers.

He felt something move against his foot and looked down to see a massive gutter rat scurry away with a piece of flesh in its mouth. A shudder went down Mubeen's spine and he felt his hair stand on end.

Further ahead he could see a glimmer of light emerging from a room. He quickened his pace to get there. As he crossed the doorway, he felt himself slipping and had to reach out and grab hold of a gurney to prevent himself from falling. He glanced downwards and realized that he was standing on a floor slick with blood, fluids, and human tissue. He pulled his hand away in shock as he realized that he was holding on to a frozen limb of a cadaver rather than the steel frame of a gurney.

"Never knew you would come so late," boomed a voice behind him. Mubeen spun around to see a man dressed in green surgical scrubs, surrounded by a few dozen more gurneys containing decaying corpses. The voice belonged to Dr. Zafar, the police surgeon. Mubeen had reached the autopsy center in the police morgue of Cooper Hospital.

The morgue received around fifteen corpses daily and a third of these were without claimants. As per official policy, the police had to search for claimants for seven days before allowing disposal. Unfortunately, this was a slow process. Disposal happened at the rate of three or four bodies per day, thus resulting in a pile-up of more than a hundred cadavers in a fifty-five-rack morgue.

Dr. Zafar looked at Mubeen and smiled. He was wearing his surgical mask so the smile was only discernible from the twinkle in his eyes. "How can you keep cheerful in a hellhole like this?" asked Mubeen as he walked across to Zafar, carefully avoiding the puddles on the floor but grateful for the immediate presence of another living human.

"A smile is a curve that sets everything straight," laughed Zafar, taking off his mask and applying some Vicks Vaporub under his nose to neutralize the permanently foul odor of the place. "I am used to this hellhole."

Mubeen quietly thanked his stars that he did not have to work in conditions like those that Zafar worked in.

"Your bodies are ready," announced the police surgeon, opening the door to the refrigeration chamber, like a baker announcing a fresh batch of bread from the oven. Mubeen helped him pull out the two tagged corpses and load them on gurneys.

"Would you like to carry out the autopsies here?" asked Zafar.

"No," replied Mubeen. "I need the equipment in my own lab. If you don't mind, I'll simply take the bodies and share the results with you by email."

"I need to be present during the autopsy, as instructed by Rupesh," replied Zafar apologetically. "Either you carry out the autopsies here or I come to your lab."

Mubeen thought about this. All he wanted was to get the hell out of Zafar's ghoulish morgue. He made up his mind quickly. "Let's get these loaded into my van. You may come with me."

"I would have got one of my assistants to help move the corpses if you had showed up before eight o'clock," explained Dr. Zafar. "Unfortunately at this time it's only me in this place."

Zafar discarded his scrubs and washed his hands with soap and hot water before helping Mubeen roll the gurneys back to the white van belonging to Private India. Both men loaded them inside then climbed in the front.

Mubeen drove out of Cooper Hospital and headed toward Colaba. On reaching Private India's office block, he drove into a parking garage at the rear of the building. The door closed behind them and lights came on automatically. He flicked a switch on his hand-held remote and the floor of the garage began slowly rising. Within two minutes the van had been transported into Mubeen's state-of-the-art medical and forensics facility in the heart of Private India's office complex.

The contrast with the Cooper Hospital autopsy center could not be more apparent. Mubeen's lab was sophisticated, modern, and spotlessly clean. Gleaming white tables illuminated by shafts of light supplied by overhead energy-efficient fixtures ran the entire length of the lab.

It was equipped with the very latest tools, including a new machine that combined multi-slice computed tomography with magnetic resonance imaging to produce a virtual autopsy in 3D that could easily detect internal bleeding, bullet paths, and hidden fractures, hard to find with a traditional autopsy. Spectrometers for detection of explosives and illegal drug residues dotted one side of the laboratory, while equipment for the analysis of bloodstains, fingerprints, DNA, hair, fibers, and other trace evidence occupied the rest. A newly acquired device that could accurately identify specific dyes in acrylics, cotton, and other fibers occupied a table of its own.

Having unloaded the corpses from the gurneys, Mubeen began by carefully examining the necks of both victims with a dermascope.

"What are we looking for?" asked Zafar, as he glanced around the facilities, somewhat awed by the infrastructure available to Mubeen.

"Inflamed edges," replied Mubeen, continuing to scan the skin surface with his dermascope and handing over another one to Zafar so that he could work in parallel.

"Inflammation is absent," he said into the cordless

microphone on his collar. "A clear sign that these victims were dead before being strung up."

Next, Mubeen and Zafar loaded each body into the MRI machine. As the neck scans of the victims showed up on the bank of high-resolution monitors, the answer became apparent.

Once again speaking into the microphone, Mubeen said, "The neck's hyoid bone usually breaks during strangulation but rarely during hanging. In both corpses the hyoid bones are found broken. It is my considered opinion that we are dealing with a strangler, not a hangman."

Chapter 15

"HAVE WE CHECKED the cell phones that were discovered at both crime scenes?" asked Santosh, turning to Hari.

Private India's core investigation team was seated in the conference room for a meeting and Santosh was reviewing their progress.

Hari cleared his throat before speaking. "Both phones were in working order. The phone belonging to Dr. Kanya Jaiyen was only used for conversations with two other numbers. On the other hand, the phone of the journalist Bhavna Choksi was used much more extensively."

"You say that the Thai doctor's phone only communicated with two other numbers. Do we know whose numbers they were?" asked Santosh.

"That was very easy to figure out," replied Hari. "One of the numbers belonged to Bhavna Choksi."

"So it's evident that our two victims knew each other," observed Santosh. He shot Nisha a gleeful look. "There's our connection."

Hari nodded. "Oh yes. Kanya Jaiyen and Bhavna Choksi had several phone conversations on the day that Jaiyen was killed," he said. "The problem is that the other number that communicated with Kanya Jaiyen was from a prepaid SIM. The name and address provided to register the SIM are false and there is simply no way to trace the actual caller."

"Given the fact that there was no sign of a break-in at either crime scene, it's highly probable that the murderer knew both victims," said Santosh. "It's very likely that the second SIM showing up on Kanya Jaiyen's call logs belongs to the killer."

"Either that or the killer knew enough about their routine to be able to get into their living spaces," said Nisha, looking up from her smartphone.

"Do we know whether either woman was sexually assaulted?" asked Santosh, directing his question at Mubeen. "Any indications of rape?"

"No sexual assault in either case . . ." replied Mubeen, "no traces of blood, saliva, or semen. At both crime scenes we have single strands of hair. The strands match under the microscope . . . They came from the same head."

"Any luck with DNA?" asked Santosh.

"No roots present, hence no DNA," said Mubeen. "I tried searching for nuclear DNA in the hair shaft but none was present."

"What about time of death?" asked Santosh, closing his eyes to think. "Do we now have a precise idea regarding when these women died?"

"Kanya Jaiyen was killed between eight and ten on Sunday night," answered Mubeen. "This can be further narrowed down by the CCTV footage, which showed the suspected killer going into her room at eight fifty-one and leaving at two minutes past nine."

"And Bhavna Choksi?" asked Santosh.

"My medical estimate is between eight thirty and ten on Monday morning. Given the fact that the cleaning lady discovered the body at nine thirty, we can safely assume that time of death is between eight thirty and nine thirty."

There was silence. Santosh got up from the table and began to pace the conference room, an action that made everyone else rather uncomfortable. He had an annoying habit of popping up behind them unexpectedly.

"Do you mind if I leave you for a moment?" asked Mubeen. "I was in the middle of a critical test and should have the results in a few minutes." Santosh nodded irritably as Mubeen got up to leave the conference room.

"Why don't we release his picture to the press?" asked Nisha.

"He is waiting for us to do precisely that," said Santosh. "Look at the crime scenes and all the props around the bodies. Consider the fact that the second victim is a newspaper reporter. The strangler is hungry for publicity. Give the murders some extra column inches and you will see the body count increase. Yes, the body count will go up."

"You're right," agreed Nisha. "It may also send the city into a panic. No one knows that there have been two women strangled in similar fashion. As of now, they are simply two unrelated murders in a city that is famous for its high crime rate. Any public disclosure could make the murderer that much more careful. We would rather have a careless perpetrator."

"We also need to keep in mind," said Santosh, "the possibility that the person in question may simply have been a visitor. We have no clear evidence linking them to the murder. On the whole, it's better that we keep this under wraps." He settled down in his chair. Within a few seconds he was up again and over behind Hari.

"For a moment," he said, "let's focus on the fact that both women were discovered with a variety of objects tied to their hands and feet with string."

"I'm stumped on that one," Nisha admitted. "A lotus flower, a dining fork, and a Viking helmet at the first scene; a rosary and a bucket of water at the second. The murderer is obviously trying to tell us something but I wish I knew what."

"Have we contacted Dr. Kanya Jaiyen's relatives?" asked Santosh.

"We have informed her husband in Thailand," replied Nisha. "Her body will be sent home via a Thai Airways flight to Bangkok this evening."

"What about the suitcase in her hotel room? Anything of importance?"

"Just personal effects—clothes, shoes, toiletries, jewelry, makeup, and medicines," said Hari. "We found her passport, some cash, and her American Express credit card. The card had not been used in Mumbai except to guarantee her reservation at the hotel."

"Have we checked relatives and employers of the journalist?" asked Santosh.

"No family. Just a boyfriend," replied Nisha. "He's an investment banker and has been out of the country for the past five days. We've ruled him out as a suspect. I'm scheduled to meet Bhavna's boss at the *Afternoon Mirror* in the next hour."

Mubeen strode briskly back into the conference room. "I have some important information," he interrupted. His face was flushed with excitement. "The fiber and dye analysis that we ran on the two garrotes used for the killings. Both are made from handwoven cotton. In both, the yellow dye is a natural one that has been used for centuries in India—*Acacia nilotica*."

Nisha looked questioningly at Mubeen. "What exactly do the fabric and dye tell us?" she asked.

Santosh cut in before Mubeen could speak, his encyclopedic memory having been spurred into action. "Handwoven cotton or silk—dyed using *Acacia nilotica*—was used by an ancient Indian murder cult called the Thugs."

Chapter 16

"THUGS?" ASKED NISHA incredulously. "Didn't the British wipe them out from India entirely?"

"Yes, but while it's easy to destroy a cult," replied Santosh, "it's far more difficult to destroy the ideology that spawns it— an ideology that has thrived for five hundred years."

"Five hundred years?" said Nisha. "I thought that the Thugs were a nineteenth-century phenomenon."

"Actually, tales of an ultra-secret cult of killers roaming India go all the way back to the thirteenth century," explained Santosh. "It's just that the Thugs became famous only after the British took over India. In the 1800s India's British rulers began getting sporadic reports of a substantial number of travelers going missing, but there was no proof to indicate that these were anything but isolated incidents of weary people becoming lost."

"What's your point?" asked Nisha, bemused by his historical digression.

"It was the discovery of several frighteningly similar mass graves across India that revealed the truth," said Santosh, effortlessly recalling from memory details of the obscure group—information that no normal individual would bother to hold on to. "Each grave site was filled with the corpses of people who had been ritually massacred and buried. The uniform method of killing was strangulation with a *rumaal*—a yellow silk or cotton handkerchief."

"Why strangulation in particular?" asked Nisha.

"Shedding blood was strictly prohibited. This was at the very core of thuggee belief. It was thus absolutely necessary that the murders were carried out in a perfectly bloodless manner."

"But why exactly did these people murder others?" said Nisha.

Santosh tapped his fingers on the conference table excitedly. "The word thug actually means deceiver," he began. "In fact the English word thug is etymologically derived from the Hindi word *thag*. The Thugs traveled across India in groups. They pretended to be pilgrims, traders, or soldiers and would mingle with fellow travelers, patiently gaining their trust and confidence. Thugs would often travel for days and miles with their targeted victims, cautiously waiting for an opportune moment to strike. When travelers least expected it, usually during camping hours at night, the leader of the Thugs would give a signal for the massacre—or thuggee—to begin."

"What sort of signal?" asked Nisha.

"The leader would usually ask someone to bring the tobacco," said Santosh. "This phrase was a signal to the other Thugs that the looting and killing could begin."

"'Bring the tobacco'? Are we now dealing with a reborn thuggee cult?" wondered Mubeen.

"This is not the work of a Thug," replied Santosh.

"Why?" asked Nisha. "How can you be so sure?"

"Thuggee beliefs forbade them from killing certain classes of humans. Women, holy men, musicians, lepers, and foreigners were not considered legitimate targets. Our first victim—Dr. Kanya Jaiyen—was a foreigner, and both victims were women."

His team digested the information. "How were the Thugs vanquished?" asked Nisha finally.

"Due to the efforts of a Bengal Army officer—Sir William Henry Sleeman," answered Santosh robotically. "He devoted his life to the annihilation of thuggee. By analyzing murder sites, Sleeman and his troops predicted future attack locations. His men used the Thugs' own modus operandi against them. Disguised as traders or pilgrims, the officers would stick around at predicted attack sites, waiting for a band of Thugs to draw near. They would be ambushed the moment they tried to attack. Information obtained through the interrogation of prisoners was also used to plan every ensuing operation. By the end of the nineteenth century, the British were able to declare that all Thugs had been exterminated."

"Had they actually been finished off?" asked Nisha.

"Many have wondered if the British were too quick to pat themselves on the back," said Santosh. "How a secret brotherhood that had withstood centuries could be annihilated in such a limited window of time has remained a puzzle. While it is true that mass murders and graves are a distant recollection, in some far-flung provinces of India rumors still persist about yellow-sashed wanderers who befriend travelers with their engaging smiles and chatter."

One voice in the room had stayed absolutely silent. Its owner remained seated at the conference table, his face now ashen white. A build-up of sweat on his forehead had begun to trickle down his face in spite of the air conditioning. Hari Padhi attempted to maintain a calm expression as he digested the information offered by Santosh.

Chapter 17

IT WAS EARLY evening when Nisha entered the offices of the *Afternoon Mirror* in the old Fort district of Mumbai. She passed through the hustle and bustle of the newsroom to a glass-walled office that was occupied by the newspaper's editor, a chain-smoking woman in her mid fifties.

Ignoring the fumes and the disconnected smoke alarm, Nisha strode in and introduced herself. After perfunctory pleasantries had been exchanged, she opened up a notes tab on her smartphone and began to ask questions.

"Were there any recent threats against Bhavna?" she said. "Anyone upset by anything that she had written?"

"Not that I can remember," answered the editor, taking a deep drag from the Virgina Slim that dangled from her lips. "Last year she wrote an article about teenage pregnancies at a famous Mumbai girls' school. The principal was very upset and stormed into her office. That was a while ago, though."

Nisha held out a photograph of the man who had been

caught on CCTV leaving Dr. Kanya Jaiyen's hotel room. "We believe that this man may have visited Bhavna at her home on the morning she was killed. Does he look familiar?"

The editor studied the photograph carefully and eventually shrugged. "You can't see his face."

"Even so . . ."

"Sorry, it doesn't ring any bells. I don't think I have ever seen this man before. I could give you a list of the names and phone numbers of contacts that Bhavna had scheduled to interview over the next few days. Maybe it could throw up a match?"

"Thanks, I appreciate that," replied Nisha. "Anything that you can tell me about her personal life?"

"As far as I know, it was quite normal," said the editor. "She wasn't married but was seeing a guy—a decent bloke. She introduced him to me during our last New Year's office party. A banker, I think."

"Were they getting along? No fights?" asked Nisha.

"Not that anyone in this office was aware of," said the editor. "As far as we could tell, she was on her way to eventually marrying the chap. She was working late during the last few days because he was on an overseas trip."

"What was the latest story Bhavna Choksi was working on?"

"Ah, now *that* I can't tell you, I'm afraid."

"Can't? Or won't?"

The editor exhaled smoke and smiled wanly through the cloud. "A bit of both, Mrs. Gandhe. Bhavna had a workstation and I dare say we could boot it up and have a look at her files, but we're a newspaper. To be helping . . . you're not even the police, are you? To be assisting a law enforcement agency such as yourselves, well, it would seriously compromise our editorial integrity. Unless . . ."

"Yes . . . ?" said Nisha carefully, thinking she knew exactly what was coming next.

The editor stubbed out her cigarette and leaned forward. "Unless we could perhaps come to an arrangement."

"And what sort of arrangement would that be?" sighed Nisha.

"Perhaps we could help you with details of Bhavna's assignment in return for details of the murder."

"Details?" repeated Nisha.

"Mrs. Gandhe, all of us are devastated by the loss of Bhavna," said the editor, "but we realize the show must go on. She would have wanted details of her murder to appear as an exclusive on the front pages of her own tabloid—not in some other newspaper. Come on now, what information on the case can you offer me?"

Nisha shook her head in disgust. "We're trying to find a killer here—"

"And I'm trying to run a newspaper," shrugged the editor. Her phone began to ring and Nisha thanked her stars. She signaled that she had to leave and made a quick retreat from the office before the editor could put down the receiver.

As Nisha left the office building she was being watched by a camera. Its telephoto lens whirred like a casino counting machine.

Chapter 18

"HARI?"

Private's tech wizard turned at the sound of Nisha's voice. "What can I do for you?" he asked, pleased to see her, and even more pleased when she perched herself on the edge of his desk.

"I went to the *Afternoon Mirror* today," she explained.

"Looking for a job?"

She chuckled. "Looking for information on Bhavna Choksi, only her editor was far more interested in what I had to tell her about the murder than actually helping us find the killer."

He pulled a face. "Newshounds, eh? Tsk."

"We recovered a laptop from Bhavna's home," said Nisha. She pointed. "That one there, I believe. Could you crack it?"

"Of course," he smiled.

"Brilliant." She eased herself off the end of his desk, departing with her jacket slung over her shoulder and her Glock at her hip. "Let me know how you get on."

"Will do," he said, watching her go. Then he placed Bhavna

Choksi's Windows notebook before him on his workstation. This was going to be fun. The hacker in him always relished the prospect of entering forbidden territory.

He plugged in a USB flash drive preloaded with a program titled Ophcrack and held down the power button until the machine powered off. He then powered up the computer, entered the machine's BIOS, changed the boot sequence, saved the changes, and exited.

Taking a deep meditative breath, Hari restarted the machine and waited for Ophcrack to load. The program used rainbow tables to solve passwords up to fourteen characters in length and Hari had found that it usually took less than ten seconds to pop one out. He began counting backwards from ten.

Exactly on cue, Ophcrack spat out Bhavna's password. Hari wrote it down on a piece of paper, unplugged the USB flash drive from the computer, rebooted it, and logged in using the password supplied by the program. He then began examining the journalist's computer for material that could be of use to Private India.

Besides previous articles on a variety of subjects, Hari began looking for Bhavna's latest web searches. Within a few minutes he knew that she had been searching for travel coordinators, stylists, pet groomers, physiotherapists, public relations managers, nutrition experts, fashion designers, beauticians, psychiatrists, and fitness instructors. Not only that, but . . .

Hari picked up the intercom handset and dialed Nisha's extension. "I can tell you what Bhavna Choksi was working on in the twenty-four hours before she was killed," he said. "She's got web searches galore, plus she was good enough to keep a list on her desktop."

"Excellent," Nisha beamed. "Apparently her most recent piece was a feature on the lifetstyles of the rich and famous . . ."

"I'm looking at it now. It's a bunch of names, lots under the heading 'possibles,' just one under the heading 'definite.'"

"All right," she said, "let's have the definite."

"It's a hairstylist. Name of Aakash—just 'Aakash'—at the Shiva Spa Lounge."

"Excellent," she said, "I owe you one," and hung up.

In his own office, Hari replaced the receiver, feeling an odd mix of emotions: pride at having recovered the information Nisha needed, but something else too, and for a second he simply stared at the silent receiver in its cradle.

Then he stood, left his office, and took the stairs to Colaba Causeway, where he lit a cigarette. As he exhaled a cloud of smoke through his nostrils he made a call.

It was answered by a husky female voice.

"Can we meet later tonight?" Hari asked her. "It's urgent. There's something I need to discuss."

Chapter 19

"IT'S NOT A hair *salon*, it's a hair *lounge*," said Aakash the head stylist, his eyes ablaze.

The difference, as far as Santosh and Nisha could see, was that the Shiva Spa had a resident DJ who played deafening music. Stylists bobbed their heads in time to the beat as they dealt with trendy clients, all of whom regarded themselves with empty expressions in the mirror, as though to show an actual human emotion might be considered uncool.

Aakash, however, was allowed to show an emotion—something to do with his artistic temperament, no doubt—even if that emotion was best described as emphatic irritation. He wore an orange tailored jacket with the sleeves pushed up. Beneath it was a T-shirt that had been artfully ripped and stressed, and tight jeans with a chain hanging off the waistband. He was hairless.

"Well, perhaps we could find a place somewhere in the *lounge* that's a little more private?" Nisha yelled over the din of a Bollywood tune.

Aakash glanced from her to Santosh, who stood at her shoulder, rolled his eyes as though the whole thing were a terrible inconvenience, then turned on his heel and strode toward the rear of the salon—sorry, *lounge*.

Nisha and Santosh swapped amused glances and followed, pleased to hear the music recede. Indeed, away from the DJ was where the place earned its spa status. Waltzing on ahead, Aakash led them through a section where slightly older patrons were being seen to by chic stylists wearing black, and back here the atmosphere was more serene. The music was classical, and the stench of hair products and eau de toilette was at least partly replaced by the smells of coffee and burning incense.

Finally they reached the office, where Aakash, still wearing an expression of exasperation, directed them to a pair of unnecessarily uncomfortable steel-tube chairs, while he sank himself into a sofa.

He kept them waiting while he studied his phone then dropped it, looked at them, sighed, and said, "Yes? What can I do for you?"

Santosh, his cane held between his legs, let Nisha do the talking.

"We're investigating the murder of a journalist, Bhavna Choksi. We believe she'd been in contact with you."

Aakash tilted his chin, thinking—or pretending to.

"No, I don't think I know the name," he said.

"She represented the *Afternoon Mirror.*"

"Oh, *her.*" He pulled a face. "Yes, she did get in touch, you're right."

"And you agreed to do an interview?" said Nisha.

"At first, but I changed my mind."

"Why?"

Aakash looked haughty. "She told me she wanted to know more about my work but it was all false pretences."

"Really? I thought she was writing a piece on those who look after the rich and famous. The support staff, if you like."

He bridled. "I'll have you know, I'm far more than 'support staff.' What I do . . ." he waved his hand airily ". . . is closer to art."

"Be that as it may . . ."

Aakash frowned. "Look, she may have pretended to be writing a soft feature, but I could tell—she was digging for dirt."

"And did she get any?" asked Nisha.

"No," he sniffed.

Nisha threw Santosh a look and he raised his eyebrows. She leaned forward. "Mr. . . ."

"Aakash," he said, affronted. "It's just Aakash."

". . . Aakash—I'm having difficulty understanding why you wouldn't want to talk to the *Afternoon Mirror*. After all, the free advertising alone surely would have made it worthwhile. I'm picturing it now, the salon—sorry, the *lounge*—featured in the *Afternoon Mirror*, waiting lists stretching off into infinity. It would appear to me to be—what do you call it?—a no-brainer."

"Well," he said defensively, "that's just where you're wrong."

"Why?" she pressed. Her voice was soft, but probing. "Was there something you were worried she might discover?"

By now Aakash was looking shifty. The office door was open. He got up, walked over, and closed it. The act was dropped a little. "Look," he said, "I may have, um, overplayed the celebrity angle of my work."

Nisha and Santosh exchanged a glance.

"In what way?" said Nisha.

"In the sense that the celebrity bit of my client list needs working on."

"You are yourself becoming something of a celebrity, are you not? The very fact that Bhavna wanted to interview you attests to that."

"I am," said the hairdresser proudly.

"And yet this reputation is built on false pretences . . ."

Aakash froze as if the walls had ears. "All right," he said, "keep it down. Don't tell the world. I do have some celebrity clients, just not lots."

"How many celebrity clients?"

"Three."

They both looked at him, eyebrows raised.

"Okay," he admitted. "None. Yet. But did you see the lounge? They'll be pouring in soon, just you mark my words."

"I see," said Santosh, the first words he'd spoken since they'd arrived at the Shiva Spa. He looked at Nisha and saw his own disappointment reflected in her eyes. "I think we're done here."

Chapter 20

THE MAN KNOWN only as Munna sat across two seats of the booth in the Emerald Bar, an illegal dance bar. Huge and perspiring heavily, he mopped his wet brow with a handkerchief every now and then, piggy eyes blinking as he spoke into his phone.

Munna liked gold. Under an open-necked shirt he wore gold-rope chains around his neck. His chubby fingers were made even chubbier by an assortment of thick gold rings. On the table in front of him was a pack of Marlboro Lights, a solid gold lighter, and a sleek gold-plated cell phone. He was rumored to carry a gold-plated Desert Eagle in his waistband.

There were other rumors about Munna. That the lake bordering his weekend home on the outskirts of Mumbai was used to breed crocodiles, an efficient and ecologically friendly means of disposing of human bodies.

In booths to the left and the right sat some of Munna's men who, as well as drinking, smoking, and pawing the girls, provided an intimidating gauntlet to run before an audience with the gangster. But in Munna's private booth were his personal bodyguards, standing to his left and right, their Glock 22 pistols in shoulder holsters under tailored cotton jackets.

Next to him a girl sat curled up. Not a day older than sixteen, she wore a tiny skirt and a bra top, had dark rings under heavy-lidded eyes, and track marks on her arms, visible if you looked close enough. With her legs tucked up beneath her she leaned into Munna and endured his wandering hands. Soon she would dance for him, once his business was concluded, and after the dance, perhaps he would bid his close protection to leave them, and they would stand outside the door of the booth and listen to her stifled screams.

Munna controlled most of the city's drug traffic, bootlegging, prostitution, extortion, and illegal betting. Growing up in the slums of Mumbai, Iqbal Rahim had fought his way to the very top of the crime ladder by bumping off his rivals and accomplices in equal measure. He had somehow managed to retain a baby face, and hence came to be known as "Munna"— or baby boy.

There was absolutely nothing that Munna could not get done in the city and he often used that power to play Robin Hood to full effect. Whether it was the school admission of a child, the medical treatment of a cancer patient, or the out-of-turn allocation of a subsidized house for someone on an endless waiting list, Munna ensured that he was both loved and feared. There was no politician in Mumbai who could hope to win an election without Munna's invisible support.

Barely two decades earlier, Mumbai had been in the throes of a deadly gang war. The police chief set up an encounter force to deal with the situation. In Mumbai police terminology, an encounter was a euphemism to describe extrajudicial killings in which a police team shot down suspected gangsters in carefully staged gun battles. It was all-out war.

The net result was that the Mumbai police had succeeded in crippling the underworld in Mumbai. Although "encounter specialists" within the police force were criticized by human rights activists, they were praised by ordinary citizens. Rupesh's boss—the Police Commissioner—had started his own career as an encounter specialist and had worked his way up to his present position.

Only the most determined gangsters had remained in Mumbai during the encounter years and Munna was one of them. His mentors had fled to Karachi and Dubai while Munna had gobbled up the residual empire left behind by them. Several corpses later, he had emerged more powerful than any previous mafia don, someone who knew the value of working alongside the enemy.

A man walked into the bar's dark air-conditioned interior. In the center of the garishly decorated place was a huge dance floor on which a few dozen young girls dressed in traditional Indian outfits gyrated to the rhythm of Bollywood songs. Seated at tables arranged around the dance floor were lecherous men who would get up every now and again to shower cash on girls who caught their fancy. Waiters unobtrusively served alcohol while quietly pocketing cash for arranging private encounters with the girls.

The man appeared at the door of Munna's booth. "Hello, Munna *bhau*," he said.

"Have you come to talk business?" growled Munna.

"Indeed I have," replied Rupesh.

Chapter 21

SANTOSH UNLOCKED THE door and entered without bothering to switch on the lights. His second-floor apartment was close to the Taj Mahal Hotel, a short walk from his office in Colaba. The bright sodium-vapor street lights outside his windows bathed his dark living room in an eerie golden hue.

In the kitchen, he took out a glass from the overhead cabinet and placed it under the ice dispenser, enjoying the reassuring clink of ice cubes in the glass. He took it into the living room where he picked up the half-empty bottle of Johnnie Walker Black Label from the side cabinet, poured the golden liquid into the glass, listened to the ice cubes crackle as the whisky settled in.

Just one, he told himself. *Just the one*. Johnnie Walker or Jack Morgan—he'd made his choice. Jack had had faith in him, helped to pick up a broken man. And this—this was the biggest case Private India had handled so far.

He wasn't going to let Jack down.

Santosh settled in too. He stretched out on the sofa, picked up the remote, and switched on the television set. He rarely watched TV but found the sound strangely reassuring. It was a news channel showing another uproar in the Indian parliament as the government and opposition benches traded charges of corruption and incompetence.

Santosh ignored the events on television, took a generous gulp of the whisky, and stared at an oversized photograph on the wall. It showed a laughing young woman holding a six-year-old boy in her arms. It was a photograph he had taken at a hill resort, a few hours away from Mumbai.

He had not known at the time that it was the last photograph he would ever take of his wife and son.

He downed the rest of his glass in a single swig and poured himself another. His drinking had increased over the past few years, but it numbed the pain. The drooping eyes, the graying hair and unsmiling face were the result of a combination of loneliness, aging, anguish, and the drinking. Santosh continued to gaze at the photograph until he fell into a slumber. Then the nightmare took over. It was a recurring theme and varied only minimally.

Santosh, Isha, and Pravir were returning from a weekend trip to the hill resort. It had been Santosh's effort to reconnect with his family. His work had kept him so completely absorbed that he had begun to feel like an outsider when he was seated at the dinner table with his wife and son. Even though Isha had never complained, the distance between them had been growing. For the moment, though, they had succeeded in forgetting about it. Santosh was driving the car with his wife seated next to him. Pravir was playing a video game, seated in the rear. Santosh took his eyes off the road for a few seconds. He did not see the tree at the crest of a hairpin turn a few yards ahead.

There was a sickening sound of crumpling metal as the car smashed into it. The screeching of tires, the car spiraling out of control, the smell of burned rubber and fuel . . . Darkness.

"You killed them, you drunk bastard," said a cop, holding out a pair of handcuffs to Santosh as he woke to the sound of alarm bells ringing in a hospital.

The alarm bells continued ringing. *Switch off those goddamn bells,* thought Santosh. The bells persisted. *Switch them off, motherfucker*, he thought, but there was no respite. The bells continued to clang noisily in his head.

Santosh woke to find his telephone was ringing. He pulled his feet off the sofa and sat up. He rubbed his eyes groggily. The clock on the wall showed three o'clock in the morning. He picked up the cell phone that was persistently ringing next to the empty bottle of Johnnie Walker and took the call.

"What's the matter with you? I've been trying to reach you for the past half-hour," said Rupesh irritably.

"Sorry, the phone was accidentally switched to silent mode," lied Santosh.

The answer seemed to mollify Rupesh. "We've got a third body," he said without pause. "You need to get yourself over to Hill Road immediately."

Chapter 22

HILL ROAD WOUND through Bandra, a posh suburb favored by Bollywood actors, musicians, and artists. The house in question was toward a quiet stretch of the street, close to Mount Mary Church.

Santosh had asked Mubeen to pick him up. His head was aching and his stomach burning from alcohol-induced acidity. He had hurriedly dissolved a couple of Alka-Seltzer in a glass of water and gulped them down before jumping into Mubeen's car.

There was virtually no traffic on the roads at this hour and Mubeen was able to get them to Bandra within fifteen minutes. They waited in the car at the closed gate for a few minutes before the steel grille was raised electronically to let them through. Mubeen parked in the private driveway of the bungalow next to several police vehicles and gathered his equipment from the boot of the car.

The house belonged to an Indian pop singing sensation—Priyanka Talati. A single song in a single Bollywood movie had fueled her meteoric rise to iconic status. That one song had made her a legend throughout India and all of South Asia. The soundtrack album had charted in sixteen countries worldwide, and the song had become the fastest-selling single in Asia. In a short career of five years, Priyanka had sung on over forty soundtracks across five languages and had won fifteen awards, including one National Film Award, two Filmfare Awards, and three International Indian Film Academy Awards.

Hari and Nisha were already at the crime scene, having been alerted by Santosh to the developments. Rupesh was there too, lips red with cardamom-flavored chewing tobacco.

"Your chap Hari Padhi has checked out the security system," he told Santosh. "It's a highly sophisticated one but it was never triggered. Either the intruder understood the technology or they were allowed in by the owner." He led them through the entrance passageway into an elegant living room.

One of the walls was covered with awards, trophies, and gold and platinum disks while another bore a huge canvas by Indian painter Syed Haider Raza, the painting having been publicly acquired by Priyanka for three million dollars during a charity auction.

"Quite obviously the killer was not interested in either the painting or its value," remarked Santosh, as he observed Nisha taking photographs of the crime scene. "Only a very wealthy individual would leave such an expensive painting on the wall. On the other hand, an intruder of modest means might not have fully appreciated its value."

He shifted his gaze from the walls to the floor. Toward the center of a vast and expensive Pietra di Vicenza marble floor lay the body of Priyanka Talati, dressed in a designer tracksuit and expensive sneakers. Around her neck was the now-familiar yellow garrote.

"What is she lying on?" asked Santosh.

"It's a faux tiger skin," replied Nisha. "Rather cheap. It's certainly not part of the expensive decor."

"So it's a prop. Yet another clue left by our killer," said Santosh grimly. *What the fuck are you playing at?* he thought. *Faux tiger skin? Why are you messing with my head?*

"Did you notice this?" asked Nisha as she bent down to take a close-up shot of the victim's face.

"Is that a rupee coin on her forehead?" asked Santosh, gripping his cane firmly in order to bend down a little.

"Yes, it's a one-rupee coin," replied Nisha. "But it's been sawed in half down the middle."

"Is that brass or gold?" asked Santosh, pointing to a small bell-shaped pendant that hung around the victim's neck on a chain.

"We will have to examine it in the lab to check the exact metallic composition," replied Mubeen, who was scanning the body with a dermascope. "Although it's unlikely that a woman occupying a twenty-million-dollar home with a three-million-dollar painting hanging on the wall would be wearing a brass pendant."

"You are right," said Santosh. "If the pendant turns out to be cheap, we can safely assume that it's a prop left by the killer. Any rough estimate of the time she died?"

"Judging by lividity," said Mubeen, continuing with his examination, "I'd say that she's been dead for at least four hours. That's all I can tell you at this stage. Let Zafar and me examine her in the lab and we should be able to give you a more precise answer."

Santosh look at his watch—3:30 a.m. If Priyanka Talati had been killed four hours ago, it would make the time of death around 11:30. Turning to Rupesh, Santosh asked, "How was her body discovered?"

"There were complaints from neighbors that the music in her house had been turned up to full volume," replied Rupesh. "The sanctioned noise limit in a residential area like Bandra is reduced from fifty-five decibels to forty-five by ten p.m. Her stereo was thumping out Bollywood numbers at over a hundred decibels. The neighbors called up the police control room to register a complaint. When the beat patrol got here there was no one to open the electrical gate. That's when the beat sergeant called us."

"What about her personal staff?" asked Santosh, eyes flitting around the room, mentally taking snapshots of everything. "Someone must have seen something."

"Priyanka Talati had lived most of her life in Singapore," explained Rupesh, who had already interviewed one of the neighbors. "She was uncomfortable keeping household staff, hence the high-tech security system in her house. She had a personal assistant who stayed with her for twelve hours in the day. A cook came in for about three hours in the morning to carry out the cooking for the entire day. A team of cleaners also arrived each day to do the housekeeping but they were usually out by eleven o'clock in the morning."

"No security guard at the gate?" asked Santosh.

"It is remotely operated from within the house," said Rupesh.

"In which case, there would be a CCTV camera at the gate, right?"

"Absolutely. There are two security cameras," explained Rupesh, "one at the gate and the other at the entrance door. Both feed into a digital recording unit inside a closet. Unfortunately the hard drive containing the recorded material is missing."

Rupesh was staring at Priyanka's body. Even though she was fully clothed, he was seeing someone else . . . a naked woman, bleeding internally from wounds inflicted by objects inserted into her body. Repeatedly raped.

Santosh bent down to examine Priyanka's forehead more closely. "Do you see what I see?" he asked Rupesh, breaking his reverie.

"A rupee coin cut in half . . ." said Rupesh tentatively.

"Yes, but look underneath," said Santosh.

Rupesh bent down to take a closer look. "Ah, I see it now. It's a single strand of hair."

"Too much of a coincidence. I am convinced that the hair is a bogey—a prop left to mislead us," said Santosh. "I'm pretty certain it will match the other two strands." He stopped talking suddenly, squinted as he attempted to focus on the coin. "See the way that it has been placed . . . It looks like a half-moon. What day of the week is it today?" he asked animatedly. "Quick! What day?"

"Tuesday. But what does that have to do with anything?" asked Rupesh, wondering how many whiskies Santosh had downed before getting there. Very little remained secret among the members of Mumbai's security establishment.

"If Priyanka Talati was killed at around eleven thirty then it means that the murder happened on Monday night, not Tuesday morning," said Santosh, ignoring Rupesh's impatience.

"What the fuck are you driving at, Santosh?" asked Rupesh, slightly annoyed by the trivial questions and statements.

Santosh turned to Nisha. "Do you have an almanac on your smartphone?"

"Yes," she answered curiously. "What do you need to know?"

"The exact phase of the moon on Monday night."

Nisha did a quick search on her phone. "Let's see. We had a full moon a week ago, a waning gibbous on Thursday night . . . and, ah, here it is. Monday night was a third-quarter moon."

"And a third-quarter moon is a half-moon!" exclaimed Santosh. Even though he did not smile, a look of satisfaction briefly crossed his face. "We have a rupee coin on Priyanka Talati's forehead that looks like a half-moon. The night of the murder turns out to be a half-moon night. The murder happens on a Monday. The word Monday means day of the moon. Think about it. Isn't it possible that this murderer is killing according to an astronomical calendar? Hmm? Isn't it?"

Chapter 23

RUPESH WAS ASKED the same question six times. On each occasion, his practiced bland reply was delivered with the utmost patience. "At this time, we have a few leads that we are working on. Priyanka Talati's murder is being treated as a high-priority case."

The conference room of the Mumbai Police Headquarters was packed with reporters, photographers, and news channel crews, and provided standing room only. A fire in the room that day would have wiped out India's fourth estate entirely.

Santosh and Rupesh had discussed the matter in great detail and had decided that not having a press conference about the inquiry into Priyanka Talati's death would seem suspicious. She was simply too famous. "Just ensure that no one can link her murder to the previous two," advised Santosh. "Let's not give our killer the publicity he craves."

"Is it true that she was strangled?" asked a gray-haired hack from a New Delhi-based news channel.

"It would hamper our investigations if we were to reveal details of the crime publicly," replied Rupesh smoothly. "We are keeping such matters private so that we may bring investigations to a satisfactory conclusion as quickly as possible. I trust that everyone in this room will cooperate with us in this regard."

"Is Priyanka's killing an isolated murder or part of a wider pattern?" asked the editor of the *Afternoon Mirror.*

"We have no evidence at this stage to indicate that her murder is anything other than an isolated incident," replied Rupesh, wondering from where this woman had obtained a tip-off.

A lady from a news channel known for its proximity to the opposition party got up to deliver a speech instead of a question. "Last year, two hundred and fifteen murders, four hundred rapes, two thousand, five hundred burglaries, almost eleven thousand thefts, and over eighteen hundred cases of cheating were reported in the city. Does the police force of Mumbai intend to do anything to stem this crime wave? It seems that more than half of the city's force is assigned to VIP duties, protecting politicians and their family members, rather than being available for crime-fighting."

"Madam, I understand your anguish," lied Rupesh, knowing full well that the woman was speaking the truth. "Please understand that Mumbai's police force is committed to reducing crime. Our Commissioner has instituted a high-level commission to find out how we can revamp our inquiry system."

"The government has become expert at appointing commissions of inquiry and doing little else," replied the woman sarcastically, ensuring that her two accompanying cameramen focused on her and Rupesh in parallel while they exchanged words.

"Have you received any information regarding the possible motive for the killing?" asked a young reporter from an Indian-language newspaper.

"At this stage we are pursuing multiple lines of inquiry and we shall have a clearer idea once all angles have been investigated," said Rupesh, revealing absolutely nothing of any value.

Watching the press conference on the television in Private India's office, Santosh smiled. Rupesh had handled it well.

Watching the press conference on television in another part of town, someone else frowned.

Chapter 24

ISOLATED INCIDENT? TRYING to snatch away my hard-earned publicity? How dare they try to make Priyanka's death look like a random killing? It's time for me to increase the pressure on you chaps. It has been rightly said that one can't make an omelette without breaking eggs. It's time for me to break a few more.

Do you like eggs? Personally, I have never cared for them but here I am in front of the stove, about to boil a dozen. I have a vague recollection of painting pretty designs on Easter eggs. I recall being told that one needed to hard-boil the eggs before painting them or else they would rot quickly.

I drop the eggs into the scalding-hot water. Do you like water? I used to hate it but now I love it. You know why? Because if you hold someone's head in a tub of water, you can stop their breathing. Like a garrote, water is also a murder weapon. Be it a *rumaal*, a tub of water, or a pillow—they are all switches. Flick the switch and you can turn life into death.

Oh dear, I have completely forgotten. Where is the ironing board? Ah, there it is. Now, let's see, how many yellow scarves do I need to steam the wrinkles from? I've already used three. The *rumaal* is such a versatile murder weapon . . . I wonder why it isn't used more often.

Yellow was my mother's favorite color, you know. She would wear yellow sarees. Ah, sarees! The Indian saree is the most sensual piece of clothing that one can wear. The six-yard piece of fabric requires some practice to drape but it hugs a woman's body in all the right places. It's exciting, not because of what it reveals but because of what it doesn't. What an incredible feeling to have the soft fabric caressing your skin at all times of the day, even the most intimate of places.

I pull out my special scarf from my pocket. Three knots are firmly tied in it. I survey my work with some satisfaction but check my contentment. I still have lots more to do.

I'm coming to get you, bitch. Wait for me. Trust me, it's worth waiting for.

Chapter 25

"THIS IS THE only store in Mumbai that sells these particular shoes?" asked Santosh incredulously.

They were illegally parked on Waterfield Road, looking warily at a line of designer boutiques, and one in particular called Michel that, according to Hari, was the city's only supplier of the distinctive black buckled shoe. As modeled by Dr. Jaiyen's probable killer in the Marine Bay Plaza.

They stepped out of the company Honda Civic and into the searing heat of Mumbai. Stopping to let a couple of stylish ladies pass, they crossed to Michel and tried to enter the store—only to find the door locked.

Santosh stepped back, puzzled. "Oh bloody hell," he said, realizing the problem. It wasn't the sort of shop where you just went inside. Oh no. You had to be *allowed in*.

Sure enough, a snooty sales assistant was watching them from a window, wearing the bored, expressionless look of the terminally trendy. Exactly the same look he'd seen on the customers at the Shiva Spa. "Aakash" would be right at home here, he mused.

"Can we come in?" he mouthed, and the bored-looking sales assistant did all but roll her eyes as she surveyed them from a distance. At last she relented and unlocked the door.

"Good day to you, sirs," she said. "How may I help you?"

Another assistant, standing at the counter, momentarily glanced up from flicking through a magazine then looked back down.

"I'm looking for information about a pair of shoes," said Santosh, casting his eyes around the shop.

The assistant smiled wanly as he looked for the pair. He found them with a triumphant "Ah!" and scuttled over to where they were displayed. "These," he said, holding them up with a glance at Hari, who confirmed that they were indeed the shoes from the CCTV footage.

"Those shoes are for display purposes only, I'm afraid," said the assistant, evidently relishing the terrible news she was about to impart. "They are custom-made to order and the waiting list is . . ." She called over her shoulder, "How long for the Oakleys, Ria?"

Without glancing up from her magazine, Ria said, "Two years."

"Two years," repeated Assistant One, unnecessarily.

"Ah, but I don't want to buy a pair," explained Santosh. "I want to know who *else* has bought a pair."

"I'm sorry?" said the assistant, eyebrows shooting up.

Santosh looked at her, his already low expectations sinking further. He could tell how this one was going to end.

Sure enough, in a matter of minutes the two Private men were back in the Honda, with Santosh cursing—cursing his luck, the two snooty assistants; whatever there was to curse, he was cursing it.

"Hey, boss," said Hari from the driver's seat, and Santosh became aware that the IT guy was making no move to drive off. Indeed, he was sitting with the laptop on his lap, lid up, tapping away.

"What are you doing?"

"The shop's router was behind the counter. That particular model came with a generic password you were supposed to change as soon as you'd set it up, but of course nobody ever does so—hey presto—we're in."

He beamed at Santosh, who craned over. "What do you mean? You've hacked into their computer?"

"No, I've hacked into the router. Now . . ." He jabbed a button with a flourish. "*Now* I've hacked into the computer. What were the shoes called again?"

"Oakleys."

"Here we go. Oakleys waiting list. God, the lying cow—the waiting list is only six months."

"Just go to the orders fulfilled," said Santosh.

A list of twelve or thirteen names scrolled up on the screen in front of him; at least half of them had been shipped overseas. Those left would all have to be checked, of course, but there was one name in particular that jumped out at him.

N. D'Souza, the Attorney General.

Chapter 26

"DOES THAT LOOK like the Attorney General, Nalin D'Souza?" asked Santosh.

In the conference room, the members of the Private team were rewatching the CCTV footage for what must have been the thousandth time. Takeout containers were spread out on the table in front of them but for the time being went ignored.

"It's difficult to tell from this angle," said Nisha, studying the 108-inch LCD screen, everything bigger and blurrier than in real life.

"This guy doesn't seem to have the AG's bearing," said Santosh, squaring his own shoulders as if to make the point.

"So it's not him," said Mubeen.

"No," said Santosh, his thoughts far away, "but that's not all there is to it. Show them, Nisha."

Nisha, perched on the edge of the table, click-clicked on the laptop trackpad, and a picture of the handsome Attorney General appeared on the screen. "Look at the hair," she said.

They looked at the handsome face of Nalin D'Souza, the dark Portuguese features that seemingly rendered him irresistible to women.

"That was taken about a week ago. Now look at his picture here." She clicked to another shot. "He's had his hair cut."

Santosh turned from the screen to address his team with eyes that blazed with excitement. "You see? He'd had his hair cut. And what did we find at the murder scenes? Strands of black hair, same shade as D'Souza. Strands of *cut* black hair."

"So he's our man?" said Mubeen, sitting forward.

"No," said Santosh abruptly. "It's all too convenient. Even so, he's the closest we have to a suspect right now." He indicated the picture on the screen. "Where was this taken?"

"At a page-three party at the Oberoi on Sunday night," said Nisha.

"The night of Kanya Jaiyen's death. Does this give him an alibi?"

"He left it early."

"Okay," said Santosh slowly. "Let's be careful about this. The last thing we want to do is ruffle enough feathers to get removed from the case, but we do need to know the AG's movements at the times of the murders."

They sat down to eat their dinner and let the screen go to TV, which was showing coverage of a function attended by a who's who of the entertainment industry. It was the annual Filmfare Awards night—India's equivalent of the Academy Awards—to host and honor the bold and the beautiful of Bollywood.

They watched it in silence, chewing their food, each of them pleased to have a respite from what had been an exhausting day. For his part, Santosh had spent most of the afternoon at the cremation ground, attending Bhavna Choksi's funeral.

The tabloid journalist's last rites had been held at Banganga

Crematorium on the shore of the Arabian Sea. Her crematation had been attended mostly by her friends and colleagues from work. Draped in a white shroud, her body had soon been engulfed in flames atop a pyre of wood, bamboo, and grass, while a Brahmin recited verses from Hindu scriptures. Some distance away, her boyfriend and a group of mourners had prayed silently as thick billowing clouds of smoke curled into the sky. From speaking to a few of Bhavna's friends, Santosh had discovered that the boyfriend had arrived on a morning flight from London in order to attend the funeral. Santosh had waited until the very end to observe and make note of each and every attendee. Experience showed that murderers often attended their victims' funerals, because it helped them to relive the excitement of the kill.

Meanwhile, Mubeen had been busy with the autopsy of Priyanka Talati. As expected, the hair found at Priyanka's home matched microscopically with the two other samples from the previous murders, but no DNA could be extracted from it due to the absence of the root. The preliminary autopsy results had been along expected lines—ligature strangulation with snapped hyoid bone. Metallurgical analysis had shown the bell pendant and chain to be of brass, thus confirming Santosh's suspicion that it was a prop.

Dr. Zafar had joined Mubeen for the examination, having brought over the body on a gurney from the police morgue. "Do you mind if I leave the gurney here and have it picked up later?" he had asked.

"You seem to be in a hurry today," Mubeen had observed curiously.

"I have visitors," Zafar had said. "I need to be home a little earlier."

"Not to worry. The gurney can be stored in this chamber."

Mubeen had pointed to a stainless-steel unit that allowed several gurneys to be placed side by side.

"I will need some time to complete the analysis," he'd continued. "Santosh wants a complete drug toxicology done on her."

"Why?" Zafar had asked. "Wasn't she killed by strangulation?"

"Sure," Mubeen had replied. "It's just that I have stopped asking why. Santosh *always* has a reason for *everything*."

"Do you need help or should I proceed?"

"You carry on," Mubeen had said. "I have collected blood from her femoral vein as well as her heart. Luckily there was some urine in her bladder too. Combined with bile and tissue samples from her liver, brain, kidney, and the vitreous humor of her eye, I should be able to do a full report for him."

Nisha had spent her time contacting the security firm that had installed the surveillance system and burglar alarm at Priyanka Talati's house. They had disclosed that they'd offered her their remote monitoring service but she had not agreed, citing privacy concerns. The security firm had simply installed the equipment—alarm system, CCTV cameras, and recording unit—and was duty bound to react if the alarm was triggered. If the recording unit was removed from Priyanka's home, there was simply no backup copy anywhere else.

There were far too many unanswered questions swimming around in Santosh's head. What did all the props left by the murderer mean? Why were they different at each scene? What was the murderer trying to tell them? What was the motive for the three killings? How were the murders related to the thuggee cult? Why had the victims opened their doors to the strangler? Whose hair was being found at the crime scenes? What was the common thread that linked the three victims to one another?

"What was the name of the security firm that installed the CCTV equipment at Priyanka Talati's house?" he suddenly asked Nisha.

She looked at her smartphone to check but was interrupted by Santosh. "Don't tell me. I'll bet you that it was Xilon Security."

"You are right," said Nisha, realizing where he was going with it. "All three murder sites have had the same security consultant."

"Find out everything that you can about Xilon," he said, "founders, owners, directors. Look into the backgrounds of all their site engineers and find out if anyone has a suspicious past." He stared blankly at the television screen, looking straight through the glitter and glamor of the Filmfare Awards.

One person stood out that night, though. Her name was Lara Omprakash and she seemed to be picking up a substantial number of awards. Lara was an elegant woman in her forties. She had been a leading lady in several blockbuster films but had bowed out gracefully a few years previously. Bollywood was always in search of the sexiest body and prettiest face that it could find, and maturity carried no premium for women. From a career in front of the camera, Lara had switched over to a career behind it. She had turned director—and how. Challenging all the norms of a formula-driven industry, she had directed the previous year's biggest hit, a cutting-edge suspense thriller about a woman leading a double life.

On the television screen, Lara stepped up on stage and gracefully accepted the award for best director. She was retaking her seat when she was requested to return on stage to receive the award for best picture also. Having delivered a short, witty, and dignified acceptance speech, Lara went back to her seat and sat down next to a familiar face.

Santosh was shaken out of his reverie as the TV cameras

panned over the audience in the VIP section. Sitting next to Lara and looking rather dapper in his tuxedo was the man who had accompanied her to the awards ceremony that night.

It was Santosh's boss from LA—Jack Morgan.

Chapter 27

SANTOSH SAT WATCHING the giant screen with his mouth agape, attempting to make sense of Jack Morgan's presence at the Filmfare Awards. Nisha, Mubeen, and Hari were equally stumped but before they could recover from the surprise, they heard a familiar voice ask: "Anyone home?"

Jack Morgan—ex-marine and head of the world's largest and most renowned investigation agency—strode purposefully into the Private India conference room, still dressed in his tuxedo but with the bow tie having been undone. His day-old stubble and rugged good looks were the ideal combination for a charm offensive, but underneath that was a smart and extremely driven individual who surrounded himself with intelligent and committed people. Jack Morgan only hired the cream of the crop and paid them the very best salaries in the industry.

Walking up to Santosh, he shook his hand and indulged in a bit of good-natured back-thumping. "Nice to see that the retina scan at the entrance still remembers me," he said, turning to give Nisha an almost imperceptible peck on her cheek. He then quickly went around the conference table to shake hands with Mubeen and Hari.

"What brings you here, boss?" asked Santosh. "Why didn't you keep me informed? I would have come to pick you up from the airport."

"No need for formality, Santosh," said Jack. "I'm here because of Lara Omprakash."

"Had I known that you know her, I would have requested you to arrange for me to meet her," said Hari, sputtering like an excited schoolboy.

"That could still be arranged," said Jack, winking at Hari, who was still a little distracted by the Filmfare glitz on the screen. "Stop staring at her! Trust me when I say that she's far prettier off camera."

"I thought that the Filmfare Awards were broadcast live. How are you in two places simultaneously?" asked Mubeen rather naively, looking at Jack's face on the screen.

"They buffer the broadcast by two hours so that they can do on-location edits," replied Jack, "particularly for the song-and-dance sequences that all Indians seem to love." He settled down into one of the chairs at the conference table.

"So, here I am in Mumbai," he continued. "I wasn't too sure if I would come but the pressure from Lara was simply too much. She almost forced me to board the flight."

"How do you know her?" asked Santosh, the investigator in him taking over.

"Ah, the interrogation has started," remarked Jack in jest. "Okay, here's the condensed version. Lara Omprakash was doing brilliantly as a heroine in Bollywood. Unfortunately most leading ladies there have rather short careers. The film industry is notoriously sexist and retires them the moment that a younger, hotter, sexier alternative emerges. Lara was intelligent. She withdrew in good time."

"That still doesn't explain how you know her," persisted Santosh, almost forgetting that Jack was his boss, not a suspect.

Jack ignored the impatience and helped himself to a kebab from one of the tandoori cartons. "She decided to switch careers from acting to direction and took two years off from Bollywood. She settled down in LA temporarily and enrolled at the world-renowned American Film Institute in order to make the transition."

"How did you meet her?" asked Hari eagerly.

"While she was in LA, she became friends with another student—a young actor from Brazil," answered Jack. "A stringer from an Indian gossip magazine took some compromising photographs of her with this Brazilian friend. She needed someone to help her retrieve those photos before they were published back home. My name was recommended to her by the associate dean of the institute."

"Were you able to help her?" asked Nisha.

"What do you think?" said Jack, licking the tandoori spice off his fingers.

"I think it's possible that Mr. Jack Morgan became better friends with Lara than the Brazilian," joked Nisha.

"Lara has never had time for anything besides her work and hobbies," said Jack, sidestepping the question deftly.

"That's one of the ironies of life," remarked Nisha cryptically.

"What is?" asked Jack.

"The fact that one woman's hobby could often be another woman's hubby," she replied.

Chapter 28

"I SAW YOUR report," said Jack to Santosh. "You seem to have a serial killer who has a fetish for yellow garrotes."

"Three victims in roughly twenty-four hours between Sunday and Monday nights," replied Santosh. "Worrying average. Unfortunately, we're no closer to finding him than we were after the first murder."

"Have you tried finding out whether there was anything to link the victims?" asked Jack. "Did they stay in the same locality? Did they work in similar professions? Did they eat at the same restaurant? Did they use the same hairdresser or dry cleaning service? Do they have a common friend or boyfriend?"

"I've been plugging data into PrivatePattern since this morning but can't find anything to link them," said Nisha. PrivatePattern was the Private organization's proprietary analysis tool. Investigators from all over the world fed case data into the system and allowed the software to throw up possible links and matches.

"The first victim was a doctor from Thailand, the second was a journalist working for a Mumbai tabloid, and the third was a famous pop singer," she continued. "I have tried cross-referencing various elements from their lives but have drawn a blank. The main link so far is the security consultant—Xilon—whose technology was in use at all three locations. The only other definite link is the fact that the first two victims spoke to each other extensively over the phone."

"What about the third?" asked Jack. "Any phone conversations with the other two?"

"Priyanka Talati—our singing sensation—did not believe in keeping an intrusive cell phone by her side. Her personal assistant answered phone calls for her but he is quite emphatic that Priyanka never received a call from either Kanya Jaiyen or Bhavna Choksi."

Santosh perked up. "The reporter—Bhavna Choksi—was writing a story about people that work with celebrities, right? Was the singer—Priyanka—on Bhavna's list of contacts?" he asked Nisha.

"No," she replied, glancing down at her notes. "There were no celebrities on Bhavna's list. Only people that worked *alongside* celebrities—helping them with their travel arrangements, physiotherapy, styling, pets, public relations, psychiatric counseling, clothes . . ."

"Okay, let's forget that angle and focus on the murders. What was common to them?" asked Jack.

"All the victims were women," replied Santosh mechanically. "None of them was sexually assaulted. All of them were killed by strangulation with a yellow garrote. The security firm at all three murder sites was the same. There was no forced entry at any of the locations. There was no trace evidence except for a single strand of hair—minus any DNA—at all three murder sites. The strangler left props—varying across the killings—at all the murder sites."

"Refresh my memory a little," said Jack. "What were the props?"

"The first victim was left with a lotus flower and a dining fork tied to her hands, and a toy Viking helmet tied to her feet. The second was found with a rosary in one hand and a bucket of water in the other. The third was found lying on a faux animal skin, half a rupee coin placed on her head, and a small brass bell-shaped pendant hung around her neck." Santosh rattled off the details from memory.

"If you can't find a link between the victims then try finding what connects the props. The killer is trying to tell you something," said Jack quietly. "Find the pattern that fits the props and you will crack this case wide open."

Under the conference table, Hari nervously clutched a small pendant in his right hand as he prayed to God that his secret would remain buried. He anxiously hoped that the husky-voiced woman he had spoken to earlier remained unaware of the latest developments.

Chapter 29

BLUE MAGIC TANTRA Records was no backstreet operation. Everything about the studio where Priyanka Talati had made her chartbusting albums screamed "big time."

Santosh felt shabby, old, and out of touch as he and Nisha were led through the swish studio then deposited in the control room. Through floor-to-ceiling glass they watched as Priyanka's music producer moved up and down a huge mixing console on a leather-backed swivel chair, his fingers dancing over sliders, head bobbing to music they couldn't hear.

In his late thirties, he wore Kai-Kai sandals, faded jeans, and a gray company T-shirt printed with the logo "Blue Magic Tantra" in electric blue. And something else—a yellow bandana.

Now that's interesting, thought Santosh, as the producer swung on his chair and waved at them through the window of the control room. *A yellow bandana. The same fabric and dye, perhaps?*

Moments later they sat down for coffee with the producer. "Priyanka was one of the most talented and versatile singers that India has ever produced," he said sadly. "I was convinced it was only a matter of time before she'd be nominated for a Grammy."

"She lived most of her life outside India, is that right?" asked Santosh, using a sip of the brew to surreptitiously study the bandana.

"Yes," said the producer. "She studied music at the Yong Siew Conservatory, part of the National University of Singapore. Her parents were divorced. Her mother lived in Singapore—working as an accountant, I think—while her father lived in Thailand from where he continued to work for the merchant navy. Priyanka's growing-up years were divided between Singapore and Thailand."

"What about her personal life?" asked Nisha. "Did she have a husband or boyfriend?"

"She married rather young—unfortunately to the wrong guy," said the producer. "He turned out to have a serious drinking problem. Even worse was the fact that he used Priyanka for target practice when he was sloshed. She'd been single for several years now but the divorce proceedings were dragging on . . . Nasty."

Santosh kept quiet. Any reference to drinking inspired loathing and longing within him almost simultaneously. Loathing for his lack of self-control. And longing for yet another drink.

"Could we have his name, please?" asked Nisha. "Any idea where he lives?"

The producer provided a name but was not sure of the exact address. He told them that the apartment was somewhere in Andheri.

"Was there anyone new in her life?" asked Santosh at last.

"Was there anything strange or abnormal in her habits or routine?"

"She had been shooting for a new music video and had been rather tired due to extended cosmetic makeover sessions as well as extra power yoga classes," replied the producer sadly. "We would have released the new album next month along with the video. The song was to be used as the soundtrack for an upcoming film." It was evident that Priyanka's death had affected him deeply.

"Which movie?" asked Santosh.

"A new thriller by Lara Omprakash," said the producer. "It had taken us almost a year to find the right sound for the film. Lara too was very excited about it."

"Would you know whether Priyanka had a drug habit?" asked Santosh suddenly.

"Why on earth would you think that?" the producer said indignantly. "Priyanka was on a perpetual high—from her music. She didn't need drugs!"

"Another question," said Santosh carefully. He had noticed the small blue logo of Blue Magic Tantra Records on the producer's yellow bandana. It wasn't the same type of scarf as the ones used in the murders. "What was your relationship with her?"

The producer looked directly at Santosh and tears welled up in his eyes. "I loved her—not only as my protégée but also as a special friend. Unfortunately Priyanka never thought of me as anything but her producer, so the matter ended there."

"I have to ask this," said Santosh. "Where were you at the time that Priyanka Talati was killed? Monday night between eleven and midnight."

"I was here all night," said the producer, not seeming to take any offense at the aggressive line of questioning. "We were recording a track for Shivaraman Mahadevan—the leader of the Indian fusion group Samudra. You can ask any of the musicians. They'll tell you that I was here from eight p.m. onwards until the wee hours of the morning."

Santosh and Nisha thanked the producer and left the air-conditioned interior of the Blue Magic Tantra office for the heat of Mumbai city.

"We will need to check the tabloid reporter's contacts list," said Santosh, "to see whether Priyanka's cosmetician or yoga instructor were on it. Also, we should find out the exact address of the former husband in Andheri and pay him a visit." Nisha nodded as she unlocked the doors of the car and got into the driver's seat. Santosh settled into the passenger seat next to her. That was the precise moment at which both of them saw it.

Tied to the steering wheel was a bright yellow scarf, identical to the ones that had been used in the three killings.

Chapter 30

HARI PADHI GOT into the driver's seat, belted up, and started
the car. On most days he did not bother to drive his car to
work, preferring to use a Meru Cab, one of the hundreds of
air-conditioned aqua-colored taxi cabs that jostled for space
alongside the older but less comfortable black-and-yellow cabs.
But today was different.

After about fifteen minutes of driving along congested roads,
he parked near a school. Locking the car, he stepped out,
passed the school, and headed down a narrow lane that led to
a famous temple.

As he drew closer to it, the lane became slightly more
crowded with holy men, hawkers, and beggars. He stopped at a
small shop to buy some incense sticks, sandalwood paste, basil
leaves, flowers, a ritual stole, and a watermelon. He then passed
through the small wooden gate that led to the Durga Temple.

It was early morning by Mumbai standards and the temple
was almost empty. It took Hari less than a few minutes to reach

the goddess. He lit the incense sticks before the large idol of Durga. Then he dipped the flowers into the sandalwood paste and placed them along with the basil leaves at the feet of the deity as part of the ritual offering. He draped the stole reverentially around the shoulders of the deity.

Next he placed the watermelon on a small platform in front of the statue. He bowed down to pray for a few moments before he lifted a pocketknife and split open the watermelon with a single swipe. The red insides of the melon lay exposed as bloody juices oozed out.

A watermelon or gourd was an acceptable alternative sacrifice in the modern age. In medieval times, an animal or human sacrifice would have been the norm.

Chapter 31

THE SCARF ON the steering wheel had left Nisha and Santosh stumped. Santosh had immediately phoned Jack and they had agreed that the cloth should be given to Mubeen for comparison. His verdict had been quick—the fabric and the dye were identical to those used in the other three scarves.

Why would he do that? wondered Santosh. *Why tie a scarf to the steering wheel of investigating detectives? Nothing about him suggested he was into playing games with cops. The ritual was his thing.*

Santosh put aside his thoughts for a moment. He had to pay a visit to Priyanka Talati's former husband, accompanied by Jack.

Nothing in his life to date had prepared Jack for the ordeal of traveling on a Mumbai Local train. Santosh had suggested that it would be more efficient to reach Andheri—where Priyanka's ex lived—by train rather than car. He was absolutely right. Making the journey by commuter train cut the travel time by half. What

Santosh had avoided telling Jack was the fact that getting on or off a Mumbai Local train at most times of the day was a test that could easily have been devised by the toughest marine.

Transporting an incredible eight million commuters daily, the train was the very lifeline of Mumbai, but the notorious Mumbai Local had the ability to make people shudder simply to think about it. Trains were usually badly overcrowded with people packed inside like sardines. The doors rarely closed and passengers were often left hanging out, clutching the guard rails for dear life.

Thankfully their journey from Churchgate station to Andheri was uneventful because it was not rush hour. Even though they had been unable to find seats for half the journey, the train was not too overcrowded and they were able to find comfortable standing room.

While they were in the train, Santosh's phone rang. Holding the overhead bar with one hand, he passed his walking cane to Jack. Using his free hand, he pulled out the cell phone from his pocket. He looked at the screen to see who the caller was. Rupesh.

"We have a small problem," began Rupesh.

"What is it?" asked Santosh.

"That editor from the *Afternoon Mirror* has been sniffing around. So far we've succeeded in keeping under wraps the fact that the three murders are related. We'll be in a mess if this comes out."

"What prompted the snooping?" said Santosh.

"She received a yellow scarf in a package," said Rupesh. "As of now, she does not know the connection between the scarf and the three murders."

"How did it arrive?" asked Santosh. "By post, courier, or hand-delivery?"

"Plain Manila envelope, postmarked Mumbai GPO. We've checked for fingerprints. There are none."

"The address was handwritten?"

"Negative. Laser printer."

"No chance of any handwriting analysis. What do you suggest?"

"I say that we call another press conference and reveal a little more, but keep the key details to ourselves," proposed Rupesh. "At least that way we'll be in control of what goes out."

"I disagree," Santosh told him. "This killer wants publicity. The clues at the various scenes are the perfect ingredients for a juicy crime thriller. It's possible that Bhavna Choksi, the *Afternoon Mirror* reporter, was killed specifically with the intention of getting front-page visibility. The yellow scarf being sent to the tabloid's office proves that the perpetrator desperately wants column inches. Provide a spotlight and you will have dead bodies piling up even faster."

After persuading Rupesh not to take any further action until they'd had a chance to discuss it personally, Santosh hung up as the train rolled into Andheri station. From there they hailed a three-wheeled diesel-fume-spewing auto rickshaw to the address that Nisha had given them. It was the last known address of Priyanka's ex.

They trudged up the stairs to the fifth floor because the building's sole elevator was out of order, Santosh keeping up with Jack in spite of the cane. They rang the bell to an anonymous-looking door that bore only an apartment number. There was no response from within. Santosh rang the bell once again but still there was no answer. He knocked on the door with no success.

"Maybe he's out," said Jack. "Or he could have moved."

"Or he could be lying dead," countered Santosh. "We need to get inside."

Without hesitation, Jack kicked in the door with ease. Once a marine, always a marine.

The shattered door revealed an unlit passage beyond. Lying slumped on the ground was a disheveled man who looked as if he hadn't bathed for a month. His face was unshaven and his muddy-brown hair was almost shoulder-length. His nails were long and filthy, and a pungent odor of dried sweat emanated from his body.

"Firoze Quadri?" asked Santosh, as the man rubbed his eyes and scratched his week-old stubble.

"What if I am?" the man asked warily, an even more terrible smell emanating from his mouth. It was obvious that Quadri hadn't used a toothbrush for a long time.

"We need just a minute of your time, sir," said Jack, pulling up the dazed occupant by the scruff of his neck and almost carrying him further into the apartment before he could object.

It soon emerged that Priyanka's ex was a down-on-his-luck alcoholic. While married to her, he had tried his hand at a variety of jobs but had never been good at any of them—writer, artist, interior designer. Eventually he had realized that his only claim to fame was the fact that he was married to Priyanka. His male ego utterly bruised, he had taken to drink and had filled the nondrinking hours with violent outbursts directed at his famous wife. One day when he had returned home after a long night of drinking at the local bar, he'd found that Priyanka had left. The next day her lawyer had gotten in touch.

The apartment was an extremely valuable piece of real estate in a city where every square inch commanded an outrageous premium. Priyanka had been attempting to evict him and take back possession of the apartment, but the case was stuck in the backlog of the High Court of Bombay.

For the present, though, the valuable property was little better than a dump with empty beer bottles and cartons of partially consumed takeout meals strewn all over the place. The stench of rotting food was sickening. Jack opened a window and attempted to switch on the ceiling fan.

"Don't bother," said the drunk. "The electricity has been cut for nonpayment of bills."

Santosh had gone into ferret mode—sniffing around and turning over bottles and packages. He was wondering whether he might find a few yellow scarves lying around. "Did you know that your ex was murdered recently?" he asked, continuing his search. The dazed expression on Quadri's face made it quite evident that he had not heard the news.

"The bitch left me penniless," he snarled, not in the least bothered by the fact that his ex-wife had been tragically murdered. On the contrary, a smile of satisfaction crossed his face. "Since we haven't been officially divorced as yet, would you know whether I can claim a share of her estate?"

"Where were you on Monday night between eleven and midnight?" Santosh demanded, ignoring the question.

"Can't remember," mumbled the ex blankly, scratching his crotch.

"You do realize that your divorce proceedings with Priyanka give you a strong motive for her murder?" said Santosh, using his cane to scare away a lizard on the doorframe nearby.

"I never leave this place," replied the drunk. "Ask the neighbors or the security guards at the gate. I am always worried that the bitch may forcibly repossess the house while I'm out."

Jack looked at Santosh and shook his head, pointing to the empty alcohol bottles scattered all over the floor. They were wasting their time with Quadri.

Santosh agreed. Quadri had unkempt shoulder-length hair. It seemed unlikely that the man would leave a murder scene without shedding some of it. Furthermore the hair samples at all three murder sites had been short strands of black hair, not the muddy brown color of Quadri's.

While one could loathe Quadri, he was quite certainly not their man.

Chapter 32

THE MUSTACHE WAS prominent, and combined with his height and build it gave him an imposing air. He used a discreet entrance next to a private hospital. There was no sign to indicate that what lay beyond the door was a maze of barriers, soldiers, and sniffer dogs. A single plainclothes officer with a pistol tucked away under his jacket directed visitors into the complex that sported the look of a well-funded university—manicured lawns, sparkling fountains, and well-tended buildings.

The imposing man occupying the chair in the central office on the top floor was the chief of the Inter-Services Intelligence—or ISI. The Director General of Pakistan's premier intelligence service was a veteran, having served as a lieutenant general in the Pakistan Army. It was a powerful job, being the head of an organization that employed over ten thousand officers and staff members, not including informants and assets.

The Chief of Army Staff was his mentor, but occupying the post of Director General was always a balancing act. If one was too successful, one became a target of the political establishment. On the other hand, if one was incapable of delivering results then there were enough people baying for one's blood in the army.

Headquartered in Islamabad, the ISI had been responsible for supporting the Afghan Mujahideen against the Soviet Union in the erstwhile communist Afghanistan and later providing support to the Taliban against the Indo-Iranian-backed Northern Alliance in the civil war in Afghanistan. Most importantly, the ISI was involved in covert operations in Kashmir and other parts of India, having nurtured and supported several outfits on the ground there that gave the ISI much-needed deniability of its own role.

Inside the Director General's office was a massive desk capable of doubling up as an impromptu conference table. The Director General was holding a meeting with the head of the CAD—the Covert Action Division of the ISI—a youthful-looking man in his early forties.

"Do we have someone inside as yet or not?" asked the Director General, his voice tinged with a Punjabi accent.

"It has taken us several months," replied the CAD head smoothly, "but, yes, I am happy to report that we finally do have access to Private."

A smile hovered on the Director General's face. "It will give me the greatest pleasure to see that outfit destroyed. Three key operations in India have been botched by the interference of that lot," he said. "The train blasts, the hotel attack and the Air India hijack . . . In all instances we've had operatives captured or killed."

"In that case, should I proceed with the next part of my plan?" asked the CAD head.

"Yes. If you have managed to penetrate the organization,

then start making arrangements for the next phase. Use the Indian Mujahideen network to handle logistics," responded the Director General, drawing in a deep breath of nicotine and tar. "By the way, who is this man who has managed to get inside the fortress?"

"He is a Muslim from the medical fraternity. He has strong anti-American leanings and is thus the perfect candidate for the job," replied the CAD man.

"Good," said the Director General. "Keep me posted regarding your progress."

Chapter 33

THE HAJI ALI Mosque was a unique structure in Mumbai's architectural landscape. Built on an islet off the coast of Worli in the southern part of Mumbai, it was only accessible via a narrow causeway that ran for a distance of five hundred meters through the sea. During high tide the mosque was cut off from the mainland when the causeway was entirely submerged. Sensibly, Mubeen had made sure that he reached the mosque well within low-tide hours.

As he neared the whitewashed structure, he could see the eighty-five-foot-high minaret—a familiar feature on Mumbai's sunset skyline. Upon arriving at the islet, he used the sculpted entrance to reach the marble courtyard containing the central shrine. He paused for a moment before the tomb, covered by a red-, green-, and gold-embroidered sheet and supported by a silver frame. He mouthed a silent prayer before making his way to the men's prayer hall. Here he stood in a corner, silently reading the ninety-nine names of Allah that made up the Arabic patterns on the marble pillars.

The prayer hall of Haji Ali gave Mubeen a feeling of comfort. It allowed him to silently grieve for his son and remember happier times with his wife. It allowed him to draw sustenance from the prayers that surrounded him. He was particularly grateful for the presence of Sufi singers who filled the air with sweet melodies in honor of Allah.

"What makes man so cruel?" he asked himself. After pondering the question for a while, he realized there was no single answer that could adequately address the question. At that moment, he kneeled down on his prayer mat, faced west toward Mecca, and raised his hands to his ears, chanting, *"Allahu Akbar,"* and thus drowning out the pain of what he had undergone in America.

Chapter 34

THE POSH SCHOOL for girls was very quiet at this hour. Even though it was a day school and none of the students remained on the premises after hours, the principal never left. The vast grounds had ceded space to accommodate a corner cottage for the principal. Separated from the volleyball court by a thick hedge and mango orchard, the cottage was a substantial perk afforded to the person lucky enough to occupy the post. Established by a Scottish missionary many years before Indian Independence, the school was one of the most prestigious girls' academies in Mumbai.

There was never any reason for the principal to worry about security because the entire five-acre plot in the western suburbs of Mumbai was cordoned off by a high wall and barbed-wire fences. There was only one gate to the entire complex and a team of well-trained security guards patrolled it around the clock.

Within the walls and barbed-wire fences were build-ings housing the classrooms, cafeteria, library, gymnasium, auditorium, laboratories, and swimming pools. A football field, cricket pitch, volleyball court, and tennis court occupied the remaining land.

Inside the principal's cottage there were two floors. The lower one contained the living room, dining room, and kitchen, the upper floor two en suite bedrooms. Adjacent to the principal's cottage were staff quarters containing a bedroom and bathroom for any domestic help that the principal chose to employ.

Inside the larger bedroom facing the front garden, the principal, Mrs. Elina Xavier—a widow in her mid fifties—was fast asleep. Given that it was the third day of the school's annual examination week, Mrs. Xavier had taken time off to visit Mahim Church. Getting inside on a Wednesday could be a test of perseverance because of the long queue of devotees waiting for admission. Mrs. Xavier had been exhausted by the visit—particularly given the fact that she was undergoing the last few chemotherapy sessions that had been prescribed by her oncologist.

The full-time maid who cooked Mrs. Xavier's meals and did the household chores was also asleep in the adjacent staff quarters. A few hours after Mrs. Xavier had slipped into dreamland, there came a very soft creaking noise in the cottage as one of the doors of the closet in the smaller bedroom opened slowly. Someone stepped out of this and tiptoed across the room to the door. The trespasser had been inside the closet for over five hours, having entered the house earlier in the day as part of the school's outsourced housekeeping team.

Crossing the narrow passage that separated the two bedrooms, the intruder opened the door to the master bedroom and glanced over to where the substantial body of Mrs. Xavier lay asleep, heaving and snoring. Wearing a maintenance boiler suit, shower cap, and rubber gloves, the intruder approached the bed, holding a yellow scarf in one hand, and in the other a plastic bag containing a carton of hard-boiled eggs.

Placing the bag on a side table by the bed, the prowler slipped the scarf around the principal's neck and pulled on both ends firmly. Mrs. Xavier woke from her dreams only to find that she was in the midst of a nightmare. She gasped for air but her windpipe was obstructed. Her terrified eyes pleaded for mercy but there was none forthcoming. She reached out with both hands to try to free her neck from the excruciating grip of the garrote but all strength seemed to have abandoned her. The strangler continued to pull until Mrs. Xavier's body went limp.

Staring at her bulging eyes, the killer felt an inner rage bubble up. Spitting on her face, the perpetrator called her a cunt and a whore. Quickly realizing the mistake, the murderer went back to the closet, retrieved a tissue, sprayed it with bleach, and used it to carefully remove any traces of saliva from her face.

The intruder then headed over to the thermostat unit near the bedroom door and adjusted the temperature to the highest possible setting. The carton was removed from the bag and each egg carefully placed on the bed. Soon Mrs. Xavier's body was surrounded by a dozen eggs, arranged in an oval around her.

Chapter 35

SANTOSH WAS LIVID. His face was flushed red and he was breathing heavily as he strode into Rupesh's office. He threw down a newspaper on the desk and asked, "How do I solve this case if you do not heed my advice?"

"No idea what you are talking about," said Rupesh, picking up the paper casually to read the front page.

YELLOW GARROTE KILLINGS, read the headline of the *Afternoon Mirror*. The article went on to reveal that three murders in the city—including one involving the newspaper's reporter, Bhavna Choksi—had been perpetrated by a strangler who left a signature yellow scarf at the crime scene. The story went on to say that the police were covering up the news in order to avoid having to answer questions about their inefficient and half-hearted investigations. The report had been picked up by Indian newswires and every hack in town was now chasing the story.

"I took your advice," said Rupesh, slowly and deliberately

chewing on a lump of tobacco in his mouth. "I did not speak with any reporter."

"I find that difficult to believe," countered Santosh. "You pick up a phone and tell me about a reporter with suspicions. I request you to avoid answering her questions. In less than a day it's front-page material."

Rupesh folded the newspaper calmly and stood up. "Think about it, Santosh," he said. "If I had given this reporter an exclusive, why the fuck would she trash the cops? This story makes it bloody difficult for me to handle the flak that will come my way from the Police Commissioner and the Home Minister. Tell me, why would I want to put myself in such a mess?"

Santosh was silent as he digested Rupesh's reasonable argument. "I would suggest that you should look within your own team and see if someone has been indiscreet," suggested Rupesh craftily as Santosh attempted a graceful exit.

As soon as he was out of the room, Rupesh picked up his cell phone and dialed a number. "*Namaskar bhau*," he said by way of greeting when Munna answered his gold-plated phone.

"Did you leak the story?" asked Rupesh, almost whispering.

Munna laughed. "When one has been sitting in the pub all day, one often takes a leak. I have no need for the other variety," he said mischievously.

Chapter 36

NOT MUCH HAD changed in the newsroom of the *Afternoon Mirror*. It was mostly as it had been twenty-five years ago when established by a wealthy Parsi industrialist. But the newsroom had been a hive of activity the previous day.

There were sixteen desks, clustered in groups of four. Each desk was designated for specific verticals—politics, entertainment, city news, business, sports and the like. Toward one corner of the newsroom was the glass-walled office occupied by the paper's chain-smoking editor.

She had picked up the receiver of her desk phone without a second thought. In her profession, it was common to spend the better part of the day on calls.

"Am I speaking to Jamini—editor of the *Afternoon Mirror*?" a male voice had asked. It had a mysterious quality to it. Commanding yet slightly nervous; strong yet wavering.

"Yes, you are," the editor had replied, stubbing out her

half-smoked cigarette into the overflowing ashtray on her desk. "Who is this?"

"Did you like the gift that I sent you?" the voice had said, not bothering to offer any introduction.

Jamini had suddenly been on full alert. A parcel containing a yellow scarf had been received by her in the morning and she'd immediately realized that the caller was referring to this.

"What is the scarf for?" Jamini had asked, trying to keep the conversation going as she signaled through the glass walls for her senior reporter to come inside. *Find out if you can trace this call*, she'd scribbled on a piece of paper that she hurriedly handed to him.

"Do not bother tracing this call," the voice had said. "It is a prepaid SIM registered to a false identity. It will tell you nothing about me."

Jamini had realized that she was dealing with a highly intelligent individual. "I'm not interested in tracing the call," she'd lied. "I simply want to know if there is a story in this for me."

"That pesky reporter—Bhavna Choksi—was killed with a yellow scarf, just like the one you received earlier today. Is that story enough for you?"

"That still doesn't explain why you are calling me," the editor had said, warming to the game. "Bhavna was no friend of mine . . . only an employee. Why should the manner of her death be a story?"

"What if I told you that the singer—Priyanka Talati—was also killed in the same manner? Is *that* a story?" the confident voice had asked.

"It could be," the editor had said, attempting to hide her excitement. Her colleague from the newsroom had returned with a slip of paper reading: *Have spoken with crime branch. They're trying to pinpoint the location. Stay on the line.*

"What more do you want?" the voice had asked.

Jamini had been about to reply when the line had gone dead. "Hello?" she'd asked, a tad desperately, but had realized that the caller had hung up.

Just as she'd thought that she had blown it, her phone had rung once again. "It's me calling from a different number," the voice had said. "I don't trust your type."

"Did you kill Bhavna Choksi and Priyanka Talati?" Jamini had asked, scribbling notes on the ruled pad in front of her.

"Absolutely. All three murders have happened in Mumbai, all executed by the same person, in the same manner. The police are covering it up to prevent panic."

"Who is the third? You mentioned Bhavna Choksi and Priyanka Talati," Jamini had said rapidly.

"A foreign doctor. Her name was Kanya Jaiyen. She was staying at the Marine Bay Plaza Hotel when she was killed."

"Why were the women murdered?" Jamini had asked.

"I have done my duty by calling you and telling you that all three murders are connected," the voice had said. "Do some part of the fucking investigation yourself!"

The second call had lasted less than a minute.

Chapter 37

THE MAN WAS extremely thin, almost gaunt. His eyes seemed to pop out of his face due to the fact that there wasn't an ounce of extra flesh anywhere on his body. His delicate looks belied his intent, though. He was the chief of the Indian Mujahideen—an Islamist militant group dedicated to carrying out attacks against the Indian state—and one of the most feared individuals among those in the know about terrorism.

Investigations by security agencies had revealed that the Indian Mujahideen was actually a front for the Pakistan-based Lashkar-e-Taiba. The avowed purpose of the Lashkar was to create an Islamic caliphate across South Asia and, to that end, it had been sponsoring acts of terror in Kashmir as well as other parts of India, having been provided with moral, strategic, and financial support by Pakistan's premier intelligence agency, the ISI.

The gaunt man exited the taxi and waited at the corner of Jai Prakash Road and Yari Road in the Versova district of Mumbai.

Less than a minute later a black Mercedes-Benz pulled up beside him. Due to the dark sunblinds the occupant within was not visible to the outside world.

The front door opened and a bodyguard jumped out. He quickly patted down the gaunt man and opened the rear door for him. The Indian Mujahideen man got inside. Already ensconced in the rear was the owner of the vehicle.

"I am only meeting you because I like to consider all business proposals," said the vehicle's owner. "So speak."

"Mumbai is your fiefdom," replied the thin man. "Anything and everything is possible once you decide to make it happen."

"What do you want?" asked Munna impatiently.

"I require thirty kilograms of RDX," explained the Mujahideen man. "I am willing to pay a premium for the right quality, delivered to the right place at the right time."

"And what makes you think that I can supply that?" asked Munna, playing innocent in his trademark style.

The thin man smiled. "Your reputation is glorious. Your name is mentioned in reverence not only in India but also in Pakistan. I am told that the only reliable source in India is you."

Munna lit a cigarette with his solid gold lighter. He took a deep puff, exhaled, and thought about the matter for a minute. Without any warning, he stubbed out the cigarette on the Mujahideen man's hand.

The man screamed in agony as the cigarette seared his skin. Munna laughed. "You can barely handle the heat of a cigarette. What makes you so cocky about handling thirty kilos of deadly explosives?"

The thin man cradled his burned hand in the other and, ignoring the pain, replied: "In your interest and mine, it is better that this transaction should remain a business one only.

You do not need to know more than I have told you. Name your price."

Within a moment, Munna's vise-like grip was at the other man's throat. Munna continued to clutch it with one hand, allowing his prey an occasional gasp for breath. Just as the thin man thought that he would pass out, Munna let go abruptly.

"I may have my faults, but I do not do business with terrorists. Got that?" he said gruffly. "Why on earth would you think I would support a terrorist attack—on Indian soil?"

The gaunt man tried one last angle. "Perhaps if I were to tell you the target?"

Munna looked at him, eyebrows raised.

"Go on," he said.

PART TWO

Chapter 38

2006

SANTOSH REMEMBERED THAT week vividly. It was impossible to forget.

Seven bomb blasts had taken place during a period of eleven minutes in Mumbai starting at 6:25 p.m. The bombs had been set off on trains running along the Western Line of the railway network and had gone off in the vicinity of suburban railway stations— Matunga, Mahim, Bandra, Khar, Jogeshwari, Bhayander, and Borivali. Pressure cookers had been used to increase the afterburn of the thermobaric explosions. During those eleven minutes, two hundred and nine people had been killed and over seven hundred injured.

The Prime Minister had called a high-level security meeting at his residence. In attendance were the Home Minister, National Security Advisor, Home Secretary, and Chiefs of the Intelligence Agencies. Accompanying the chief of RAW to that meeting was a much younger and less wise Santosh.

"Around three hundred and fifty people have been detained for questioning," the Home Minister informed the Prime Minister.

"But do we have any serious leads?" he asked.

"The Indian Mujahideen is our strongest suspect," said the RAW chief. "Telephone intercepts show a very high volume of calls between India and Pakistan during the period leading up to the blasts."

"But can we be sure of Pakistani involvement?"

"May I say something, sir?" asked Santosh. The Prime Minister looked at the young man, paused for a moment, and then nodded. Santosh avoided eye contact with his boss, who had specifically instructed him to remain quiet throughout the meeting.

"Sir, the forensic science laboratory has carried out chromatography and has confirmed that a mixture of RDX and ammonium nitrate was used for the bombings. We are also fairly certain that all the explosives were planted at Churchgate railway station, the starting point of all the affected trains."

"What is your point?" asked the Prime Minister.

"My point is that the presence of RDX indicates that there would have been some support from the ISI."

The meeting at the Prime Minister's residence lasted less than an hour. It wound up when an email was received by a TV channel claiming that sixteen terror operatives had been used to plant the bombs and that a local subgroup of the Indian Mujahideen had claimed responsibility.

A memorial service was held a week later in Mumbai at 6:25 p.m. local time, the exact moment that the blasts had started. The President of India raised his hand to his forehead in salute and led a two-minute silence as candles and wreaths were placed at all the affected railway stations. Santosh was at Bandra railway station at that time, his head bowed in silence.

In front of him was a crowd of people who had gathered to pay *their respects to the victims. A little boy ran from his father's grip and was about to fall from the platform onto the tracks when a young woman in uniform managed to catch him.*

"Thank you—a million times," said the grateful father to Nisha as Santosh looked on.

"Listen to your dad," she said to the young boy. "He loves you. Just ask an orphan and she will tell you how empty life can be."

Chapter 39

TODAY, SCHOOL WAS out. The ring-round system had been implemented and the girls told to stay at home. Those who'd slipped through the net had turned up to find a notice on the school gates—and beyond the gates police cars littering the drive. And perhaps, if they looked very carefully, the black Honda Civics of the Private India team.

Inside the school, Santosh took a deep breath, leaned on his cane, and stared at the body on the bed. Nisha stood by his side, waiting for her boss to speak, for the cogs of his mind to start turning. Cops moved around them, Mubeen directing them. Camera flashes strobed the room.

"Name is Elina Xavier," said Nisha by his side, "she's the school principal. Or was."

"His fourth victim," said Santosh, almost to himself.

"He's really getting a taste for it, isn't he?"

"No," said Santosh, almost sharply, "this has nothing

whatsoever to do with a taste for killing. The deaths themselves . . . look at it . . ."

He took a step forward, indicating the body on the bed with the point of his cane. "The killer enjoys the act of killing, and I dare say it excites in him intense emotions, but he hasn't changed his modus operandi. There is no experimental edge to them."

She looked at him. "'Experimental edge'?"

"If you enjoy painting, do you paint the same picture every time?" he asked her. "Does a photographer take the same photo?"

"But he doesn't do the same thing each time," said Nisha. "Each time the ritual changes."

"Exactly," said Santosh. His eyes gleamed. "But the ritual is post-mortem. The murder is the same each time. The art is in the ritual, and that is very important, Nisha. That tells us something. It tells us that we should be paying very close attention indeed to the ritual."

"The eggs," said Nisha.

"Indeed, the eggs. And the heat. You notice how hot it is in the room?"

Nisha nodded.

"It's a story he's telling us, Nisha," said Santosh, turning to leave. "And he'll keep on going until he reaches the end of his tale."

Chapter 40

JACK MORGAN WAS seated on a folding director's chair while the director herself ran around barking instructions like a woman possessed. The movie involved a star-studded cast and Lara Omprakash was at her cajoling best, attempting to squeeze the finest performances out of her actors.

Lara had suggested that Jack drop in and spend the day with her at Film City, an integrated complex boasting several studios, recording rooms, gardens, lakes, theaters, and open ground for larger custom-built sets.

The shot neared completion. Lara shouted: "Cut! It's a wrap," and high-fived the executive producer.

"Let's have some lunch while we still can," she said to Jack, leading him away from the buzzing set to her luxurious vanity van. "I have to shoot a cameo appearance for the film and will be needed by makeup and wardrobe in a short while."

The van had been customized for her on a truck chassis fourteen meters long that could be compressed to half the size when it was on the road. The vanity offered Lara the comfort of a lounge, kitchenette, gym, office, bedroom, and washroom.

The driver of the van—Bhosale—switched on the generator that powered the beast and asked if she needed anything. Lara tipped him and told him to go have his lunch as she and Jack settled down in the lounge. She opened the refrigerator and took out a chilled beer for Jack and an orange juice for herself. "My cook has prepared Greek salad, quiche, chicken and mayo sandwiches, and banana bread," she said, pulling out the food and placing it on a walnut-veneered dining table.

Jack helped himself to the beer and settled into a plush leather massage chair. Lara laughed. "You always loved being massaged," she joked.

"And you were always happy to offer the service," retorted Jack, smiling. It was evident that the two had shared substantially more than a business relationship.

Lara put down her glass on the table and sat next to Jack on one of the arms of the massage chair. She reached over and began to knead his shoulders. Jack felt the tension in his muscles easing.

"Why didn't you stay on with me in LA?" he asked softly.

"You knew that I would eventually leave," replied Lara. "Mumbai, Bollywood . . . this is my life. Yes, what we had was great while it lasted, Jack, but I could never have made LA my life."

She slipped into the chair until she was in Jack's lap. He held her in his arms as she snuggled into his body. A moment later their lips were locked in a passionate kiss. Jack's hands moved toward Lara's breasts. Unexpectedly, she broke away, got up, adjusted her clothes, and ran her fingers through her hair.

"What happened?" he asked, slightly bewildered.

"This place isn't private enough," said Lara. "I feel as though we're being watched. Let's meet for dinner at my place where we can carry on our conversation." She smiled.

"What conversation?" asked Jack playfully, reaching for a sandwich.

Fifteen minutes later, he was comfortably ensconced in the chauffeur-driven Mercedes-Benz that Santosh had arranged for him, and around an hour later he was back at the Private India office.

In Santosh's room he plonked himself down on one of the visitors' chairs. Santosh was his usual gloomy self. He began to pace around the moment Jack sat down.

"What's the matter?" Jack asked curiously.

"Were you just with Lara Omprakash?" Santosh inquired.

"Yes. I left her about an hour ago. I'm meeting her later tonight though."

Santosh remained quiet and contemplative. After a substantial pause he said, "I need to tell you something, Jack."

"Sure, Santosh, what's the matter?" asked Jack, leaning forward in his chair.

"I have just had a call from Rupesh," replied Santosh, choosing his words carefully. "Around thirty minutes ago, Lara Omprakash was discovered—strangled—inside her vanity van."

Chapter 41

THE DRIVE TO Film City passed in silence. Jack was in shock. A part of him was simply unable to believe that Lara had been killed. He had tried to convince himself over many years that what they had was just a casual fling, but seeing her in Mumbai had awakened feelings that he could not understand. He was not in control of himself, and Jack Morgan—ex-marine—hated that.

Jack, Santosh, and Nisha reached Lara's vanity van and saw that the police had taped off the entire area. Rupesh was standing at the door, barking orders to his men. The place was swarming with khaki-clad policemen.

Rupesh wordlessly made way for them to enter. On the sofa inside the lounge of the vanity van was the body of Lara Omprakash. She was dressed in the same clothes that she had been wearing during the morning shoot—jeans with an Indian-silk kurta top. The familiar yellow garrote was around her neck and a bluish hue in her skin at the point of strangulation was discernible. Her body had been left in a semi-upright position on the sofa.

"What's that on her lap?" asked Santosh, his eyes scanning the crime scene almost in slow motion. "What is it?"

Nisha kneeled down near Lara's body and looked at the object on her lap. It was a plastic baby doll. One of the hands of the doll had been tied to Lara's with string so that it would not fall off.

What's inside your sick, perverted mind? thought Santosh. *Why was Lara Omprakash your fifth victim? Is there a predetermined order in which you are proceeding? How are you choosing them? What do these symbols mean? How do you . . . ?*

Jack's voice brought Santosh out of his trance. "Where is the driver?" he asked. "When I was here earlier, Lara tipped him and told him to go have his lunch."

"He's missing," replied Rupesh. "We've put out an alert to trace him."

There was an uncomfortable pause. Turning to Santosh, Rupesh said, "I cannot allow this investigation to remain with Private India any longer."

"Why?" asked Santosh.

"Your boss—Mr. Morgan—spent the first half of the day with Lara Omprakash," replied Rupesh. "He was in her vanity van for quite some time before he left. I have no option but to include him as a possible suspect. That being the case, leaving this investigation with Private India would create a conflict of interest."

"You've got to be joking, Rupesh," said Santosh. "Jack was not even in India during the previous murders. He reached here only on the day of the Filmfare Awards."

"Ah, but that isn't true," said Rupesh. "Information I have received from immigration authorities at Chhatrapati Shivaji

Airport shows that Mr. Morgan arrived a full two days before the Filmfare Awards. In fact, he was here in town when the first murder was committed—Sunday night."

"Is this true, Jack?" said Santosh softly.

His boss nodded silently.

"What brought you here on Sunday? And why did you keep it a secret from me?" asked Santosh.

"I'm not at liberty to discuss that at the present moment," said Jack, staring intently and rather defiantly at Rupesh.

The policeman had a triumphant look on his face. "I shall need you to surrender your passport to me, Mr. Morgan. You are not at liberty to leave the country till such time as our investigations are complete. Is that clear?"

Jack reached inside his jacket and handed over his passport to Rupesh without demur.

"I will need all the evidence and investigation reports that you have accumulated so far in this case," Rupesh instructed Santosh. "Where are Mubeen and Hari?"

"They're still bagging evidence at the principal's cottage in the girls' school," explained Nisha. "They should be back in the office within an hour."

"Fine. I shall expect all information to be fully shared with my team at headquarters no later than today," replied Rupesh, placing Jack's passport into his pocket and simultaneously searching for something else. He was unable to find what he was looking for. Calling out to one of his constables, he barked an order.

"Bring the tobacco," he said as he escorted the Private India team out of the van.

Chapter 42

THE TWO MEN strolled along Chowpatty Beach. It was evident that they were not friends, more likely business acquaintances. Chowpatty Beach, though, was an odd choice of location for a business meeting.

Apart from Juhu Beach in the suburbs, Chowpatty had always been Mumbai's favorite leisure area. During working hours it remained the haunt of the contentedly jobless, who would nap under the canopy of its dwarfish trees. At sunset, though, its character turned distinctly carnival-like, with children screaming for Ferris wheel spins and pony rides. There was entertainment for adults too. Pavement astrologers, palmists, and fortune-tellers would target hapless tourists and for a fee tell them whatever they wanted to hear. Monkey shows, street plays, tightrope walkers, and gymnasts displaying incredible yogic positions would take over the beach, while at the other end a row of *bhelpuri* shops selling Mumbai's most famous street snack—roasted puffed rice and fried semolina, drenched in sweet-and-sour chutney—would do brisk sales as hordes of hungry visitors took time off from the drudgery of their day-to-day lives.

It was unexpected to catch sight of Santosh strolling along the beach with an unidentified man. His companion was enjoying a *kulfi*—a traditional Indian ice cream—on a stick. The man was neatly dressed in a short-sleeved shirt, casual cotton slacks, and soft leather loafers. He wore all the accessories of a privileged lifestyle—designer sunglasses, expensive wristwatch, and pen. Such things usually acted like magnets for the pickpockets and petty thieves that dominated the Chowpatty stretch, but this particular man would never be a target. Every beggar, performer, and pickpocket in the crowd knew that it would be foolish to target the man in question.

There was only one peculiarity that made him distinct from the rest. It was the fact that his left arm had been amputated at the elbow. The story of the man's rise to his present position was almost the stuff of legend and the street dwellers talked of it with awe.

Escaping from a drunk and violent father in the rural heartland, he had arrived in Mumbai on a train as an eleven-year-old boy. When he had got off the train at Mumbai Central station, he had been tired, disoriented, and broke. He had spent the next couple of hours begging for food until, miraculously, a middle-aged couple had approached him. They had given him hot tea and samosas, promising him that they would help him earn a better life. Unfortunately, he had not realized that the food was drugged.

He had soon been placed in a taxi and taken to one of the municipal hospitals of Mumbai, where a doctor had been bribed to amputate his healthy arm. He had been deliberately handicapped so that he could be used as an object of pity, begging at street corners, traffic lights, and the religious sites of Mumbai. This was part of an organized racket known as the begging syndicate, and the boy spent the next five years of his life doing precisely that. At the end of each day, his handler would round up the unfortunate kids he had put on the streets and siphon off the daily take, leaving them with next to nothing.

Unlike the hundreds of other kids who were mutilated, blinded, or maimed so that they could be used in this way, this particular boy had a unique talent. He was a great team leader. He was soon able to organize all the teenage boys of his area into a cohesive group and was thus able to send their handler packing. When the bosses of the syndicate got word of this, they sent in their thugs to intimidate the kids. It was the thugs who ended up with wounds inflicted by acid-filled bulbs flung at them by the kids. The boy who had started out as a victim had himself morphed into a gang leader.

The boy, however, had remained a Robin Hood at heart. Unlike the ruthless customs of the begging syndicate, the boy's methods included sharing fifty percent of the take with each beggar. If the weekly take was lower than average, then the beggar would have to make up the loss the following week. Repeated drops in take meant expulsion from the group and being permanently barred from those areas that they controlled. In effect, it was old-fashioned carrot-and-stick theory, a management system of incentives and disincentives. The beggars who worked in his team were not allowed access to solvents, alcohol, or *charras*—Afghan hashish laced with opium—whereas under the syndicate glue-sniffing, drink, and drugs had been encouraged so as to keep the kids under control.

Over the next eight years, almost all key areas of Mumbai

became his territory and the beggar unwittingly turned CEO. Santosh had met him while investigating a case during his days at RAW and had cultivated him as an important resource. The well-dressed amputee—along with his team of over ten thousand beggars—now constituted Santosh's eyes and ears in Mumbai. He was the reason that Santosh could walk the streets at any time of the day or night without having to watch his back.

Santosh silently handed over a photograph of the cap-wearing individual caught on CCTV exiting Kanya Jaiyen's hotel room. "Could you pass that around to the boys and let me know if this chap shows up?"

The man did not look at the photograph. He simply folded it and placed it in his shirt pocket.

"Any information regarding our mutual friend?" asked Santosh.

"That rascal Rupesh has tried everything in the book to break me but he has been spectacularly unsuccessful," said the other man, grinning broadly. "He thinks that I don't know about his dealings on the side with Munna. But I know for a fact that Munna wants to control not only Mumbai's drugs, gambling, liquor, and prostitution but also the city's begging network. I ain't ceding my territory quite that easily."

"Rupesh is on Munna's payroll?" asked Santosh.

"Can't be sure, but they have met a few times," said the young man slyly, accepting a packet of cash from Santosh. "Munna met with a man who is known to be a member of the Indian Mujahideen. My boys told me that Munna told him to fuck off . . . almost threw him out of his car."

Why would an Indian Mujahideen member wish to meet Munna? wondered Santosh as he continued strolling along the beach with his amputee associate.

Chapter 43

I ALLOW THE water to run. It fills the old tub noisily. The sound of splashing reverberates through the room. I shut off the faucet once the water reaches the brim and kneel down in front of the tub, placing my hands on its edge. I lean forward and allow my face to touch the water. I allow my head to be immersed entirely. I leave my eyes open so that I can see beneath the surface and feel the sensation. Baptism!

The truth is that human lungs were never designed to squeeze oxygen from water. But for someone struggling below the surface, it is an instinctive reaction to draw water into the larynx. The irony, of course, is that the water intake only serves to cut off the supply of life-giving oxygen, thus resulting in death. Birth, death, and rebirth . . . baptism!

I hold my breath to prevent the water from hitting my lungs and force myself to stay immersed. There is no struggle, no panic. I am fully conscious and entirely in control. I count the seconds quietly in my head. These days I can count to two hundred and fifty without passing out. I pull my head out of the water and suck in air gratefully.

One only realizes the value of air when one is deprived of it and one only begins to value life in the face of death.

I actually feel sorry for Jack Morgan. So many raging hormones within . . . desperately yearning for union with the warm, inviting body of dear Lara, only to be served up her cold corpse instead. Deprivation yet again. What a tragic turn of events!

I look up at my wall. The front-page story is fixed on it with sticky tape. I am in the limelight now . . . that gift to the editor did the trick. Someday I will be even more celebrated and they will worship me like a deity. My mother always predicted that I would be famous.

One day a neighborhood child snatched my toy. My mother held me to her chest and calmed me down. She then made me look into her mirror. "Do you see your face?" she asked. "It's so very beautiful. It will take you places."

But those moments were few and far between.

Yes, Mother, I am famous now. Just like you predicted. I am living my dream . . . or is it your nightmare?

Chapter 44

THE MOOD AT Private India was somber. The senior team had assembled in the conference room at Jack's request.

"First of all, I must clarify the fact that I knew Lara from her days in LA," he began. "My initial contact with her was on a case, but once the assignment was over we ended up becoming friends and soon we were romantically involved. There was absolutely nothing I wouldn't do to protect Lara."

"Jack, you are embarrassing us. Not a single person in this room believes that you are a suspect," said Santosh, absent-mindedly playing with his walking cane. "The suspicion is only in Rupesh's mind."

"The news from the grapevine," began Nisha, "is that Rupesh's boss—the Mumbai Police Commissioner—put pressure on him to hand over the investigation to Private India initially even though Rupesh personally was against it."

"That seems strange," said Santosh. "Rupesh called the Commissioner while I waited. It was he who sought permission for us to take the lead."

"Rupesh wanted to retain control of the investigation," said Nisha. "It was the Commissioner who was keen to pass it on to Private India."

"Even so, how does that make a difference?" asked Jack.

"Well," replied Nisha, "the Commissioner has now been kicked upstairs and will soon be taking over as Director General of Police—a nonjob if ever there was one! Rupesh was simply waiting for an opportunity to snatch the case from us. With the Commissioner going, your presence in Lara's van on the day of her murder was the perfect excuse for him to act."

"Be that as it may," said Jack, "this case is no longer just another investigation for Private India. This is now personal. I have lost one of my dearest friends and we are not going to give up on finding the perpetrator, irrespective of whether we're officially on the case or not."

"Rupesh wants us to submit all our findings and reports to him in the next few hours," Nisha reminded them.

"And so we shall," interjected Santosh. "Give him whatever he wants, but make sure that you have copies and backups of everything so that our own investigation can continue—with or without Rupesh's blessing."

"What about the evidence collected from Principal Elina Xavier's murder scene?" asked Mubeen.

"Expedite your analysis so that you can return the physical evidence to Rupesh. As usual, retain copies of your findings," replied Santosh, nudging Jack to get up.

He wanted their boss to return to his hotel and get some rest. Jack was staying at the Taj Mahal Hotel and Santosh's apartment was close by, less than a ten-minute walk from the Private India office in Colaba.

The streets wore a festive look because most of Mumbai was celebrating Navratri—the Festival of Nine Nights—an extravaganza to honor the power of the Hindu mother goddess Durga. All along their route, small kiosks and makeshift temples had been erected and were decked out with flowers and bright electric lights.

"C'mon, I'll show you what Navratri celebration is all about before I drop you off at the hotel," said Santosh, grasping Jack's elbow to steer him into some open ground. Hundreds of young men and women had gathered there to dance the *Dandiya*—a form of dancing traditionally performed during the festival. Jack noticed that the men and women, each holding two short sticks in their hands, were dancing in concentric circles. On every fourth beat the sticks would clash together in order to complement the music in the background.

In one corner of the ground a huge canopy had been constructed, under which sat a massive statue of Durga. Around the statue hundreds of worshipers sang devotional songs, danced, lit earthen lamps or incense, offered flowers, and recited prayers. The expression on Durga's face was angry. Jack was curious despite his dazed and drained condition after Lara's death.

"Durga, despite the terrifying imagery with which she is depicted, is not a malevolent deity," explained Santosh patiently. "For the ancient Hindu seers she was simply the goddess of time and transformation, who could help one understand the cycle of creation, life, death, and rebirth. To the uneducated, however, she was something entirely different. The Durga of medieval times was thirsty for human blood and could only be satisfied through human or animal sacrifice."

Santosh continued to explain the characteristics of Durga

to Jack as he stood transfixed before the large statue. At that moment Santosh saw something that he had been missing all along. It sent shivers down his spine.

Chapter 45

"WHAT'S THE MATTER, Santosh?" asked Jack, realizing suddenly that they had been standing in front of the statue for a long time. Santosh seemed to be staring fixedly at the idol's hands.

His heart was beating wildly as he grabbed Jack's arm like a man possessed, hurried out of the celebration grounds and hailed a cab—wildly waving it down with his walking stick. He was still waving it inside the cab, urging the driver to get a move on.

"I thought you wanted to walk," began Jack, but Santosh ignored his boss.

"Take us to the Town Hall, and there's an extra fifty in it for you if we're there within five minutes . . . five minutes!" he instructed the cabbie. He then took out his cell phone and dialed Nisha, barking instructions. Jack was left wondering if there was some truth in the rumors that he had appointed a lunatic as his Indian bureau chief.

With its vintage parquet floors, grand spiral staircases, wrought-iron loggias, and exquisite marble statues of forgotten city fathers, the white-colonnaded Town Hall was perhaps one of the most splendid and imposing of Mumbai's heritage monuments. The cabbie dropped them off at the base of the stairs leading up to the magnificent building. Nisha arrived at the same time in another cab.

"Why have we come here?" she asked breathlessly, having run part of the way due to the urgency of Santosh's summons.

"It's not the Town Hall that we're interested in," he said as they began walking up the stairs. "This particular building also houses the Asiatic Society, which has a collection of close to one million books, some of them priceless antiques. We should easily find the one that I need."

The Asiatic Library had separate sections housing different treasures. An impressive numismatic collection of over a thousand ancient coins including a rare gold *mohur* belonging to the most famous Mughal emperor—Akbar—was also housed in the building. Of course, the collection was not open to public view but the library was accessible to all. Santosh ignored the direction signs and headed for the reading room, the fading grandeur of which attracted many senior citizens who sat under the ancient ceiling fans poring over local newspapers.

"What are we looking for?" asked Nisha, as they entered the library and headed toward the central desk.

"Tell the chief librarian that we need a book by M. D. Jayant and Naveen Gupta," replied Santosh. "I can't remember the title but it's an illustrated book that explains the nine avatars of Durga." Nisha returned a couple of minutes later with a slip of paper on which the librarian had written the rack number where the book could be found.

Having located *The Nine Durga Avatars of Hinduism*, they sat down at an illuminated desk. Nisha began to read aloud the relevant passages to both men as softly as she could.

"The mother goddess—Durga—has three basic forms and each of these has three manifestations thus resulting in a total of nine avatars. Each night of the nine-day festival of Navratri is dedicated to one of the nine avatars—"

"Yes, yes, I know that," said Santosh impatiently. "I want to know what each avatar looks like."

Nisha quickly leafed through the book and found the chapter that described the first avatar of Durga. She was known by the name Shailputri. Turning the pages further, they saw an illustration showing what Shailputri looked like. There was a moment of hushed awe when they saw the image of the avatar holding a trident in one hand and a lotus flower in the other.

"Look at that," said Santosh, pointing to the mount of the goddess. Nisha and Jack looked at the picture more closely. Santosh was spot on. Shailputri was shown mounted and seated on a bull. *The first victim at the Marine Bay Plaza.* Nisha felt her heart racing as the theory that Santosh was proposing dawned upon her.

Chapter 46

"THERE IS ONLY one way to find out if my instincts are correct," said Santosh. "Let's check out each of the nine avatars of Durga. Each one!"

Nisha quickly flipped the page and found that the second avatar was called Brahamcharini. She was pictured with one hand holding a water pot, and another holding a rosary.

"This ties in perfectly with the murder of Bhavna Choksi," said Nisha excitedly.

"Let's go further," instructed Jack, realizing that Santosh's insight might possibly have cracked the case wide open.

Nisha browsed the pages to find the third avatar, Chandraghanta. This avatar of Durga was shown riding a tiger. She was holding a bell and had a semicircular moon painted on her forehead.

"Priyanka Talati," whispered Nisha to Jack.

"Actually, it turns out I was right in another little observation too," said Santosh.

"In what way?" asked Nisha.

"The name Chandraghanta is a combination of two words—*chandra* and *ghanta*," he replied. "The first means moon and the second bell. The murder of Priyanka happened on a Monday—the day of the moon. The night of the murder as per the almanac was a half-moon night. The half-moon is also a symbolic representation of a bell."

Jack took the book from Nisha and turned the pages to check the fourth form of Durga. The avatar was called Kushmanda. Below the image in the book was a brief explanation.

"The name Kushmanda is derived from two separate Sanskrit words," Jack read out, *"kushma, which means warmth; and anda, which refers to the cosmic egg. So Kushmanda is considered to be the creator of the egg-shaped universe."*

"Elina Xavier was left on her bed with a dozen eggs placed in an oval pattern around her," Nisha confirmed.

"There was something else about that murder scene," said Santosh. "The temperature in the room had been set as high as possible, remember? Which ties in with the association with warmth."

Jack hurriedly turned the page to the fifth form of Durga. Her name was Skandamata. She was depicted as holding her son—an infant—on her lap.

"Lara . . ." Jack sighed, slumping in his seat.

"What are the remaining forms of Durga?" asked Santosh. "After all, we know that she has nine forms, right?"

Nisha took the book back from Jack and hastily turned the pages to find the next avatar. "Here she is." Nisha was pointing to an illustration of a goddess mounted on a lion. "Apparently this form is known as Katyayani."

She flipped over the pages and showed Jack and Santosh the next image—Kaalratri—a terrifying form of Durga. With a bluish-black complexion, long and disheveled hair, and seated on a donkey, this form was shown holding a bunch of thorns in her hand.

The eighth avatar was Mahagauri, depicted with a fair complexion and holding a drum. Finally, the ninth incarnation—known as Siddhidatri—was shown with four arms holding a discus, a mace, a conch, and a lotus.

"Four forms still left. It means that we should expect four more murders," said Santosh grimly.

Chapter 47

"IF WE KNOW that the murderer is killing according to the nine incarnations of Durga, can't we use this information to warn people?" asked Nisha.

"How?" replied Santosh. "Knowing what the symbols mean tells us absolutely nothing about how the killer is choosing his victims. Nothing! For all we know, the bastard could be standing in a supermarket or on a street corner, randomly choosing targets."

"So what deductions can we make from what we know?" asked Jack.

"Well, one thing is certain," said Santosh. "Given that all the victims are depicted as incarnations of the goddess Durga, we can be fairly certain that all the future targets will also be women."

"All five previous killings have been in Mumbai, which means that the city constitutes a comfort zone for the killer," added Jack.

"There's something in the thuggee story that is also relevant to our investigation," said Santosh. "For most of the cult members, killing was a religious duty. They often saw their murders as a means of worship. Almost the equivalent of human sacrifice."

"Why the yellow scarf?" asked Nisha. "What does that have to do with Durga?"

"I think I know the answer to that one," replied Santosh. "I remember my grandmother recounting to me a legend in which Durga once fought a ferocious demon. Unfortunately, each drop of the monster's blood would spawn yet another monster. Durga finally created two men, each armed with yellow scarves, and ordered them to strangle the demons—in effect killing the monsters without allowing them to multiply. I assume that the thuggee tradition of yellow scarves has its genesis in that story."

He took a deep breath as he tried to clear his head. "We know that at the first three murder sites the security apparatus belonged to Xilon. There was no CCTV system at the girls' school or in Lara's van. What have we found out about Xilon?" he asked Nisha.

"The company was created by a retired armed forces man— squeaky-clean track record. The reason that Xilon was at all three initial murder sites was because they have a monopoly of sorts . . . they control around two-thirds of the security business in Mumbai."

"What about the company's employees?" asked Santosh.

"I am still looking into individual employee records," said Nisha. "Two of the senior engineers are on leave and one hasn't reported in for a couple of days."

"Find out about the missing employee," said Santosh, his antennae picking up on a possible angle.

"Sure, I'll get on it first thing tomorrow."

The library was almost empty at this hour. Most of the senior citizens who had been perusing newspapers and magazines in the public reading room had left. Any sound made within the imposing space was amplified by its high ceilings and marble pillars. Santosh's excitement caused his voice to rise and echo. In the center of the generously proportioned room the old librarian sat in his wooden chair, dozing off intermittently, absorbing snatches of conversation emanating from the table occupied by the Private India team.

They fell silent as Jack and Nisha stared across the table at Santosh, who seemed to be lost in thought, his lips moving as his mind chewed over the latest developments.

As they waited for the great detective's next pronouncement they cast amused glances at each other. Nisha, aware of Jack's hugely magnetic charm, felt herself redden all of a sudden, and was grateful when Santosh looked up from the book at them, his eyes shining with excitement.

"He's not being worshipful to Durga," he told them. "The trinkets he attaches to them, they're not respectful tokens, they're silly toys. A Viking helmet, for God's sakes. This is not some kind of veneration, it's a *desecration*. Why? Because our man hates women. He's not just killing women, he's killing womankind."

Chapter 48

THE SEA OF humanity dressed in white was overwhelming. It was high noon and the weather was hot and muggy but that had not deterred over a hundred thousand devotees from gathering in open ground on the outskirts of Mumbai. A roar of approval erupted from the crowd as Nimboo Baba pressed his palms together and greeted his followers with the traditional Indian greeting, "*Namaste.*"

Nimboo Baba had been born Nimesh in the holy city of Benares, by the banks of the Ganges. His family had moved to Delhi and Nimesh had been placed in a municipal school from which he had dropped out in the fourth grade. Having run away from his parents, he did everything he could in order to survive on the streets. He had sold newspapers on the pavements, washed cars at parking lots, prepared tea on railway station platforms, and even picked pockets. One day he had met a wandering ascetic and had been miraculously transformed.

The stories cranked out many years later by Nimboo Baba's PR machinery would go on to say that a sage had visited Nimesh's parents on the day that he had been born and had gifted them with a lemon. Apparently he had told them that, while a lemon was sour, it had incredible curative properties. "Your son shall be like a lemon—a healing medication—for the world," the sage had supposedly said.

In Hindi, the word for lemon was *nimboo* and thus Nimesh the pickpocket would soon become Nimboo Baba the great spiritual master. He opened his first ashram—a meditation center—in Delhi. His evening sermons, during which he would use ordinary examples and simple language, began to be attended by ever-increasing numbers. Over the next two decades, Nimboo Baba would open over a hundred such ashrams in India and would claim to have over twenty million disciples, including followers from the United States, Europe, and the Far East.

The man waited in the cool, air-conditioned interior of his black Mercedes-Benz for Nimboo Baba's sermon to be over. When it was time for the Baba to exit the grounds and head over to the luxury suite that was permanently booked for his comfort at a prominent Mumbai hotel, he chose to get into the waiting car instead.

Munna offered Nimboo Baba a bottle of chilled mineral water from the small refrigerator built into the armrest. The godman accepted it and quickly gulped down the contents. "These sermons leave my throat parched," he complained.

"Given the amount of land and money that you have amassed from your sermons, I imagined you would never thirst for anything," replied Munna, with a twinkle in his eyes. Nimboo Baba laughed. The only one who could speak to him so openly was Munna.

What was never mentioned in the PR material published by the Baba's marketing machinery was the fact that his outfit acted as a massive money-laundering center for Munna's ill-gotten wealth. Millions of rupees from illicit operations found their way as "donations" into Nimboo Baba's ashrams, from where they were converted into legal assets such as land, buildings, bank balances, and legitimate businesses. A perfect instance of Hindu–Muslim partnership.

Munna's association with Nimboo Baba went back several years, to the time when Munna had been attempting to establish his supremacy in Mumbai's underworld. On one particular evening he had been injured during a shoot-out with a rival gang. Wounded and bleeding, Munna had sought refuge in one of Nimboo Baba's ashrams. The Baba had kept the police away and ensured that Munna was provided with medical attention. That day had been the genesis of a symbiotic relationship between the two men, the guru providing occasional advice and spiritual wisdom—besides a nifty way of laundering Munna's money—and Munna providing financial support to the Baba.

"How is my special disciple getting along?" asked Nimboo Baba. "I hope you are assisting in every way that you can after the Thailand return."

"Getting along rather well, I would say," replied Munna. "And yes, I am happy to help. How are your dealings with the Attorney General progressing?"

Nimboo Baba laughed. "He's up to his neck in gambling debts. I have been bailing him out whenever he needs me to."

"Good," replied Munna. "With him so indebted to you, we continue to have leverage. I must tell my betting managers to keep taking wagers from him."

"He was the country's top-earning lawyer before he accepted

the Attorney General's position. Where did all his money go?" asked Nimboo Baba.

"Men who are very active in their professional lives tend to be equally active in their personal ones," offered Munna sagely. "He changes his woman almost every month. Expensive proposition."

Chapter 49

RUPESH LEFT HIS Jeep to navigate the last few yards on foot. His team briskly jogged ahead of him. Rupesh felt his shoes squelch in the muck along the banks of the canal. Scrap-metal houses bordered the sewer that lazily flowed through the slum, carrying a thick sludge of floating plastic bags, bottles, chemicals, garbage, and tons of human and animal excrement. Asia's largest slum—Dharavi—was spread over a square mile of Mumbai and over a million wretched souls called it home.

"Do we know the exact house where he was spotted?" asked Rupesh, keeping up with his men.

"Yes, we do, sir. This lane is the recycling area of Dharavi, full of small workshops that reprocess paper, tin cans, plastic, and cardboard. Toward the end of the lane is the bootlegging operation that our informer told us about. He's holed up there." Rupesh looked at his watch. It was ten minutes past midnight.

They reached the target shed in a few minutes. It was single-storey and ramshackle with a footprint of less than a couple of hundred square feet. Patched together from rusting and mismatched corrugated-metal sheets, the windows and door were simply jagged holes cut through the tinwork. The stench from the brew could be detected from far away in spite of the overhanging and all-pervading stink of sewage that thickly enveloped Dharavi.

Rupesh's advance party had already brought the operation to a standstill and all the men working there had been rounded up. In the center of the shed stood a massive vat in which country liquor was being adulterated with industrial methylated spirit, batteries, cockroaches, cashew husks, and orange peel. Rupesh placed a kerchief over his nose and mouth as he headed over to the single man who had been cuffed and made to stand apart from the others.

"Thought you could get away, eh?" asked Rupesh, delivering a near jaw-breaking slap to the terrified man's face and drawing blood from his mouth.

"Believe me, sahib, I ran because of fear. I am innocent," protested the cuffed man nervously. It was Bhosale, driver of Lara Omprakash's vanity van.

A crowd had gathered outside the bootlegging hut and Rupesh's men were using batons to keep them at a distance. Among the rounded-up men was one who looked more menacing than the others. Rupesh motioned him over.

"Your shithole of an operation only functions because I choose to look the other way," he said, carefully avoiding using Munna's name. "But if I find you harboring a murderer again, I shall crush your balls with a walnut cracker. Is that fucking clear, motherfucker?"

The leader nodded warily. No point getting busted by the cops. The stock of deadly hooch that was inside the premises had a street value of a million rupees.

"Tell your goons outside to clear the way," instructed Rupesh to the bootlegger as he seized Bhosale by the scruff of his neck and shoved him toward the waiting police Jeep.

Once inside the vehicle, Rupesh cranked up the engine and the Jeep took off like a rocket. There were a sub-inspector, two constables, and Bhosale inside it with him. The vehicle weaved through the dark and empty streets of Mumbai as they headed toward the distant suburb of Mira-Bhayandar.

"Where are we going?" asked Bhosale nervously, sandwiched between the two constables on the back seat of the Jeep.

"It's party time, my friend," replied Rupesh. "I do not want you to think that the Mumbai police are poor hosts. We are capable of showing our guests a good time."

Most of the development of the Mira-Bhayandar area had happened on the eastern side of the railway line, whereas to the west it was still covered by mangroves and salt pans. Rupesh brought the vehicle to a halt in the compound of a construction site on the east side. At this time of night it was empty.

Rupesh got out of the Jeep and signaled his subordinates to follow along with Bhosale. They passed cement mixers, earth movers, piles of construction materials, and stacked-up scaffolding beams until they reached a temporary construction elevator, which was little more than an iron cage boarded up with plywood.

Bhosale anxiously surveyed his surroundings, his eyes darting about like frightened mice, as the rickety contraption creaked its way up to the seventh floor—the last to be constructed thus far.

"Laundry time," barked Rupesh. He took a large pinch of tobacco from his pouch and placed it in his mouth. The two constables removed Bhosale's handcuffs, grabbed him by his underarms, and swung him over the side of the incomplete building.

"Hang him out to dry," said Rupesh with a grin on his face. The constables allowed Bhosale to grasp the edge of the concrete slab with his fingers as his body dangled from the seventh floor.

Bhosale looked down at the distant earth beneath his suspended feet and felt a warm sensation in his crotch. He had peed involuntarily. "Help!" he pleaded, feeling his fingers losing strength. "I beg you to spare my life, sahib."

Rupesh and his men watched Bhosale's fingers turn white as he struggled to keep himself alive. Rupesh moved to the edge and gently placed one foot on the prisoner's left hand.

"As of now, I have only rested my foot on your hand," he said softly, enjoying the kick of the tobacco in his mouth. "In the next few seconds your fingers will feel my entire weight. I shall then step on your right hand. You will howl for mercy but I shall not listen. You are scum and I shall be overjoyed when you fall into your muddy grave."

"Please, sahib," howled Bhosale. "I'll do anything. Mercy! Please!"

"I simply want your confession, nothing more, nothing less. Give me a full disclosure and I shall step away," promised Rupesh. He then began to apply more pressure to Bhosale's hand.

Chapter 50

THE WEATHER WAS hot and humid when Ragini Sharma, the opposition MLA—Member of the Legislative Assembly— from Alibaug constituency and a potential aspirant for the post of Minister for Women and Child Development, gathered along with thousands of women supporters at Chowpatty Beach and marched to Azad Maidan. The march was a protest against a violent gang rape that had taken place a few days previously in Mumbai. Ragini Sharma was demanding the resignation of the state's Home Minister.

Ragini's party only had permission to hold a protest meeting at Azad Maidan—an open area of ground in the heart of South Mumbai—not a rally. Ragini Sharma had chosen to defy that ruling and declared that her supporters would march along with her even though it would lead to road blockages and traffic snarls at several places during peak travel hours in the country's commercial capital.

Addressing a crowd of over a hundred thousand supporters —men, women, and children—at Azad Maidan, Ragini Sharma took center stage with confidence and grace. After greeting her supporters, she said, "According to the government's own statistics, a woman is now raped in India every twenty minutes. Even though the number of sex offenses has increased, the number of convictions is falling. Why do we have an incompetent Home Minister at the helm? Isn't it time for us to send this spineless government packing?"

The crowd roared its approval as Ragini warmed to her theme. "Two days ago, a young woman of twenty was gang-raped by seven men from her neighborhood. Her attackers filmed the assault on their cell phones. Should we allow such monsters to walk the streets of Mumbai? When will we be in a position to guarantee safety and security to the women of this city?"

Ragini waved to the gathered crowd and raised her folded hands in a gesture of humility. She knew that this political rally was a reaffirmation of her own strength. Assembly elections in the state were less than a year away and Ragini realized that she stood a fighting chance of becoming an influential voice in the fractured political landscape.

She looked at her watch. She had to be back at her constituency within a couple of hours. She nodded to her team that it was time to bring the public meeting to an end. Toward the rear of the crowd stood a young man dressed simply in an open-collar shirt, jeans, sneakers, and cap. He realized that Ragini Sharma's public gathering was winding down and decided that he needed to move quickly so that he could reach her destination before she did.

Chapter 51

THE RELATIONSHIP BETWEEN hunter and prey is unique. It's almost like unrequited love because one party hardly feels anything at all. Ask a stalker about his relationship with the one he stalks and you will begin to understand the intense yearning that I have to live with.

I have been stalking you but you do not seem to notice my presence. What a shame! Later tonight, my face will be firmly emblazoned on the retinas of your eyes. You will be incapable of forgetting it—forever.

I was seated in the visitors' gallery of the Legislative Assembly when you rose to address the speaker during question hour. I was among the crowd that listened to you with rapt attention at Azad Maidan. You have so much concern in your heart for the poor and downtrodden women of Mumbai! Your words almost brought tears to my eyes! You know that I'm fibbing, right? Just like I know that you don't give a rat's ass about the exploited women who live in this hellhole.

I was way ahead of your car with the flashing red beacon as I drove from the public meeting to your constituency home in Alibaug, on the outskirts of Mumbai. So very nice of you to drop in and check on your constituents. I wonder how many of them will attend your funeral, Ragini Sharma?

I am quietly working along with the team that is planting saplings in the front garden of your bungalow. Luckily, all the workers are temporary hires and do not recognize each other. I am wearing a casual labourer's dirty clothes and my head is covered with a soiled cap to protect me from the harsh sun. I ensure that I keep my cap lowered so that my face remains mostly hidden from the prying eyes of the policemen in your security detail. I am invisible to you and your men.

Your arrival in the constituency results in a long line of people queuing up to request favors and dispensations. It is late by the time you retire for the night. By that time I have already moved into your bedroom.

You are completely unaware of my presence. A good hunter must wait patiently for hours, not allowing the prey to pick up the slightest suspicious scent. I am lying in wait for you—right under your bed—up toward the headboard so that my feet are not visible.

Your maid walks in to deliver your customary glass of milk and then leaves. You toss and turn for a while, reading a Mills & Boon in bed, but after twenty minutes you switch off the lights.

I wait for another hour to ensure that you are fast asleep before I crawl out from under the bed. In one rubber-gloved hand I hold a yellow scarf and in the other I carry a rolled-up wall calendar and a specimen bag. It's time for me to get some work done.

Sleep, whore, sleep, slut . . . deeper . . . deeper . . . breathing shut.
Sleep, bitch, sleep, cunt . . . deeper . . . deeper . . . while I hunt.

Chapter 52

YELLOW GARROTE STRANGLER arrested, screamed the headline of the *Afternoon Mirror*. The byline was that of Bhavna Choksi's chain-smoking editor, Jamini.

Rupesh leaned back in his swivel chair and placed his feet on his desk. He peered through the angle formed by his shoes to observe the expression on Santosh's face as the Private India chief perused the article. Besides the other details, special prominence had been given to the photograph of ACP Rupesh Desai, mentioned as the no-nonsense cop who had captured the killer.

"Policing is about keeping as many balls as one can in the air while simultaneously protecting one's own," remarked Rupesh as he smiled at Santosh.

"This is crap, and you know it," Santosh replied, throwing down the newspaper on the desk.

"Is it only crap because I solved a case that your fancy team with all its sophisticated methods couldn't?" asked Rupesh slyly.

"It's not about that—" began Santosh.

"Then what exactly is it about, my friend? I thought we had a clear understanding that all credit for solving this case would be mine alone. Since when did you begin to fancy the spotlight?"

"I am more than happy to let you have all the publicity you want, Rupesh," said Santosh. "But please do remember that I know what extra-legal methods are used to extract confessions. Most importantly, the driver—Bhosale—had no motive for murder at all." He thumped his walking cane on the floor to emphasize his point.

"He may have been blackmailing his boss, Lara Omprakash," argued Rupesh. "He may have known some of her secrets. Possibly he wanted more money and she refused. He killed her in a fit of rage." Rupesh seemed determined to make the jigsaw puzzle pieces fit together even if he had to hammer and chisel them into place.

"Nisha has managed to get hold of an extract from the security register in Film City, where Lara's movie was being filmed," Santosh told him. "It would be worthwhile for you to have a look at it."

Rupesh took the list and glanced at it casually. "What exactly do you want me to see?"

"The list shows the date and time that any given vehicle passes through the main gate of Film City," explained Santosh. "The security agency is duty bound to log all registration numbers, time in, and time out."

"So?" asked Rupesh.

"Look at the registration number highlighted in yellow. It's Lara Omprakash's vanity van. You will see that it was there several times during the past few days," explained Santosh.

"Why are you wasting my time like this?" complained

Rupesh. "The city wanted the killer nabbed. He's safely in a lock-up."

Santosh ignored this comment. "The problem," he continued, "is that your hypothesis is unable to explain how the fuck this man—your prime suspect—could have been driving Lara Omprakash's vanity van in and out of Film City on Sunday night when Kanya Jaiyen was murdered, as well as on Monday night when Priyanka Talati was killed!"

Chapter 53

THE THICK GREEN strip that separated most of Mumbai's coastline from the Arabian Sea was almost entirely submerged at high tide. It was only when the waters receded that the band of vegetation would become visible. Clusters of densely packed trees criss-crossed by slender creeks constituted Mumbai's natural defense barrier against floods—the mangroves.

A small fishing boat dropped anchor near the trees with their dark, waxy leaves and finger-like aerial roots. Two men jumped off the boat into the knee-deep water and began wading toward land, holding a basket between them. To any casual observer they would have resembled fishermen hauling their catch back to shore. Their actual purpose was a lot more sinister.

Once safely on land, they were greeted by a third, delicate and gaunt-looking man who had been patiently awaiting their arrival. "As-salam alaykum," said the waiting man to the two boatmen.

"Wa alaykumu s-salam," they replied, carefully lowering the basket onto dry ground.

"Do you have the entire consignment with you?" asked the waiting Mujahideen man.

"Thirty kilos. Have a look," said one of the boatmen as he pulled off the plastic sheet that covered the basket. Inside it were several small wrapped parcels containing a white crystalline solid. It was not a drug-smuggling operation that was underway in the mangroves of Mumbai. The cargo was far more deadly: a consignment of a nitramine commonly known as RDX.

The three men quickly lifted the basket and hauled it over to the waiting vehicle. "Are you sure you will not be stopped by the cops?" asked one of the boatmen.

The Mujahideen man raised his hands to the heavens. "*Insha Allah,* there should be no problems. We're hoping to rid the world of a satanic organization that prevents us from achieving our holy and pure aims. With Allah on our side, how can there be any obstacles in the way?"

"Is your access in place?" asked one of the boatmen.

"He is ready and willing. He hates the Americans more than we do," said the thin man, getting into the driver's seat of the vehicle.

The two boatmen took their leave and waded back into the water. The small craft would help them reach a fishing trawler anchored in the Arabian Sea. The trawler would take them back to their point of origin—Karachi, Pakistan.

Chapter 54

THE HOUSE BELONGING to Ragini Sharma, the Honorable MLA from Alibaug constituency, was a hive of activity. A company of armed police had been deployed around the perimeter in order to keep her political supporters at a distance. Unfortunately rumors of her death had leaked out and a mob of Sharma's constituents stood shouting slogans of support near the gate.

Within the bungalow grounds were parked several police vehicles, some marked and some unmarked. All the staff, including security personnel, gardeners, cook, and maid, had been assembled by Rupesh's subordinates and were being questioned. The bungalow had been cordoned off with security tape and a further roll of police tape had been unfurled outside Ragini Sharma's bedroom door.

Inside lay the corpse of the politician, her bed sheets showing clear signs of a struggle. Ragini Sharma had fought back, it seemed. Like many middle-aged women in India, she slept in the blouse and petticoat of her saree, finding these inner garments much more comfortable than nightclothes. Around her neck was the now-familiar yellow garrote embedded within a bluish band of discolored skin.

Santosh looked around the room. "Did we find any surveillance equipment?"

"Negative," replied Hari as he continued checking the room. "The Alibaug region has erratic power supply. It would not have been possible to run sensitive cameras and data recorders. The killer possibly knew that this house did not have an electronic security system in place."

"Any luck with trace evidence?" asked Santosh. He walked over to Mubeen, who was busy swabbing Ragini Sharma's face. Nisha watched from the sidelines, staring intently at the victim's face.

Noticing her concentration, Santosh said, "What's the matter? Seen something?"

Nisha remained quiet. Where had she seen this woman before? Was it simple familiarity with the face of a public figure or was it a faded memory? The harder she tried, the more her memory seemed to fail her. Her thoughts were interrupted by Mubeen.

"The killer spat on the school principal's face," he announced. "I'm checking to see if there has been a repeat performance here."

"You never told me that you found saliva on Elina Xavier," reprimanded Santosh, his usual contemplative expression turning into a scowl.

"In addition to the usual strand of hair," replied Mubeen. "The saliva sample was infinitesimally small so I wasn't sure if it would lead to anything. Furthermore, there is no guarantee that it actually belonged to the killer. Someone had tried to clean it off with bleach but missed an exceedingly small trace that landed on one eyebrow. The chances of finding the killer's DNA here are much greater. This victim fought back, so there's a chance we may find interesting evidence under her fingernails. Hello, what have we here?"

"What have you found?" asked Santosh, forgetting his irritation.

Mubeen bent down to look at the pillow with a magnifying glass. Pulling out a pair of forensic forceps, he placed his find into a small specimen bag. Holding it up proudly to Santosh, he said, "We now have something that could help us. We have a strand of hair!"

"Big deal," retorted Santosh. "We've found the same god-damn hair at all the murder sites."

"Yes, but I can see that this one seems to be almost complete. I think that some part of the root is intact," said Mubeen.

Santosh took the bag from him and looked carefully at the hair inside. It was short and black with nothing unique to mark it out. Turning his gaze toward the pillow and pointing with his cane to a piece of paper sticking out from underneath, he asked, "What is that under there?"

"I haven't had a chance to examine it closely because the victim's head is still on the pillow," said Mubeen, "but it seems to be a page from a wall calendar."

"Pull it out," instructed Santosh. "I need to see it."

Even though Mubeen would have preferred to wait and carry out each task in scientific sequence, he did not wish to aggravate his boss, who already looked irritable and impatient. Mubeen took a photograph of the position of Ragini Sharma's head on the pillow and then gently lifted it. Reaching out with his other hand, he pulled out what Santosh wanted. He handed it over wordlessly to his boss, who took hold of it in his rubber-gloved hands.

Santosh stared at the paper. It was indeed a wall calendar—a cheap one that had no glossy photographs or aesthetic value. It simply set aside a page for each month. Working days were shown in black numerals and weekends and national holidays in red. The calendar had been left with the pages turned to the month of July.

Rupesh appeared behind Santosh and looked over his shoulder. "What have you found?" he asked. It had been a tough decision to allow Private India back into the investigation but pragmatism had won, for the moment at least. The clincher had been Munna's phone call: "Get them back into the investigation. Don't ask me why."

"It's a wall calendar," replied Santosh. "It was left under her pillow with the pages turned to the month of July. If you notice, the days starting from July twenty-third have been circled."

Why these dates? thought Santosh. *Why July, not January or June? And why the twenty-third in particular?* His mind went into overdrive as he attempted to figure out the answer to the riddle. Rupesh took the calendar from him and looked carefully at the circled dates.

Santosh suddenly spoke up. It was as though a light bulb had gone on inside his head. "I'm willing to bet that all the dates in the next month up to the twenty-second of August are also marked like that," he said, leaning on his walking stick to ease the strain on his injured leg.

Rupesh flipped the page of the calendar and saw that Santosh was right, as usual. All the dates up to and including August 22 were circled.

"What is the significance of these dates?" he asked in frustration. "They have nothing to do with the dates of our murders. It's currently October."

"Ah, but these dates have everything to do with this particular murder," replied Santosh. "They are the IAU boundaries within the tropical zodiac."

"IAU?" asked Nisha.

"International Astronomical Union," replied Santosh, "the internationally recognized authority for assigning designations to celestial bodies." He found nothing strange about the fact that he was aware of that particular obscure piece of information.

"Zodiac?" asked Rupesh incredulously. "This nut job is killing according to astrologically auspicious dates?"

"No," replied Santosh, exasperated by Rupesh's lack of intellect. "The period from July twenty-third to August twenty-second constitutes the tropical zodiac of Leo. What is the symbol for Leo? The lion! This is the killer's sixth victim. The sixth manifestation of Durga is Katyayani and she is always depicted seated on a lion!"

Chapter 55

THE STRETCH OF the city from Bhendi Bazaar to Mohammed Ali Road was entirely illuminated each night during the holy Islamic festival of Ramadan. Food lanes were doing brisk business at the end of the day's fasting. They would continue turning out copious quantities of their wares throughout the night.

In a small workshop a few yards away a blacksmith was firing up his acetylene torch, the tip glowing incandescent as the old man welded metal tubes back in place. Standing watch over the process was the thin man from the Indian Mujahideen and his partner.

"I still cannot understand why you need the sealed ends of the tubes to be openable," said the blacksmith, clamping the tube with tongs over his anvil in order to strike it.

"I'm not paying you to fucking ask me stupid questions," said the Mujahideen angrily. "Just get the job done so that we can get out of here." He winked at his partner, who seemed overly nervous.

"This is not going to happen quickly," the blacksmith retaliated. "It can take multiple rounds of heating and reheating. I suggest you come back in a day or two. Leave the material here with me."

"We're not going anywhere," said the Mujahideen. "Just keep hammering away. We'll sit here and watch."

"I can't afford to hammer when the metal's cold. It will end up creating a cold shunt that weakens the work," argued the blacksmith earnestly. The Mujahideen man exhaled in exasperation. Why the fuck did the best workmen always turn out to be a pain in the ass? Why was this old man asking questions that would put him in danger of being killed? The thin man counted slowly in his head, forcing himself to calm down. His first priority was getting this stuff fabricated. He would decide how to deal with the blacksmith later.

He glanced at his partner, who was fidgeting nervously. These educated types were the worst of the lot. No guts, no glory. Just lots of jittery arguments and spineless behavior.

As the two men watched the blacksmith they fell into a sort of trance. There was a Zen-like beauty to hammering hot metal into shape. It was evident that the blacksmith was a perfectionist, hammering, heating, and polishing until he achieved a perfect factory finish. Every few minutes he would clean the anvil and unclutter his surroundings before going back to his painstaking work.

"Take your time," said the Mujahideen. "We can't afford mistakes."

"There are no mistakes in my profession, sir," replied the blacksmith, sweat trickling down his face. "Unlike a piece of wood which can turn out too short when you cut it, if a piece of metal is botched, we simply wait, reheat, and give it another go. There are always second chances—both in metal and in men."

Chapter 56

"WHERE ARE YOU, Jack?" asked Santosh over the phone. "I have been trying to reach you all morning."

"I'm at the Willingdon Club," Jack replied. "Enjoying a glass of beer after playing eighteen holes of golf."

"You never play golf," said Santosh suspiciously.

"I figured that I needed to start," shot back Jack. "Especially given the fact that an old friend invited me over."

"How many old friends do you have in Mumbai?" asked Santosh, persisting with his interrogation of his boss.

"What did you want to talk to me about?" asked Jack, changing the subject smoothly.

"Do you have your cell phone scrambler with you?" asked Santosh.

"Yes. Give me a sec," said Jack, plugging the unit into the USB port of his phone. All employees of the Private organization globally used the encryption tool. Governments and agencies around the world were snooping on every form of communication and they could ill afford the possible consequences of any leak.

"A sixth victim has been discovered," began Santosh, and detailed the findings for him.

"The killer is working quickly," Jack observed grimly.

"True," replied Santosh. "Dr. Kanya Jaiyen was killed on Sunday night, Bhavna Choksi on Monday morning, Priyanka Talati on Monday night, the school principal—Elina Xavier—on Wednesday night, Lara Omprakash on Thursday afternoon, and the MLA, Ragini Sharma, last night—Friday."

"Why the hurry, I wonder?" said Jack.

"The Festival of Navratri is a celebration of nine nights. The murderer clearly hopes to be done before the end of that period," replied Santosh. Jack could detect a note of worry in the normally imperturbable voice of his India bureau chief.

Chapter 57

"LARA OMPRAKASH, VICTIM of ligature strangulation," said Mubeen into his microphone as he completed the autopsy with Dr. Zafar by his side. "Victim has a tattoo of a Hindu deity on her right upper arm. Her pelvis shows signs of contraction from a previous injury.

"As regards the school principal, Mrs. Elina Xavier," he continued, "I have been able to find trace amounts of saliva on her eyebrow. It's possible that there may have been more on her face but that has been wiped off with bleach. I cannot use RFLP, an accurate and reliable test but one requiring a relatively large amount of DNA material. I now plan to use the PCR method, which allows for testing on very small amounts of DNA from biological samples.

"The sixth victim—Ragini Sharma—seems to have fought back. Extraction and amplification of cellular material found under her fingernails is being carried out. It is my hope that the biological material transferred during the struggle, if any, may be adequate to genotype reportable mixtures.

"Yellow scarves used for strangulation have been recovered from all six victims. In addition, a seventh was found in the car belonging to Nisha Gandhe and an eighth was sent to the editor of the *Afternoon Mirror*. All eight scarves have been passed on to Hari Padhi to conduct microscopic, stain, burn, and solvent tests, in order to be sure that all of them belong to the same fiber, dye, and manufacture family."

After shutting off the microphone, he and Zafar scrubbed up and placed the gurneys in the lab storage unit. Zafar headed back to Cooper Hospital while Mubeen left the lab for Hari's office. Knowing the speed at which his colleague worked, it was quite possible that he would already have results to share, reasoned Mubeen.

Hari's office was empty, though, and according to the receptionist he'd stepped out half an hour earlier for a smoke in the alley. Long smoke. Back at the empty office Mubeen swept his gaze over the tangle of cables, wires, computers, and instrumentation, wondering how Hari was able to make any sense of it all. He scanned the desk to see if his colleague had typed up a report containing his forensic analysis of the yellow scarves. No luck.

Mubeen tried the desk drawer but it was empty except for an electronic frame displaying a digital photograph of a pretty woman. Hari was unmarried. As far as Mubeen knew, there was no serious relationship either. The woman had been photographed seated casually on a couch with legs crossed, holding a coffee mug. She was wearing a black vest and a pair of faded jeans. There was something very sensual about her. Mubeen wondered whether it was her dusky complexion or her shoulder-length curly black hair that gave such an impression.

He put away the digital photo frame and closed the drawer. Next he opened the small cabinet beneath to check Hari's files. On a lower shelf were specimen bags containing the eight scarves that had been given to Hari for testing. Mubeen took them out and placed them on the desktop.

Each specimen bag had been clearly marked with the name of the victim and the date and time of the sample collection— Kanya Jaiyen, Bhavna Choksi, Priyanka Talati, Elina Xavier, Lara Omprakash, and Ragini Sharma. One more specimen bag contained the scarf that had been found tied to the steering wheel inside Nisha's car, and yet another held the one that had been sent to the tabloid editor. Mubeen counted the bags. That was odd . . .

"What are you up to?" demanded a voice behind him.

He spun around to see Santosh in the doorway, looking suspiciously at Mubeen. "Why are you looking through Hari's stuff?"

Chapter 58

MUBEEN STUTTERED, "I—I came to find Hari but he's—he's out."

"That still doesn't answer my question," said Santosh, continuing to stare suspiciously at him.

"I came looking to see if he had completed his examination and analysis of the scarves. There should have been eight specimen bags in all," replied Mubeen. "Surprisingly, there are nine."

Santosh crossed to the desk where the bags had been laid out, counting them for himself. Indeed there were nine bags, not eight. He put aside the bags containing the scarves that had been used for killing the six victims. He then separated the bag containing the scarf that had been found in Nisha's car and the one sent to the newspaper editor. He stared at the ninth specimen bag. It was slightly bulkier than the others and was unmarked.

Santosh held up the ninth specimen bag for inspection.

"The bag contains three scarves, identical to the other eight," said Mubeen. "These three seem to be freshly laundered and pressed. I'm wondering . . . where did Hari get them from?"

And I'm wondering whether the extra sample bag was placed here by you, Mubeen, thought Santosh to himself, angry that he was beginning to suspect one of his own team.

Chapter 59

"HIS PHONE IS switched off," said Nisha as she put her smart-phone on the table and looked at Santosh.

He, Jack, Nisha, and Mubeen sat in the conference room. The discovery of the extra scarves in Hari's office had created a dilemma. Was there an innocent explanation or was he now a suspect?

"We could activate the chip," said Santosh, looking at Jack.

All employees of the Private organization were required to be fitted with a small locator chip embedded under the skin of the upper back. It had helped save countless lives because it enabled their team to locate them during emergencies. In order to prevent misuse, however, only Jack Morgan had the power to activate and authorize tracking.

"What if there is a simple explanation? What if he went out and bought additional scarves in order to use them as comparison samples? What if he isn't absconding but has simply decided to take some time off for a romantic tryst with the woman whose photo is inside his desk drawer?" was Jack's response. Turning to Santosh, he asked, "What is your opinion? Should I activate Hari's RFID chip?"

Santosh pondered the question. *Was there an innocent explanation—or was Hari a suspect? And what about Mubeen?* Santosh remained thoughtful and silent for a minute before replying. "On the night when Nisha and I went to meet Priyanka Talati's producer at Blue Magic Tantra records, I invited Hari to join us. He asked to be excused, saying he had to meet someone. My gut tells me that he needed to be on his own so he could place the yellow scarf in Nisha's car while we were inside."

"That is circumstantial evidence, Santosh," replied Jack. "We can't suspect one of our own based upon conjecture."

"Where is the digital photo frame from Hari's desk?" asked Santosh. Mubeen passed it over. The rest of the team watched as Santosh ran his fingers over the frame containing the picture of the young woman in Hari's life. He was at his obsessive and compulsive best, and Jack knew better than to ask too many questions.

Within a few minutes Santosh had found a small, almost imperceptible toggle switch. The electronic frame could be used to display either a single photo in static mode or several sequentially in presentation mode. The toggle switch on the rear of the frame determined the mode.

Santosh flicked the toggle and the frame blinked and reset itself. It then went into presentation mode. Hari did not have too many pictures—only two, actually. They appeared on the frame alternately. One was that of the pretty woman on the couch. The other was a representation of the Hindu goddess Durga holding a human head in one of her many hands.

Chapter 60

THE MAN KEPT his head down as he made his way toward passport control, his leather satchel slung over his shoulder. Holding his ticket, boarding card, Indian embarkation form, and passport in one hand, and a switched-off cell phone in the other, he presented his papers to the immigration officer.

The officer looked at the passport, plugged some information into the computer terminal in front of him, and asked the passenger to move to the center of the counter so that a digital photograph of him could be dumped into the database. He then picked up a rubber stamp and proceeded to stamp the passport and embarkation form. Handing back the papers, he wished the passenger a pleasant flight.

His flight had already been announced and the man hurried along to clear the long security queue. He presented the security officer with a small laminated card that indicated he was fitted with a pacemaker, thus avoiding the X-ray scanners. It was another ten minutes by the time he'd cleared security and his flight listing had begun to blink green on the information displays.

The man ran toward gate 11A. He hurriedly presented his boarding card to the Emirates Airlines representative, who smiled at him and requested him to board immediately, given that they were running late.

Relieved at having boarded the flight, the man found his window seat in the economy section and settled down after placing his leather satchel in the overhead luggage bin. He looked at his watch. The flight should have taken off twenty minutes earlier but the aerobridge had still not been pulled away. He took off his shoes and closed his eyes. A little nap would prepare him better.

He felt the irritation of a mild rash caused by the adhesive tape on his upper back. Under his shirt was a piece of thick metallic foil around five inches square. It was held in place by duct tape. RFID tags—used as implantable devices for humans and pets—were relatively resistant to shielding, but thick metallic foil could prevent detection in most cases.

Chapter 61

HE WAS SEATED on a damp concrete floor. The heat and humidity of the cell coupled with total darkness was claustrophobic—almost terrifyingly so. Hanging over the place was the conspicuous stink of stale piss.

He felt something brush his toes. He squinted his eyes to catch a glimpse of a furry rodent, its eyes gleaming red in the dark. He hated rats and kicked away the pest only to be greeted by several squeaks. The area was infested with them and it seemed as though they were getting ready to gang up on him.

He shuddered as he felt sweat trickle down his naked back. He realized then that he had no clothes on. The sudden loud clanging of the steel gate being opened was strangely comforting for a moment, although a strong sense of foreboding bubbled within him.

"Welcome to the Mumbai Hilton," said Rupesh, switching on a naked light bulb inside the cell. "I thought you might like a little room service." Hari screwed up his eyes to cope with the sudden brightness. His heart was racing wildly and he could hear every thump it made in his chest. Thankfully, the bright light and additional human presence sent the rats scurrying off to more secure territory.

Hari desperately tried to recall the events that had brought him here. He had been comfortably ensconced in his aircraft seat, having a catnap while awaiting a take-off that never happened. "Any idea what's causing the delay?" he had asked the passenger next to him when he woke from his slumber. Before the gentleman could reply, one of the flight attendants had come up to Hari's seat, greeting him by the assumed identity on his ticket and passport. "Mr. Hari Pandit?" she'd asked. "There are some police officers on the aerobridge just outside the entrance to this aircraft. They say that they must talk to you immediately." A couple of minutes later, he had found himself being led away in handcuffs from the aircraft and into a police van.

Rupesh was holding a small portable DVD player in his hands. He bent down and set it on the cell floor next to Hari. "This is a small orientation video that will help you understand what we do with people who do not cooperate," he said, pressing the play button. Hari felt the pit of his stomach give way as he saw ghastly images of inmates being beaten till they coughed blood, prisoners being administered electric shocks on their genitals, and detainees being suspended from ceiling fans or forced to drink gallons of water. He had thought that police brutality was only the stuff of Bollywood movies—reel life, not real life. Apparently he'd been mistaken.

Ten minutes later Rupesh snapped the DVD player's lid shut. "I hope you enjoyed the inflight entertainment, even though your flight to Dubai had to be abandoned. Now, will you confess to these murders?" he asked as he rolled up his sleeves. "Or do I need to make you the star attraction of a future video clip?"

Chapter 62

SANTOSH SAT SLUMPED over his desk. The decision to put out a red-corner alert for Hari through Rupesh had left him drained.

Apparently Hari had adopted an alias to book his airline tickets, using a fudged passport created for him by a dodgy travel agent in Lamington Road. He had kept his cell phone powered off and had cloaked his RFID locator chip with a strip of metallic foil. For several hours Santosh and his team had lost all contact with him, but then Santosh had remembered something. Calling a number from his phone's speed-dial, he had spoken to his amputee friend. "Tell me, if I wanted to flee the country under a false identity, who would be the best chap for a passport?"

He knew the way that Rupesh and his men worked once an arrest was made. He shut his eyes in a vain attempt to block out thoughts of what the police would do to Hari.

There was still a part of Santosh that wanted to trust Hari.

He opened his eyes, stood up, opened the cabinet behind his desk, and pulled out a bottle of Johnnie Walker. After pouring three fingers of the golden liquid into a glass, he gulped it down like a thirsty desert traveler arriving at an oasis. Back at his desk, Santosh placed the bottle in front of him. He slipped into a stupor and his nightmare returned.

The soundtrack to it was from a Broadway musical, *The Phantom of the Opera*. It was playing on the car stereo because Isha loved it. The drive back to Mumbai was a picturesque one with a monsoon mist hanging over the distant hills. Pravir had insisted on buying a new cartridge for his hand-held game console and was contentedly battling demons on its tiny screen. Santosh was happy. It had been a peaceful break. He looked across at his wife. Even after ten years of marriage she looked as ravishingly beautiful as the day that he had married her. She smiled back when she realized that he was staring at her. Santosh tried to set aside his worries about the emotional distance that had developed between them. He would balance work and family going forward and would ensure that his wife had no reason to feel isolated or abandoned.

"Papa, look at—" Pravir began to say from the rear of the car when the hairpin turn appeared from nowhere. The car smashed headlong into the thick banyan by the edge of the road. After a few seconds of screeching tires and a gut-wrenching sound of collision there was silence. Santosh remained slumped over the steering wheel. Then darkness. Hospital corridors. "Another ten units of blood, stat! I'm losing him . . . blood pressure is dropping!" Running alongside the gurney was a cop holding a pair of handcuffs. "You killed them, you drunk bastard!"

"No, I did not!" shouted Santosh, a thin trickle of saliva dribbling from the corner of his mouth and onto his desk.

He struggled with the policeman who had pounced on him.

The cop was trying to pin him to the ground and cuff his hands behind his back. "Let go of me," yelled Santosh as he fended off his assailant.

"Wake up, boss!" urged Nisha as she attempted to take hold of his flailing arms. He woke from his ordeal, embarrassed that Nisha had seen him in that state. He was relieved that the nightmare had ended but also knew that it would return. It always did.

He clumsily attempted to remove the bottle of whisky from his desk, forgetting the obvious fact that Nisha would have observed it while he was in deep slumber. "Mubeen has some important information for you," she said, helping Santosh up from his chair. "Let me get you some coffee before we go to the conference room, though," she said, a hint of concern in her voice.

Twenty minutes later Santosh was in the conference room with Jack, Nisha, and Mubeen. "Even if Hari is involved, he must have had an accomplice," said Mubeen.

"Why?" asked Santosh. He gratefully took a gulp of the scalding black coffee that Nisha had placed in front of him.

"You remember that there was bleach and saliva on Elina Xavier's eyebrow? Well, I managed to extract DNA from it. Given that India has no national DNA database, I'm now trying to run a match against several other databases, including one belonging to the Mumbai police as well as Private's own directory."

"But why the accomplice theory?" asked Santosh.

"While I cannot yet positively tell you whose DNA it *is*, I can definitely tell you whose it *isn't*," replied Mubeen. "The DNA is *not* Hari's. We already have his sequence on record. The person who killed Elina Xavier and left DNA on her face was someone else."

"It could belong to the victim herself," suggested Nisha.

"The DNA is not that of Elina Xavier, nor does it match that of any other victim. It is completely different. Either Hari is not involved, or if he is then he is working alongside someone else."

"What about the previous injury to Lara Omprakash?" asked Nisha. "Any thoughts on that?"

"What previous injury?" asked Santosh.

Nisha read aloud from the report: "*Lara Omprakash, victim of ligature strangulation . . . Victim has a tattoo of a Hindu deity on her right upper arm. Her pelvis shows signs of contraction from a previous injury.*"

"Ah, let's not read too much into that," said Mubeen. "Women can often injure the pelvis during childbirth."

"Childbirth?" said Santosh. "That's interesting."

"Because she had no children?" said Mubeen. His eyes were soulful. The two men, both left childless by a cruel fate, shared an unspoken moment.

Santosh looked away. "No," he said, "Lara Omprakash had no children. Or at least, none that we know of."

Chapter 63

NISHA GANDHE WAS no fool. Perhaps there were times when her looks had held her back; when she'd been seen as nothing more than a pretty face, but she'd had to work hard to overcome that, and after all, there were more difficult crosses to bear.

There were also times when her looks could be a distinct advantage. And she wasn't above using them to get what she wanted.

Like now. At home in her apartment in Mumbai's Cuffe Parade, a desirable abode that was testament more to her husband's stockbroker salary than to what she received from Private, she ended the call with Santosh. Then took the phone to the study in order to make her next call. It was a call that required her to be . . . well, she hesitated to use the word "flirtatious," but it was as good a word as any. And innocent though it was, she didn't particularly want to Sanjeev to hear. After all, why rock the boat? Family life was her solace. As an

adopted child who thanked the Almighty for her loving husband and a beautiful daughter, she knew its importance better
than anyone.

"Nisha Gandhe," said the voice on the other end of the line.
"Would that be the same Nisha Gandhe, ex of Mumbai CID?
Gorgeous smile? Tragically unavailable?"

She grinned. "If that is the same Ajay, municipal records
wizard, then yes, indeed it is. It's good to hear your voice, Ajay."

"And yours. Especially if you've dumped your rich husband
and decided to take up with a lowly municipal fixer?"

"Sadly not, Ajay. I was thinking more along the lines of a
favor."

He made pretend-grumbling sounds but she imagined him
reaching for a pen and paper. "You could have come to the
office to request this, you know. Then I would have had the
benefit of the famous Nisha perch."

She felt herself color. "That's a thing?"

"What can I say? It's a thing."

"Okay," she smiled, "I don't really think I want to know. But
the reason I can't come in person is because this is strictly off
the record, just you and me."

"I see," he said. "*Private* and confidential, eh?"

"Very good. Don't give up the day job. Are you ready?"

"Fire away."

"It's the director Lara Omprakash."

"As in, the recently deceased director Lara Omprakash."

"The very same. She was apparently childless, but the post-
mortem examination reveals she may have given birth."

"Got you."

"Thanks, Ajay."

She left the study. Tonight the family was watching
television in the living room and sharing a pizza. Sanjeev was

indulging in his favorite pastime—channel surfing—much to the chagrin of Nisha and her daughter. Why were men never interested in what was happening on the selected channel but always interested in what else could be happening on some other channel?

"Hold it right there," said Nisha before Sanjeev could change the channel once again. It was the local news carrying a bulletin regarding the life and times of Ragini Sharma. The bulletin was less than two minutes long but the file footage was supplemented by black-and-white photographs of the early days of the politician.

"Why are we watching this?" complained Nisha's daughter. "I want to watch *Hannah Montana*."

"Just a minute, sweetheart. I need to see this because of work."

She continued to stare at the screen as old photographs appeared within the montage, accompanied by melancholy music and a hushed voiceover. Where had she seen that face before?

And then the penny dropped.

Chapter 64

"SHE WAS NO social worker," said Nisha emphatically. "Unless 'social worker' is a euphemism for 'madam.'"

"Think carefully, Nisha," said Santosh. "The incident that you mentioned was a long time ago. You could be mistaken."

"I am absolutely certain. I never forget a face. It was her," replied Nisha adamantly.

"Let's go over this once more," he said slowly. "Take your time and don't leave out even the smallest detail."

Nisha took a deep breath and began narrating her story once again. "When I had just joined the police service, I was initially posted to the Anti-Vice Squad. I distinctly remember we received a tip-off that a batch of young girls was being held captive at one of the establishments in Falkland Road, in the notorious red-light district of Mumbai."

"And what happened next?"

"We raided the establishment," answered Nisha, "and found several girls—most of them minors—inside the place.

Some of them had already been forced into sex with male customers."

"What did you do once you were inside?" asked Santosh.

"We rescued the girls and took them to a remand home. A couple of them were found in possession of drugs and were arrested. We also filed charges against the owner of the brothel—the madam."

"And you believe that the madam was none other than Ragini Sharma?" asked Santosh incredulously.

"She was little more than a prostitute with an entrepreneurial flair," said Nisha. "She had succeeded in networking with several powerful politicians whose perverted needs she served. It was because of her political clout that the charges against her were subsequently dropped, much against my wishes."

"How did she leave behind the brothel and become a member of the legislature?" asked Santosh.

"She claimed that she was protecting the girls and offering them shelter," replied Nisha. "A massive cover-up exercise was undertaken to reinvent her profile. I remember reading a newspaper report that referred to her as a social worker, someone who helped poor and downtrodden women."

"And you think that it was all a cover? That she was actually encouraging prostitution?" asked Santosh.

"Oh, absolutely," said Nisha, nodding her head vigorously. "The transformation from prostitute to brothel owner, then from social worker to politician, was a gradual one. At each stage she was careful to erase as much of her past as possible. I would never have made the connection if I had not seen those old photos of her on the news. Over the past few years she's consciously cultivated a different—more mature— look. Shorter hair, traditional sarees, spectacles . . . but the photographs of her in her youth gave her away."

"I still find it hard to believe that a mainstream political party would accept her as a candidate, given her past," objected Santosh, rubbing his chin thoughtfully.

"Stranger things have happened in Indian politics," argued Nisha. "Over thirty percent of Members of Parliament have criminal cases pending against them. The figure is even higher in the state assemblies. Phoolan Devi, the famous Bandit Queen, who had killed twenty-two villagers in cold blood during her life as a *dacoit*, was subsequently elected to parliament even though she had thirty criminal cases conducted against her. Ragini Sharma pales in comparison."

Chapter 65

IT WAS LATE and Mumbai's oldest red-light district hummed with activity.

Kamathipura had begun life as a "comfort zone" for British troops in the 1880s and was now a fourteen-lane district densely packed with dilapidated buildings and precariously balanced hutments, almost every one of them a brothel. They teemed with young girls, many kidnapped from country villages or sold into the sex trade by their own families. Drug addiction, alcohol abuse, STDs, and HIV—they all abounded in an area that over fifty thousand prostitutes euphemistically called home.

"Do you recall which one it was?" asked Santosh, as they weaved through a street overcrowded with vendors, tea stalls, and beggars.

"I shall never forget it," Nisha replied. Some of the girls that she had rescued that night had been less than twelve years old. She pointed him in the right direction.

"I know that you are perfectly capable of taking care of

yourself, but in this area any woman who makes eye contact with a male is considered fair game. Walk quickly and keep your head down," instructed Santosh. They hurried toward the premises Nisha had already pointed out.

A few minutes later they entered a near-derelict building and began to climb a precarious staircase that creaked with each step they took. On the landing, a group of gaudily dressed women stood with dubious male companions waiting for bedrooms to be vacated.

"Hey, babe, how about a blow job?" asked a drunk with bloodshot eyes. He reeked of sweat and alcohol and ogled Nisha with a smirk. He held a bottle of cheap liquor in one hand, and as they passed he reached to grab Nisha's behind with the other . . .

Nisha whirled, brought her knee into his groin and stepped away as the boozehound doubled over with pain, groaning on the bare boards. She shot Santosh a look, as though to say, "How's that for fair game?" and he just managed to suppress a smile in return, hurrying her on instead. There wasn't time for all this.

Now she led them to a room where, seated on a large red artificial-leather sofa, was the brothel's queen bee, busy stuffing a mixture of betel nut and tobacco into her mouth. She looked suspiciously at Santosh and Nisha as they approached, then raised painted eyebrows as Santosh delved for his wallet and placed five crisp thousand-rupee notes into her hands.

The madam looked at the cash. She looked back at Santosh and Nisha, standing before her, and slowly smiled, revealing betel-nut-stained teeth.

"What sort of girl do you want?" she asked Santosh. "Someone to provide a threesome along with your girlfriend?"

"I'm not here as a customer," he replied. "I just need a few simple questions answered."

The madam looked at him distrustfully. "You a cop?" she asked. "If you are, you can have your money back."

"I'm not a policeman," said Santosh. "My colleague and I are writing a book about women who made it big but started out in the world of prostitution. I was wondering whether you could tell us something about Ragini Sharma."

The madam eyed them both as though she didn't believe a word they said, but even so she tucked the cash into her blouse. Leaning over the arm of the sofa, she spat chewed-up betel nut into a brass spittoon on the floor then wiped brown slaver from her mouth.

"That bitch!"

"I take it you knew her personally?" said Santosh, resting on his cane to ease the pressure on his bad leg. He wished his head would stop pounding. That his mouth wasn't so dry.

"You could say that," blurted the madam. "She took extra pride in getting her thugs to 'inaugurate' the new girls. I was one of the girls broken in by her goons. She may show herself off as being a mighty respectable politician these days, but she's just a dirty whore! She used to fuck her clients; now she's trying to fuck the entire country!" The madam had obviously not watched the evening news or read the news reports regarding Ragini Sharma's death.

"Why didn't you leak her story to the press?" asked Nisha. "Why did you keep quiet?"

She curled a lip. "When I first came to Kamathipura, I was fifteen. I was abducted, caged, abused, beaten, and raped repeatedly until I was broken in. There was nothing that I wanted more desperately than to be reunited with my family. Each night I would sob uncontrollably as I remembered my parents, my siblings, and my home in Uttar Pradesh."

The madam took another betel leaf and delicately layered it with lime, catechu, betel nut, cardamom, and tobacco. She placed it in her mouth contentedly and continued: "One night, I was able to escape from my imprisonment. I ran to Mumbai Central railway station and boarded a train for my home village. But when I reached home, my parents refused to acknowledge that I was their daughter. They said I was a woman of loose moral character—a liability. I realized that I had not been kidnapped. It was they who had sold me into prostitution. I took the first train back to Mumbai and returned to the very establishment that had pimped me. There was no looking back for me after that."

"Ragini Sharma accepted you back?" asked Santosh.

She nodded. "A bitch she may have been. But she took me back when I had no home. I owed her for that at least."

"And then?" pressed Nisha.

"I became one of her best-earning girls," recalled the madam. "I was often sent to take care of her special political friends too. She welcomed me with open arms . . . so long as she knew I'd welcome new customers with open legs!"

"What prompted her to enter politics?" asked Santosh.

"She was especially close to someone high up in the government. She was soon serving the needs of several other politicians. I suppose it's possible that she called in a favor," replied the madam with a yawn.

She leaned and spat betel-nut mulch into her spittoon, the interview over.

On their way back down the creaking stairs they passed Mr. Blow Job, still nursing his swollen nuts and bruised ego. As they left the depressing and hopeless place and made their way toward Grant Road, they each privately breathed a grateful sigh of relief.

"It is said that politics is the second-oldest profession in the world but that it bears a close resemblance to the oldest," said Santosh. "It seems that Ragini Sharma mastered both."

Chapter 66

"YOU'RE NOT GOING to like this," said Mubeen, entering Santosh's office.

"Go ahead," replied Santosh. "I'm a big boy."

"The hair we found on Ragini Sharma's pillow? I was able to extract DNA from the root. I then ran it against several databases. I ended up with a match, but you're not going to believe whose it is," said Mubeen anxiously.

"Given that the root was intact," said Santosh, "I would have expected the hair to belong to the victim, Ragini Sharma."

Mubeen handed over a single A4 printout to him: details gleaned from a database at the . . .

"*India Fertility Clinic and IVF Center*?" Santosh started. "You found a match using a *hacked database*?" Mubeen had been right. He didn't like it.

Mubeen shrugged. "There's no national database, so . . ."

"You hacked."

"It's called cooperation, not hacking," replied the medical examiner defensively.

Santosh shook his head then looked at the printout once again. Sure enough, they had a match. The DNA from the hair found on Ragini Sharma's pillow—it belonged to a clinic sperm donor.

"There's something else you need to know," said Mubeen.

Santosh looked up from the printout. "Yes?"

"In the entire series of killings we only found two DNA samples—the hair on Ragini Sharma's pillow and the saliva on Elina Xavier's eyebrow. We thought we had a possible third sample under Ragini Sharma's fingernails because she seemed to have fought back, but the material turned out to be dirt."

"Go on," said Santosh curiously.

"I expected the DNA from the hair to match the DNA from the saliva on Xavier, given that both murders were apparently committed by the same killer," continued Mubeen.

"They're not the same?" queried Santosh.

"They're not," replied Mubeen. "But they *are* related."

Santosh's eyes traveled down to the bottom of the page. Saw the name there.

Nalin D'Souza.

Chapter 67

THE PROPERTY WAS long abandoned, its grounds so mud-soaked and choked with weeds that she was forced to park the car by the side of the deserted road and cover the last mile on foot.

And she wished that time wasn't against them, and that she could have made this trip in the daylight hours.

Ahead of her loomed the crumbling building, painted gray by the moonlight. The roof had caved in, she realized as she came closer. The rear of the building seemed to have been burned down, the walls black with the marks of an inferno. All the windows were either cracked or covered in a thick coat of dust and grime. Behind them was utter darkness and a strange eeriness.

A solid door made from Burma teak had been subjected to years of adolescent graffiti. A rusted chain and padlock held it shut and a couple of speckled lizards stood guard on the smooth stone framing the teak. Nisha's torch beam sent them scurrying for cover as it illuminated a faded signboard above the door.

Bombay City Orphanage, it said, and below that in smaller letters: ESTABLISHED 1891 BY THE SIR JIMMY MEHTA TRUST. She snapped a picture of it with her smartphone.

There was part of her that wanted to turn away from this sinister place. It dredged up memories of her own childhood, of a dead mother and an absent father. Adopted by a loving couple with strong middle-class values, she had been well educated and her adoptive parents had supported her endeavor to join the police force. But privately she always felt the absence of her biological parents.

Anyway. Enough. She shrugged off the memories to focus on the task at hand.

Would there be anything worth examining inside the ramshackle place? She could almost hear her own thoughts in the ominously silent ruins of the neglected establishment. Except for the chirping of crickets there was no sound to be heard, the nearest dwellings over a mile away. The land that had been donated to the orphanage trust was along the fringes of the long stretch of dark and forbidding mangroves that bordered Malad Creek.

She didn't have a warrant but given the building's state of disrepair she decided to take her chances and picked a rock from the ground to hammer against the rusting padlock. The blows reverberated in the stillness, shattering the creepy calm, and the rusted lock fell with a clunk to the porch floor.

Taking a deep breath, Nisha kicked open the door then slipped inside, listening. All was quiet.

So how come she had the feeling that she wasn't alone?

She ran her flashlight beam over what turned out to be a colonial-style entrance lobby. Years of neglect had resulted in a heavy layer of dust everywhere and she brought a kerchief to her face as she moved the light. To her right was a doorway leading to smaller office rooms; to her left empty hooks and patches of fading plaster spoke of pictures removed from the wall.

In front of her was a wide staircase leading to the floor above. She stepped toward it, then jumped as startled pigeons suddenly took to the air, the flapping of their wings loud as explosions in the damp silence.

Her heart hammered in her chest and she fought to control her breathing, almost laughing. She decided that if it came to a straight choice between a drunk demanding a blow job and pigeons, she'd take the drunk any day.

Now she took the steps, gingerly, praying the creaking floorboards wouldn't give way. She reached the first floor where a large room was filled with old rusting bed frames. Once upon a time it would have been a dormitory filled with children— children with no parents. Children like her.

Lost in thought, she didn't sense what was behind her until it was too late, and a blow from behind sent her sprawling to the floor.

Chapter 68

SURROUNDED BY HIS entourage, the Attorney General made his way across the plaza outside the courtroom of the Chief Justice with an almost majestic swagger.

The legal guardian of the rights of 1.2 billion Indians and occupying a constitutionally mandated rank devised to keep him at one remove from the contemptible politics of New Delhi, the Attorney General was known to be an inexhaustible worker with an incredible memory for facts, a complete mastery of the law, and an ability to direct senior judges effortlessly.

He was also a master at negotiating his way through the corridors of power. Having arrived in New Delhi as an outsider, he had taken to the country's political capital like a fish to water. Realizing quickly that one often had to play the man rather than the ball, he had become good friends with the Prime Minister's political advisor. And having achieved that, seemingly there was nothing and no one that the Attorney General could not maneuver in New Delhi and beyond.

He crossed the plaza, headed to his white Ambassador car bearing a red beacon on the roof, and asked his driver to take him to his chambers at Motilal Nehru Marg. His entourage bundled themselves into a second car and followed. As he settled into the uncomfortable rear bench seat—standard government issue—his phone rang. He looked at the number flashing on his screen. It was the Director of the CBI—the Central Bureau of Investigation.

He took the call.

"We have tried our best," began the Director. "In my opinion nothing can be traced back to you."

"How sure are you?" asked the Attorney General softly.

"I've had several men assigned to the matter. Unfortunately it's like looking for a needle in a haystack."

"I cannot afford to have this come out. The stakes are too bloody high."

"I understand completely," said the Director. "I shall do my best to keep it under wraps."

"I appreciate that," the Attorney General told him.

It was fortuitous that the Director of the CBI was under a cloud and needed all the help he could get to hold on to his position. The Attorney General had promised him he would speak to the Prime Minister's political advisor and swing matters his way.

The Attorney General smiled as he disconnected the call. It was always good doing business with people whose interests were aligned with one's own.

Chapter 69

HURT, NISHA TWISTED and in the bouncing beam of the flashlight caught a glimpse of her assailant. A grubby man wearing filthy shorts and a ripped vest, his hair was long, reaching his shoulders. In his upraised hand was a short club of some kind, ready for another attack.

"Who are you?" he demanded, advancing on her.

But she was in no mood to answer questions. The pigeons were terrifying, but grimy guys with big sticks she could deal with.

As he advanced she dazzled him with the torch and pivoted at the same time, sweeping his legs from beneath him.

The club spun off as he fell badly, and with a shout of pain so loud she didn't even bother drawing her gun. In a second she was astride him, pinning him to the floor and dazzling him again with the flashlight. Now she saw him for what he was: a grimy, broken-down old man. She felt mildly nauseous as she was hit by the stench of his unwashed body and bad breath.

On his clothes was the odor of cheap alcohol and stale tobacco smoke.

"We can do this either the easy way or the hard way," hissed Nisha. "Answer a few questions for me and I leave you with enough cash for a tipple. Play tough and I leave you with busted kneecaps."

He blinked in the light, his eyes adjusting. "Why? Who are you?"

"My name is Nisha Gandhe and I'm an investigator," she replied, out of breath. "I was hoping that a visit to this place would help me find out a little more about Elina Xavier."

"Why do you want to know?" he asked cautiously.

"She was murdered a few days ago and research into her background showed that she had once been the headmistress of this orphanage," replied Nisha. "Why don't you begin by telling me who you are and what you're doing here?"

"I used to be the night guard for the orphanage," he said, lips loosened by the promise of more booze. "I stayed here until the place shut down during the Mumbai riots."

"Why would the riots affect an orphanage?"

Pinned beneath her, he still managed a shrug. "Riot's a riot. Riot doesn't care what it destroys."

"And what are you doing here now?"

Again he shrugged. "It's here or the streets."

"And you were an employee during the years when Elina Xavier was the headmistress here?"

"Sure," said the man. "I was officially employed here at that time. She was a real tight-ass, that one."

"What do you mean?" asked Nisha curiously.

"She had all the trustees wrapped around her little finger. She could do whatever she wanted and get away with it because they were all on her side. She was arrogant and bossy with everyone here."

"How was she with the children?"

"She was a harsh taskmaster, demanding discipline, courteousness, and hard work from the kids."

"Anything else that I should know?" asked Nisha, tightening her grip on his wrists.

"There were rumors . . . but I never saw it happen," said the man suddenly.

"Rumors about what?" asked Nisha.

"That she beat the children," he said uncomfortably. "I remember hearing them crying and screaming at night, but I was never sure whether it was because of Xavier."

"Was there any evidence to suggest that she abused the children?"

"The housekeeper who cleaned the dormitory would talk of soiled sheets and bloody welts," replied the man cautiously, "but then that woman hated Xavier. I could never be sure what to believe."

"Why didn't the trustees take action? Why would they sit by quietly if there were instances of abuse?"

"The chief trustee was a powerful man. I can't remember his name now but he was very well connected, the bugger. Xavier was bonking him. In her younger days she was quite a looker," winked the deadbeat.

Nisha thought about what the man had just said and released his arms. Getting off him, she reached into her pocket and pulled out a five-hundred-rupee bill that she handed over to him wordlessly. She then turned around and made her way out of that dark and evil place that still seemed to echo with the cries and screams of orphans.

Chapter 70

ON THE WEDNESDAY that Elina Xavier, the school principal, had been murdered, she had spent the better part of the day in Mahim Church.

She had shuffled her way through the crowds gathered for prayers. Although it was a Catholic parish, few people in Mumbai called it St Michael's Church. For the average Mumbaikar—as Mumbai residents called themselves—it was simply known as Mahim Church after the area in which it was located, a place where not only Christians but also Hindus, Muslims, Parsis, Buddhists, and Sikhs could gather to pray.

It was believed that visiting the church on nine consecutive Wednesdays would result in wishes being granted—and this was Elina's ninth. She had been diagnosed with leukemia a year previously but her doctors were now telling her that the disease was in remission after bone-marrow transplants, dialysis, and multiple rounds of chemotherapy. All she had wanted was her life back. Hence her desperate call for help to the Lord each Wednesday.

Father Luis had seen Elina Xavier and looked at his watch. She had specifically requested to say confession today. It seemed as though she had needed to get a few things that were bothering her off her chest. He had gestured to her to enter the confessional. Elina had pulled herself together, taken a deep breath, and followed him to the box, taking her place on the opposite side of the screen.

Wearing a pale blue dress and dark blue shoes, she had carried a smart white calfskin handbag and had had a dignified air about her. It had been obvious that she must have been eye-catching before age and illness had taken their toll.

She had pulled a piece of paper out of her purse.

"Bless me, Father, for I have sinned. It has been many years since my last confession," Elina had said, kneeling down.

"Go ahead, Elina," Father Luis had said.

"As you know, I used to manage the Bombay City Orphanage that was established by the Sir Jimmy Mehta Trust," she had begun.

"Yes, I do recall that," Father Luis had said through the screen.

"I did not do my duty, Father," Elina had said, her eyes welling up.

"Why do you say that?" he had asked gently.

"I was in love with the chief trustee. He was a married man and I was determined to break up his marriage and become his wife. Our adulterous relationship continued for a couple of years."

"I sense there is something more than this that you wish to confess," Father Luis had said. He spoke with the experience of many years.

"I was so caught up in the affair that I allowed the orphanage's funds to be embezzled by him. Eventually it had to shut down and is closed to this day," Elina had replied.

"Be that as it may, you continued looking after the children while the orphanage lasted. That must count for something," Father Luis had said sympathetically.

"But that's just it. I was terrible to them. In particular, after I found out that I had been used like a whore by the chief trustee, I was overcome by rage. I began taking it out on the children who were in my charge."

"How?" Father Luis had asked.

"I would beat them with a rod, often till the welts bled. I would hold their heads under water to discipline them. Sometimes I would fly into a fit of rage if they had wet their beds and would almost strangle them. I was worse than a witch."

"If that was the case, how did you get your present position as the principal of such a well-respected girls' school?"

Elina's hands had trembled. "I blackmailed the chief trustee. I told him that the orphanage had closed down because of his financial misdeeds. I also had evidence of our sexual relationship, which I threatened to expose to his wife."

"And in return, he managed to get you a plum post so that you would keep your mouth shut?"

"Precisely—at the girls' school. Luckily for me, there had been an instance of teen pregnancy there and a reporter from the *Afternoon Mirror* was chasing the story. I went to her office, screamed at her, and told her that I would get the girl's parents to sue her for defamation if she printed anything. The threat worked and the paper dropped the piece. I became the darling of the board of trustees."

"And was your old friend among them?"

"Yes," Elina had replied. "He is still on the board but we

rarely talk. I got married to the gym instructor at the school but my husband died a few years later from cirrhosis. I settled down into my role and made a new life for myself."

"So why this confession, then?" Father Luis had asked.

"I was diagnosed with leukemia a year ago. Don't worry . . . it's in remission. I realize that I need to make a full confession so that I can stop walking around bearing the guilt of my past sins. I need a fresh start, Father."

He had nodded. "And are you actually repentant for your sins?"

Elina had picked up the piece of paper that she had pulled out of her purse and had begun reading: "O God, I am heartily sorry for having offended Thee and I detest all my sins because of Thy just punishments, but most of all because they offend Thee, my God, who art all good and deserving of all my love. I firmly resolve, with the help of Thy grace, to sin no more and avoid the near occasions of sin. Amen."

Father Luis had thought about what Elina had said for a moment. He had sighed before making the sign of the cross, closing his eyes, and speaking.

"Do you reject sin so as to live in the freedom of God's children?" he had asked.

"I do," Elina had replied.

"Do you reject Satan, father of sin and prince of darkness?"

"I do."

"Do you believe in God, the Father Almighty, creator of heaven and earth?"

"I do."

"Do you believe in Jesus Christ, His only Son, our Lord, who was born of the Virgin Mary, was crucified, died, and was buried, rose from the dead, and is now seated at the right hand of the Father?"

"I do."

"Do you believe in the Holy Spirit, the Holy Catholic Church, the communion of saints, the forgiveness of sins, the resurrection of the body, and life everlasting?"

"I do."

"In that case, may our Lord Jesus Christ absolve you; and by His authority I absolve you from every bond of excommunication . . . I absolve you of your sins in the name of the Father, and the Son, and the Holy Spirit. Amen."

The priest had opened his eyes to look though the screen at Elina. She had already left.

Chapter 71

HARI PADHI LOOKED up at the naked bulb hanging from the ceiling and wondered whether the wire would support his weight if he tried to hang himself. Doing that would be preferable to the alternatives on offer.

If only he could get to it.

He lay naked and spreadeagled on the bare table, his hands and feet tied securely to the corners with prickly jute twine. After tying him down to the table, the disinterested cop had left, the cell door clanging noisily shut.

And now he counted the seconds and minutes as he waited, staring at the bulb. The silence in the cell was deafening and intense fear coupled with exhaustion began to tell on him. Softly, he wept.

Suddenly there was a loud noise, a flurry of activity, and Rupesh appeared by his side. Noticing the tears, the cop took out his kerchief from his pocket and wiped Hari's face almost tenderly.

"Shhh. Don't worry," he whispered. "In a short while it will all be over," he said, his tobacco-scented breath wafting into Hari's nostrils.

Rupesh's assistant plugged something into the power outlet immediately next to the prison cell. It was a simple yet brutally effective device—a long electrical cord with a plug at one end and splayed copper wires at the other.

"Are you ready?" asked Rupesh as he waited for the constable to turn on the power supply. The worried-looking constable ran over to him and wordlessly handed over the naked end of the long cord.

Holding the wire in his hand, Rupesh looked at Hari's terrified face. He then began patiently to explain what he was about to do. "My electric prod has two electrodes of different polarity a short distance apart so that a circuit will be created via your testicles. You will feel extreme pain and distress because I shall keep the voltage high and the current low. I shall keep increasing the current if I do not hear what I want from you.

"Shall we begin?" asked Rupesh rhetorically as he placed one of the wires on Hari's privates. Hari shut his eyes in terror as he waited for the circuit to be completed.

The ringing of the phone was almost deafening. Muttering a few choice expletives, Rupesh was forced to hand over the electrical cord to the constable in order to take the call. He listened carefully to the sub-inspector who was calling from a house in South Mumbai.

Hanging up, Rupesh looked at Hari and began to laugh almost demonically. "You have the devil's luck, my friend," he said as he left the prison cell hurriedly, his constable in tow.

Chapter 72

MUNNA SAT IN a comfortable recliner in a private VIP box at Wankhede Stadium. This was the usual venue for premier cricket matches in Mumbai and where one sat was a clear indicator of where one stood in the city's pecking order.

Wankhede was packed to capacity today. Forty-five thousand spectators crammed the seven stands around the field. The high and mighty, however, were seated in thirty-seven special air-conditioned boxes.

Seated in Munna's private box were politicians, businessmen, and movie stars. Money had the ability to make everyone and everything look respectable—including Munna and his shady organization. For the forty-five thousand cricket fans seated in the stands, cricket was all about passion and entertainment. For Munna, it was simply business. He chuckled to himself as he thought about the fact that very little happened on the pitch without his say-so.

Munna's betting syndicate controlled the spot-fixing market

in Indian cricket. Spot-fixing was different from match-fixing, given that it related to isolated incidents as opposed to the entire outcome of a match. With years of experience Munna had fine-tuned the art. For instance, a no-ball, wide delivery, or getting out for single-digit runs did not require all eleven players to be part of the fix. A single player was sufficient to achieve that. Munna's gambling and betting empire ran by receiving bets on such individual events within a match. The result was that India had become the biggest hub for cricket betting across the world.

Seated next to Munna was a short, dark, and chubby man, wearing designer sunglasses. Munna flicked open his box of Marlboro Lights, but before he could reach for his gold lighter the man in shades had reached out with his own.

Public places were designated no-smoking zones but no one dared point that out to Munna. The chubby man nodded respectfully as his boss took a few more puffs and stubbed out the cigarette when his cell phone began to ring.

"*Bol*," said Munna in Hindi. "Speak."

The voice at the other end said something that seemed to upset Munna, but only momentarily. He recovered quickly as he spoke firmly into his phone.

"Signal that motherfucker batsman that if he does not get bowled out in the next twenty seconds, his wife will receive the photos we took of him with the shady lady from Romania."

Disconnecting the call, he turned to his deputy from Thailand and said, "Who was the great man who said that if you've got them by the balls, their hearts and minds will follow?"

Chapter 73

THE ATTORNEY GENERAL waited on the phone for his bookie to register the bet. A minute later the man was back on the line.

"I have cleared it, sir. Your credit limit is back in place," said the bookie. "What type of bet would you like to place? Head to Head, Top Runscorer, Next Man Out, Highest First Ten Overs, Race to Ten Runs or Innings/Match Runs?"

"Next Man Out," said the Attorney General.

"Currently Sriram and Rajmohan are the two batsmen at the wicket," said the bookie, looking at his television screen.

"Sriram," said the Attorney General.

"Odds are three to one," said the bookie.

"One million," said the Attorney General.

"Done," said the bookie.

When the Attorney General had hung up, the bookie informed his boss of the additional bet. "Keep Nimboo Baba informed," said Munna. "He will finance it."

Chapter 74

THE BUNGALOW ON Narayan Dabholkar Road in tony South Mumbai had been built in the colonial style. It provided generous accommodation for whoever happened to be occupying the post of Chief Justice of the High Court of Bombay. The current resident was the Honorable Mrs. Justice Anjana Lal. Unfortunately, she was dead.

Her Honor had not appeared in her chambers on Sunday morning. She was one of the rare judges who worked for a couple of hours each Sunday in order to review the week's cause list. It was common for Her Honor to arrive in her chambers by 10 a.m. and to spend the morning going through affidavits, petitions, replies, and appeals until noon, at which time she would proceed to her club for a weekly game of bridge accompanied by lunch.

Her court clerk, a plump, red-faced man, had tried to reach her on the phone but had failed. He had driven over to her bungalow because it had been so uncharacteristic of Her Honor to not inform him of any deviation from her printed schedule.

Upon reaching her official residence, he had found the guard at the gate in a deep slumber. No amount of prodding could stir him and the clerk had huffed his way into the house to find it empty except for the senior butler, busy preparing tea in the pantry. The clerk had asked the butler's help in forcing open Her Honor's bedroom door after repeated knocking had failed to elicit a response from within.

They had found her lying on the floor, dressed in loose, white, hand-woven cotton pajamas and top, the clothes that she usually wore in order to complete her morning yoga and meditation. Her body had been placed on the floor, her hair deliberately disheveled and her face blackened with charcoal. Tied tightly around her neck had been a yellow scarf. The court clerk had collapsed from shock upon seeing the corpse and it had been left to the butler to inform the Malabar Hill police station of events.

The sub-inspector had arrived within five minutes of the phone call, given that the crime involved a high-ranking dignitary of Mumbai. Seeing the yellow garrote, he had phoned Rupesh and awaited his arrival before allowing his men to touch anything. Rupesh had arrived a few minutes before Santosh, Nisha, and Mubeen.

Santosh circled the body like a sniffer hound. It didn't help because it disturbed Mubeen, who was attempting to take high-resolution photos of the late judge.

"See her hands," Santosh said to Rupesh excitedly. "She has been made to hold a tangle of barbed wire."

Before Rupesh could respond, Santosh used his cane to point to a small piece of paper sticking out from underneath the corpse. "Roll her over slightly and check that," he instructed Mubeen.

Trained to work in a scientific and methodical manner,

Mubeen retorted, "Let me get the photos done first. I'll move her as soon as I have documented her position."

"You will do as I ask," replied Santosh sternly. "I really don't care what sequence you have planned . . . tell me what's on that piece of paper, hmm . . . donkey?" It was a meant to be a question but sounded like a derogatory remark. Santosh was an obsessive–compulsive pain in the ass, but he had never used disparaging terms toward colleagues in the past.

Feeling irritated, Mubeen bent over in order to examine the paper that Santosh was pointing to. "It has been taped to a safety pin and the pin has been fastened to her pajamas."

"Can you discern if there is anything printed or written on the paper?" asked Santosh, the urgency in his voice palpable to all.

"It seems like a picture . . . an image of an animal's tail," replied Mubeen, gently lifting the paper at the corner with his forceps so that he could look at the side facing the floor.

"Precisely!" exclaimed Santosh triumphantly. "That image isn't just any animal's tail. It's the tail of a donkey. As a kid, did you ever play pin the tail on the donkey?"

Chapter 75

DID YOU EVER play pin the tail on the donkey? It's rather common at children's birthday parties. A picture of a donkey with its tail missing is taped to a wall at a height that can easily be reached by the kids. Each child is blindfolded turn by turn and handed a paper tail with a pushpin poked through it. The blindfolded child is then spun around until disoriented and left free to make their way to the wall and pin the tail on the donkey. Interesting game, isn't it? I never played it as a child but decided to play it as an adult this morning.

Getting into the judge's house was child's play. They leave a single guard at the gate to provide security for a colonial mansion! Usually the guard is fast asleep by the early-morning hours. Placing a chloroform-soaked kerchief over his nose required no effort at all on my part. He was out for the count within a few seconds.

The judge's downfall was her precise routine. It was common knowledge that she was an early riser and woke each morning at precisely 6 a.m. to complete a one-hour schedule of yoga and meditation. She spent the next hour reading legal briefs until 8 a.m., when her butler would bring her the newspapers along with her tea. By 9:30 a.m. she would be showered and ready to step into the official car that would take her to the High Court in the old Fort district of Mumbai. Anyone observing the judge's schedule would know that she was at her most vulnerable at 5 a.m. when the house was entirely devoid of staff.

The seventh avatar of Durga is Kaalratri. She has a dark complexion and frizzy hair, and in one of her hands holds a bunch of iron thorns. She is depicted as seated on a donkey, hence my pin-the-tail joke! In any case, Her Ladyship was devoid of any intellect and had simply risen through the ranks because of her influential network of friends. If you ask me, she was nothing more than a donkey herself.

Chapter 76

"WASN'T JUSTICE ANJANA Lal married?" asked Santosh.

"Yes, but her husband and daughter were in New Delhi attending a wedding in the extended family," replied Rupesh.

"So it's possible that the perp has been keeping track of the family and chose a day when the judge would be alone at home," reasoned Santosh. "Our strangler also knew when Bhavna Choksi's boyfriend was out of India."

"The killer stalks the targets beforehand?" asked Nisha. "Or was it simply someone who knew the judge?"

"The butler—what do we know about him?" queried Santosh.

"He's a permanent fixture here," replied Nisha. "He is the chief caretaker of the bungalow and has been attached to the property for over twenty-five years. He personally takes care of every Chief Justice who occupies this residence. Apparently he has served seventeen during this period. He has a staff of ten—including a cook and several gardeners—serving under him."

"Any visitors either yesterday or today that we know about?"

"I spoke with the butler," replied Nisha. "The judge was feeling slightly under the weather yesterday and her GP had dropped in to see her in the evening. I have obtained his name as well as the address of his clinic."

"Anyone else?"

"The judge was very particular about her yoga sessions in the mornings. Usually her teacher came in at six a.m. three days of the week. We have no idea whether her instructor came in today or not," said Nisha.

"What about her cases?" asked Santosh, turning to Rupesh. "Do we know which were currently being decided by the judge?"

"I have asked for a full list from her clerk," Rupesh replied. "She was a tough judge and showed little leniency in her pronouncements. It's possible that she may have created a few enemies along the way."

"I would suggest that we should look at not only the pending cases but also recent judgments delivered by her," said Santosh. "Someone who felt wronged could have done this."

"Sure," replied Rupesh. "I'll put someone from the High Court Registrar's office on to compiling the information." He took leave of the Private India team and got into his Jeep. Instead of going to HQ, he headed toward Arthur Road Jail, also known as Mumbai Central Prison.

Mumbai's largest and oldest prison, it was built in 1926 to occupy around two acres of land in the congested area between Mahalaxmi and Chinchpokli railway stations. The prison was originally designed to accommodate eight hundred prisoners, but densely packed with inmates the average population at any given time exceeded two thousand. Cells designed to house fifty prisoners were crammed with two hundred each. Inmates were forced to sleep in awkward positions on lice-infested blankets and the result was a high rate of tuberculosis among the prison population. Arthur Road was India's most feared jail because of the notorious cruelty of its overseers. While petty criminals were routinely mistreated, incarcerated members of crime syndicates were able to bribe guards and officers and even remotely manage their underworld activities from within. Arthur Road was nothing short of hell on earth.

Rupesh entered the cell that held Hari Padhi in solitary confinement. He was lying semi-comatose on a moth-infested blanket. Rupesh kneeled down near him, yanked him up by his hair, and whispered into his ear, "You got lucky, thuggee boy . . . a murder happened while you were enjoying police hospitality."

Exhausted and terrified, Hari nodded mutely, staring at Rupesh with tired—almost lifeless—eyes.

"I'm letting you go, but you should know that I can have you back here in no time. And, with your background, no one will believe you—including that pretty little thing you are fucking on the side. Do you understand?" asked Rupesh.

Hari nodded meekly.

"So you are now a free man. But here are the terms on which I'm letting you go . . ." explained Rupesh patiently.

Chapter 77

NISHA REACHED THE office in Worli a few minutes before closing time. What she would do for an Ajay-type figure now. She looked once again at the board that read *Office of the Charity Commissioner*, and crossed her fingers that she would be able to find what she was looking for. As was to be expected, most of the staff had left before closing hour. It was a well-known fact that Indian government servants reached their offices late and made up for it by leaving early.

A solitary senior clerk was still at his desk and looked up from the file on his desk as she approached. "I was hoping that you could assist me," said Nisha tentatively, slipping a couple of thousands into his hand.

The man looked at the cash and pocketed it quickly. "What do you want?" he asked.

"Do all charitable trusts have to be registered here in this office?"

"Under section eighteen, sub-clause one of the Bombay

Public Trusts Act of 1950, it is the duty of the trustee of a public trust to make an application for the registration of the trust at the Office of the Charity Commissioner," replied the clerk mechanically. "So the answer is yes, registration is mandatory."

"And is it possible to access the records of a given trust?"

"All trusts are required to submit their audited statement of accounts with this office. Information about income, expenditure, asset block, and trustees can be gathered from the annual audited statements submitted to the authority," replied the clerk, almost rattling off the rule book. "What type of trust are you looking into?"

"I don't understand," replied Nisha. "You mean that there are various types?"

"There are Hindu religious trusts, Muslim trusts, those registered via trust deed, Parsi trusts, and Christian trusts. If you tell me the name of the trust in question, I should be able to assist you."

"It was established in 1891 and called the Sir Jimmy Mehta Trust," said Nisha, pulling up the photograph of the orphanage signboard on her smartphone and handing it over to the clerk.

He scrutinized the photo for a moment. "Ah, that's a Parsi trust. It would have been registered under the previous act—the Indian Trusts Act of 1882. Accessing information on that one is a little more complicated."

Nisha pulled out some more cash that she handed over to him. "I was hoping that you could make it simple for me," she said. The clerk smiled. It would be a happy Diwali season for him.

"Wait here," he said. "I'll need to consult the index first. From that I should be able to pull the file number. What sort of information are you looking for?"

"I need to know when the trust shut down and why. I also need to know who the trustees were," said Nisha. Then she sat down on one of the uncomfortable visitors' chairs and waited.

Chapter 78

THE ATTORNEY GENERAL entered his bedroom on tiptoe to avoid disturbing his wife. His aim was to avoid having to answer any awkward questions. A quick shower was in order.

He was out of luck. "Is that you, baby?" asked his wife, sitting up in bed and switching on the bedside lamp.

"Yes," he replied. "Sorry, I got delayed in the office. That oil-exploration block case comes up tomorrow in the Supreme Court. The entire team had to work late."

"What's her name, you bastard?" asked his wife furiously. "Elina Xavier, Ragini Sharma, Devika Gulati, or something else?"

"That's unfair, dear," he answered. "I have had an extra long workday and I don't need this badgering."

"Oh, poor thing! You must be so tired . . . having fucked every woman inside your office and outside of it!"

"I'm going for a shower," said the Attorney General.

He was heading to the bathroom when a small vase whizzed

by him and smashed into the door. "You are an animal! Strange thing is that whenever *I* want it, you can't seem to bloody get it up!"

"Is everything my fault?" he asked. "We did try for a child several times through the IVF route. What more do you want of me?"

"Love," said his wife, dropping her head back into the pillow and breaking down.

Nalin stopped in his tracks for a minute, wondering about his next move. Then he went over to the bathroom door, opened it, and went inside for a shower.

Chapter 79

"ANY LUCK ON finding the missing employee at Xilon Security Services?" asked Santosh as he continued to read the note prepared for him by Nisha. It concerned the thuggee cult and the subsequent discrimination that they had faced in India, even a hundred years after their downfall.

"I just saw a Reuters piece indicating that an unidentified body has been discovered in Shakti Mills," Nisha said.

"Shakti Mills? Isn't Xilon's office close by?" asked Santosh.

"Absolutely. Xilon has refurbished an old industrial shed that lies along the road that is now called Shakti Mills Lane."

"Text Rupesh," instructed Santosh. "There is a high probability that the body is that of the missing employee."

"How can you be so sure? There wasn't even a yellow scarf at the murder scene or Reuters would have headlined it," Nisha objected.

Santosh shrugged his shoulders. He often found it tiresome to explain how he had figured out certain things that eventually panned out to be true. "This particular killing is not for public consumption, thus no scarf."

He went back to reading the note in front of him.

The Criminal Tribes Act refers to various pieces of legislation enforced during British rule in India, the first of which was enacted in 1871 for North India. The Act's provisions were extended to Bengal in 1876, and to Madras by 1911. The Act went through several modifications during the next decade and, finally, a comprehensive blanket legislation was passed in 1924.

Under the sweeping provisions of the new Act, the government was required to register all ethnic or social communities perceived as being inclined to the systematic commission of theft and murder. Given that these communities were described as habitually criminal, the government also imposed restrictions on their movements and compelled adult male members of such groups to report weekly to the local police station irrespective of whether they had actually committed any offense or not. In effect, criminal behavior was viewed as hereditary rather than habitual. Biological reasons were assigned to unacceptable social behavior. Crime became ethnic.

At the time of Indian Independence in 1947, there were thirteen million people in one hundred and twenty-seven such earmarked communities. Consequently, anyone born in these social categories was presumed to be a criminal irrespective of their precedents. This gave the police sweeping powers to arrest, control, and monitor their movements. Once a tribe was officially notified, its members had no recourse to repeal such notices under the judicial system. From then on, their movements were monitored through a system of compulsory registration and passes, which specified where the holders could travel and reside, and district magistrates were required to maintain records of all such people.

The Act was repealed in 1949 but it did not change the social ostracism of members of these tribes. In fact, from 1961 onwards, state governments of India began regularly releasing lists of such "criminally inclined" tribes. To date, there are three hundred and thirteen Nomadic Tribes and one hundred and ninety-eight Denotified Tribes of India, yet the legacy of the Criminal Tribes Act continues to haunt the majority of the sixty million people belonging to these tribes, especially as their notification over a century ago has meant not just alienation and stereotyping by the police and the media, but also economic hardship.

"Are you telling me that Hari belongs to one such tribe?" asked Santosh, looking up from the note at Nisha, who had been busy texting Rupesh.

"Precisely," she replied. "His surname is *Padhi*, right? But his birth certificate doesn't show that. His name is given there as Hari *Paradhi*. And Paradhi is the name of one of the criminal tribes listed by the British in 1871."

"Are you certain?" asked Santosh. "Absolutely sure?"

"Paradhis, Kanjars, Nats, Sansis, Kabutras, Banjaras, and countless others feature on the list. Hari changed his surname later in life so that he would be able to escape discrimination," Nisha explained. "The truth is that he could not have murdered Mrs. Justice Anjana Lal. He was in custody when the murder happened."

"But he could have been part of a team that is jointly executing these murders, couldn't he?" asked Santosh. "The Thugs were known to work in groups, right?"

"Hari's DNA was not present in either of the two samples at the crime scenes," said Nisha, placing a small shopping bag on

Santosh's desk. "Have a look inside."

Santosh picked up the bag and peered in. It contained several scarves, all of them identical to the ones that had been used in the murders. They were also indistinguishable from the extra scarves that had been found in Hari's desk by Mubeen. "Where did you get these?" asked Santosh curiously.

"Outside a famous Durga temple in Mumbai," replied Nisha. "Hari goes there every week to pray. A scarf or stole is a very normal offering to the deity. It is not unusual for Hari to have extra scarves lying around."

"Why didn't he simply tell us that? Why hold back and increase suspicion where none was required?" wondered Santosh, getting up from the desk and pacing the room in his usual hyperactive manner.

"Because he was ashamed of belonging to one of the so-called criminal tribes," replied Nisha. "He is having an affair with a young woman—the one whose picture we saw in his photo frame. It's possible that he didn't want her to know his background."

"Fool!" muttered Santosh. "In this day and age, does any-one care that your ancestors may have belonged to a criminal tribe?"

"Simply repealing a discriminatory law has not changed the fact that members of these communities are still treated unfairly. The ones who manage to become educated and find employment usually try to dissociate themselves from any-thing that could link them to their own communities."

Santosh turned very quiet. He limped over to the couch in the corner of his office, lay down, and shut his eyes.

"What are you thinking?" asked Nisha, slightly worried.

"Figuring out how to apologize to Hari and convince him to come back to Private India," replied her boss softly.

Chapter 80

I AM SIPPING from my cup of freshly brewed coffee as I scan the morning newspaper. *The body of an unidentified man was found inside the abandoned Shakti Mills premises in Lower Parel,* reads the article.

> The unidentified male victim, reportedly in his late twenties or early thirties, was found inside a disused tank of the erstwhile spinning and dyeing shed. This particular shed could be accessed directly from the main approach, Dr. E. Moses Road. Officers from the N. M. Joshi Marg police station are conducting the investigation.

Alas, Mr. Patel is not one of the trophies that I can publicly take credit for. For every act that happens onstage, some events must happen behind the scenes. This was a backstage event.

In fact, Mr. Patel was one of my first victims. It's just that the incompetent cops did not find his body until several days later, hence the news item today.

Patel was very punctual, though. He had promised to be at Shakti Mills by seven o'clock in the evening and he was there a few minutes before that. I was waiting for him inside the shed, leaning against an old concrete tank that once must have contained dyes and pigments of all hues for fabric to be dipped in. He approached me hesitantly.

"Do you have it?" I asked.

"Do you have the money?" replied Patel.

I quickly opened the brown Manila envelope and showed him five neat bundles of one-thousand-rupee notes, a grand total of half a million.

Patel reached into his pocket and took out a 128GB USB flash drive. "It contains the plans and wiring of all the locations that we manage in Mumbai," he said. "It also contains the passwords and master codes that allow remote access where such access is permitted."

I wordlessly handed over the Manila envelope to him as I pocketed the flash drive.

"Don't you want to verify the contents?" asked Patel.

"No," I lied. "I trust you."

He thanked me for the money and turned around, walking toward the exit. I attacked the moment that he had his back to me. The rock I held collided with the back of his head. The envelope containing the cash fell from his hands as he tumbled to the ground. He gasped for air as I bent over him and gripped my hands tightly around his neck.

"I don't need to verify the contents because I have no intention of paying you," I said sarcastically as I let go of his neck for a moment and pulled him up by his arms. He had been stunned by the ferocity of my initial attack and was babbling incoherently, pitifully pleading with me to spare his life.

I pulled him to the edge of the concrete tank that was filled with old rainwater. It was covered with a thick sludge owing to the abundant moss that had grown on the surface among the nasty-looking engine oil, turning to neon-green slime. Holding his head in my hands, I pushed his face into the murky water. Patel struggled valiantly and I allowed him to raise his head for a few quick gasps before forcing it back into the tank.

"Holding your breath?" I asked mockingly, obviously not expecting a reply. Patel's respiratory system, in an attempt to protect itself, had initiated involuntary holding of breath but it was evident to me that water would soon enter his mouth, forcing his epiglottis to close over his airway. It was a matter of time before his body would shut itself down due to oxygen deprivation.

I suddenly felt him give a few violent jerks. Hypoxic convulsions. In a few seconds it was all over. I pulled him out and laid him on the ground in order to empty his pockets of his wallet, visiting-card case, kerchief, keys, and coins.

I looked at his visiting cards. *Mr. Mayank Patel, Senior Engineer, Xilon Security Services.* Pity that someone who brags about protecting hundreds of homes and establishments could not protect himself, I thought to myself as I quickly lifted him by his legs and tipped his corpse into the filthy slime of the tank.

Chapter 81

SANTOSH ANSWERED HIS phone immediately when he saw that the caller was Rupesh.

"What the fuck are you guys at Private India up to?" yelled Rupesh angrily. Santosh moved the phone some distance away from his ear and switched to speakerphone mode so that Nisha could also hear the conversation.

"I don't know what you are talking about, Rupesh," said Santosh truthfully.

"Why didn't you tell me that you were investigating the god-damn Attorney General of India?" Rupesh demanded. "Why must I get a kick in the nuts from the Home Minister with a suggestion that I should lay off?" Santosh could visualize Rupesh's face, his lips red with tobacco, the spittle shooting forth from his mouth as he yelled.

Santosh shrugged. "I wouldn't say he was *investigated*, as such . . ."

"Then what's this I hear about you having illegally accessed his DNA records?" asked Rupesh.

"We had no idea that the hair on Ragini Sharma's pillow would throw up a match. In previous crime scenes the hairs that we found could not be used for DNA extraction," Santosh answered calmly. "It was a matter of chance that our database search produced a match with the hair found at Ragini Sharma's home. It happened to be the DNA of a sperm donor at an IVF clinic. That donor turned out to be the Attorney General. His sequence was on the clinic's computer because he and his wife had been trying to have a baby through the IVF route. It's not like we specifically went out looking to pin the blame on him."

"You should have informed me of all developments," insisted Rupesh. "The political shit from above lands on me, not you!"

"Since we are talking, Rupesh," said Santosh gently, "there is something else that you should know."

"What?" asked Rupesh, cooling down.

"You arranged for us to obtain a list of all case files that Mrs. Justice Anjana Lal had either delivered orders in or partially heard. You remember?"

"Yes. What of it?"

"Well, it seems that one of the cases she had been hearing pertained to a case of corruption brought against the twelve trustees of a charitable foundation called the Sir Jimmy Mehta Trust."

"And?" asked Rupesh, curious now.

"The foundation was established by a wealthy Parsi banker. It ran several charitable projects including a children's orphanage in Mumbai. Unfortunately, the trustees were accused of siphoning off a substantial part of the endowment."

Santosh could see Nisha scribbling on a piece of paper. She passed it to Santosh. It read, *AG was chief trustee.*

"What does that have to do with our case?" asked Rupesh, faking ignorance.

"One of the twelve trustees was the Attorney General. In fact, he was the chief trustee in later days. The case was pending in Justice Anjana Lal's court and if she had found the trustees guilty, such a ruling would have invalidated his appointment to the office of the country's highest law officer."

There was a pause at the other end of the line. Rupesh was figuring out how he would get himself out of the mess they had created by their investigation.

"Are you still there?" asked Santosh, knowing full well that Rupesh was still on the phone.

"Yes, I'm here."

"What do you suggest that I should do in this matter?" asked Santosh innocently.

"Give me some time to think it over," replied Rupesh. Santosh knew that he meant: Let me discuss the matter with my political masters.

Chapter 82

"THE YOGA INSTRUCTOR," gasped Nisha, looking up from the computer on which PrivatePattern, the organization's analysis tool, had created several relationship maps.

"What?" asked Santosh.

"The yoga instructor who visited the judge's home three times per week was also the instructor to Priyanka Talati and Lara Omprakash."

"Interesting," murmured Santosh, getting up from his chair and walking over to check the output on Nisha's computer.

"Even more interesting," said Nisha, "is the fact that our murdered journalist was scheduled to meet this same yoga instructor—Devika Gulati—as part of her investigation into people who work alongside celebrities."

"Do you know where we can find her?"

"She has a yoga studio in Walkeshwar," replied Nisha. "And there's something else," she added, reading an email from police HQ. "The overall build and clothing of the unidentified man at Shakti Mills matches with the description of the missing engineer from Xilon Security. Could this be our perp?"

"He's not our perpetrator. Let them find out the extent of decomposition of the corpse," replied Santosh. "I'm pretty certain that this engineer would have been killed before the other murders happened. He was used by the perp to obtain CCTV, security, and access details, and eliminated after he was no longer of any use."

"Should I ask Hari to go to N. M. Joshi Marg police station and check the man's belongings and crime-scene report?"

"Sure," replied Santosh. "Speaking of Hari, how is he doing?"

"He's come to work today after your chat with him yesterday," said Nisha. "There's still an uncomfortable silence between us, though. I'm feeling lousy that we allowed Rupesh to arrest him and subject him to the third degree."

"I know what you mean," said Santosh. "It will take a while for him to open up to me. In the meantime, please try to communicate with him. Ask Mubeen to help."

"Sure, I'll try."

Chapter 83

DEVIKA GULATI RAN Yoga Sutra, a stylish studio in upmarket Walkeshwar.

Nisha parked outside, giving the building an appraising look. Under Mumbai's property development rules, it was illegal to build within five hundred meters of the coastline. Yet Yoga Sutra was almost on the edge of the sea, no doubt with glorious views of Marine Drive and the Arabian Sea.

"So how did you swing that, eh?" said Nisha to herself, getting out of her car.

But she already knew the answer. In Mumbai any rule could be broken—as long as you had the right friends. A quick Google search had shown her what Devika Gulati looked like. And with those looks and that figure, she probably had no difficulty making friends.

Catty, Nisha, she thought. *Catty. (But true.)*

Not just one of Mumbai's most exclusive areas, Walkeshwar was also surprisingly quiet. The governor lived here. So did several Mumbai billionaires. Even so, what little street noise there was disappeared as Nisha stepped into the serene inner sanctum of Yoga Sutra.

In the reception area, a large statue of Buddha had been adorned with flowers and Japanese incense, while faint strains of eastern meditative chants created a soothing vibe. Through tastefully frosted glass, Nisha could see the main studio, where women on yoga mats were making the traditional bridge pose. Urging them on, even more curvaceous in the flesh than she had been on Google Images, was Devika Gulati.

Nisha's gaze traveled further. She'd been right about those amazing views.

"Devika's class finishes in ten minutes," smiled the receptionist. "I'll inform her you're here."

"Thank you."

She took a seat opposite a wood-paneled wall and studied autographed photographs of Devika with an assortment of celebrities—actors, musicians, authors, politicians, businessmen, and bureaucrats. Among the photographs were images of Lara Omprakash and Priyanka Talati. Reaching forward, Nisha picked up a Mumbai society magazine from a coffee table and began to flick through it, stopping when she came across a familiar face.

She almost didn't recognize him without the expression of irritation on his face, and then it clicked. It was Aakash, "just Aakash," brandishing a comb and a pair of scissors as though they were deadly weapons. According to the magazine he was Mumbai's "Hot Shot Hair Guru," with an "ever-expanding celebrity client list."

So they'd fallen for it too, she thought, smiling. And then something occurred to her. Unless . . . what if he'd been lying to her and Santosh? What if he really did have a celebrity client list? And then she was dragged from her thoughts as the door to the main studio opened and yoga students began to leave.

Devika Gulati appeared. Seeing off the last of her pupils with a smile and clasped hands, she turned her attention to Nisha, and though her poise remained, the smile faded, and she became businesslike as she moved across reception to greet her guest. The two shook hands and Devika gave Nisha a deliberately appraising up-and-down look that ended with an almost imperceptible tilt of the nose, as though she . . . *approved* of Nisha.

"Sorry I kept you waiting," Devika said politely, leading the way to a private office. She seemed to waft rather than move, Nisha noticed.

Devika settled into a patterned sofa that bore handwoven Hindu motifs on the cushions. She waved a hand at a slightly less comfortable-looking chair opposite and Nisha took it, suppressing a smile, knowing they were playing games here.

"So, how may I help you?" asked Devika. One arm was across the back of the sofa, and her legs were crossed at the knee. She was so . . . *arranged*.

"Mrs. Justice Anjana Lal," began Nisha. "Were you with her on Sunday morning?"

"No. I visited her on Mondays, Wednesdays, and Fridays," replied Devika. "She performed her yoga routine independently on the remaining days of the week."

"Could you please tell me where you were on Sunday morning?"

"That's easy. I returned on Sunday evening from Bangalore where I had gone to conduct a health and wellness seminar for a spa," replied Devika. "My secretary will be happy to share my travel itinerary and ticket copies with you."

"Did you know Priyanka Talati and Lara Omprakash?" asked Nisha, taking notes on her smartphone.

"Lara was a regular. I had known her for many years," replied Devika. "Priyanka was a newbie. I had been assigned by her music company to help her shape up for a music video that she was getting ready to shoot. It's terrible what happened to both ladies," she added, almost as an afterthought.

"Where were you during the night that Priyanka Talati was killed?" asked Nisha. "Monday, between eleven p.m. and midnight?"

Devika stood, crossed to a desk and punched a number on the intercom. "Fiona, please check my diary and tell me what my schedule was on Monday evening," she requested.

Within a few minutes the receptionist walked in with Devika's diary. "You were attending the launch of the new spa at Hiranandani Gardens," she said, leaving the diary with Devika and withdrawing.

"Ah, yes," said Devika. "It was a dinner hosted by the owner of the Gordon Crest Hotel to celebrate the opening of their new spa. I am a consultant for the project so my presence was required."

"Until what time were you there?"

"I left a little after midnight."

"Did you go straight home?"

"No, I was with a friend and we stopped for a drink at the J. W. Marriott Hotel before he left me at my house."

"May I know the name of your friend?" asked Nisha.

Devika smiled thinly. "Everyone knows his name. He is Nalin D'Souza, the Attorney General of India."

Chapter 84

NISHA LEFT YOGA Sutra, her mind fizzing. Not only did she now know how Devika Gulati had secured such a prime piece of Mumbai real estate, but the name of the Attorney General had cropped up once again—surely too much of a coincidence?

As she reached her car her phone rang. It was Ajay calling from the BMC—Bombay Municipal Corporation—office.

"Hello, Nisha," he said.

Her eyes went automatically to the steering wheel where the yellow scarf had been tied. Next she craned over her shoulder to check the back seat was empty. Satisfied there were no surprises in store, she clicked the central locking.

"Well," she said, "if it isn't my favorite municipal fixer. I was thinking about you just the other day . . ."

"In the shower, I hope."

"Ajay," she chided. "I'm a married woman. No, it was in the Charity Commission."

"Oh, those bent bastards. Let me guess. Good looks and a winning smile got you nowhere?"

"It was cold, hard cash or nothing."

"What if I were to tell you that my services come with a price too?"

She pulled the seatbelt across herself, clicking it into place. "I'd tell you to stop pushing your luck and tell me what you've got to tell me."

"Okay. Are you ready for this? Your Lara Omprakash child-birth query. Now, it took a bit of digging because it turned out that Lara Omprakash is a stage name. Her real name was Jamuna Chopra."

"Right . . ." said Nisha.

"And Jamuna Chopra did indeed have a child when she was just out of her teens. June twelfth, 1984."

"You're a genius," said Nisha.

"I'm glad it's been recognized at last."

"What else? Who was the father?"

"Father unknown. Child's name Aditi Chopra."

"Oh?" said Nisha. "A girl?"

"Absolutely. Gender: female."

"Okay. I wonder if you could—"

"Tell you if Aditi has married or died?"

She grinned. "You know me too well."

"I'm wasted in this job, aren't I? The answer's no. Not under that name anyway."

"Ajay, I think I love you," she said.

"If only . . ." he sighed.

"But Lara Omprakash was childless," said Santosh moments later when she called him, still parked in the road outside.

"Obviously not," she said.

"So what happened to the child?"

"Maybe nothing. Maybe Lara just kept her out of the lime-light and Aditi Chopra is living with a husband and kids somewhere nice, enjoying the good life."

"Maybe," said Santosh doubtfully. "And maybe not. Our victims seem to specialize in double lives. I've just been looking at the Mumbai crime records and it turns out that Devika Gulati is not what she seems either. She spent several years in prison on account of drug charges."

"Really?" Nisha gasped, trying to marry the two images. On the one hand, a jailbird. On the other, the diaphanous, model-like creature she'd just met.

What's more . . .

"She's friends with the Attorney General," added Nisha.

"Now there's a name that keeps cropping up."

"Exactly. He's her alibi for the night."

"And she is his."

"You think she's covering for him?"

"It's possible," said Santosh. "I tell you what. Go back in there, confront her with what we know about her criminal record, and that name—Aditi Chopra—put it to her."

"Got it," she said.

"And Nisha?"

"Yes?"

"Be careful."

"Will do, boss."

Chapter 85

SANTOSH WAS THOUGHTFUL when he ended the call, his pulse quickening, feeling that familiar buzz—not of having cracked the case, but of being about to. A sense of the pieces falling into place.

He stood and leaned on his cane as he limped over to the magnet board. He'd kept it updated since the first two murders, record cards bearing the victims' names, placed in the order in which the bodies had been found. There had been an average of one a night for the past seven nights. And if he was right, and the murders were an obscene caricature of the goddess Durga, then there would be two more, an eighth and a ninth victim. Tonight and tomorrow night.

Connections, he told himself. *Look for connections.*

Moving over, he gazed at the name *Lara Omprakash*. Her tattoo made her the only victim with a direct connection to the goddess Durga. The fact that she'd had a baby—this Aditi Chopra—might or might not be significant.

Double lives. Victims with double lives.

He moved the name *Lara Omprakash* to one side, placing it at the top of the right-hand side of the board.

What if Lara Omprakash had her child, Aditi, but for whatever reason had given the girl up? Where might she have taken the girl?

To an orphanage? He reached for the name *Elina Xavier*, taking it out of the victims' order and adding it to the new one on the right-hand side.

But the orphanage had been gutted during the Mumbai riots, and the orphans presumably turned out onto the streets, where they would have been easy prey for pimps and human traffickers. People like . . .

Ragini Sharma, perhaps?

He stood gazing at what was looking less like a roll-call of victims and more like the beginning of a life story, wondering if he was on to something or if it was just the workings of a tired and overactive imagination—

"Ahem," came a voice from the door.

Santosh snatched for his cane as he whirled, seeing Rupesh in the doorway.

"Rupesh," he said, carefully, "you surprised me."

"So it would appear," said Rupesh. His hands were thrust into his trouser pockets as he stepped into the office. "Your man Mubeen let me in. That boy needs his beard trimming." He stopped. "Hard at work, I see," he said, gesturing with his chin at the magnet board.

"Working on some ideas," said Santosh, waving a hand as though it were nothing, when in fact his brain simmered with possibilities. He stepped over to his desk. "What can I do for you?"

"You could start by giving me the promised case updates,"

smiled Rupesh, looking carefully at the magnet board. He glanced out of the open door. "Is the lovely Nisha not here?"

"She's chasing a lead."

"Is she?"

"I think we're close to cracking this, Rupesh. If you could just wait a day or so for the status report."

"How about you tell me who your number-one suspect is? And please, Santosh, don't say the Attorney General."

"It's the Attorney General," said Santosh, enjoying the look that passed across Rupesh's face.

Chapter 86

NISHA RETURNED TO the yoga studio, passed Fiona the receptionist, saying, "Just one more minute of her time if I could," and ignoring the protests, knocked quickly on the door of Devika Gulati's office, waited for "Come," then let herself in.

Devika, who had been expecting Fiona, looked startled to see the investigator return. "Did you forget something?"

"No. Did you?"

"I'm quite sure I have no idea what you mean."

"What I mean is, why didn't you tell me you'd spent time in prison on drug charges?" asked Nisha brightly.

Devika gave a short dry laugh. "You never asked," she replied. "Why on earth would I *volunteer* information like that?"

"But now it's out in the open," said Nisha, "why don't you tell me about it?"

Devika's eyes were hard. "You seem very well informed. Why do you need me to tell you?"

"I could pull the file," fibbed Nisha, "but I think I'd like to hear it from you."

Devika's smile widened. "I don't think so. I don't think you could 'pull the file' just like that. That, after all, is the sort of thing policemen do, and . . ." she gave Nisha a look of fake sympathy, "you're not a policeman. So be a good girl and leave my office."

"Sure," said Nisha with a grin, "I'll do that, go home, log on to social media, start spreadin' the news . . ."

Devika's face flared, a look in her eyes that made Nisha glad of the pressure of the Glock at her hip. And then, as quickly as it had appeared, the yoga guru's anger died down and she gave a quick, gracious nod, as though defeated by a superior opponent. She waved Nisha to a chair opposite.

"I was young. And a fool," she began. "A terrible combination. I left home and joined a psychedelic rock band. Headzone, they were called. Drugs, booze, and sex were all part of the territory. So much so that I was busted for possession."

"Possession of what?" said Nisha.

"Smack."

Nisha made a surprised O with her mouth.

"A kilo of it," added Devika.

"A *kilo*?" said Nisha. "Why so much if you were just a user?"

Devika stood and walked behind Nisha's chair. Nisha felt herself tense, grateful that she was able to see Devika's reflection in a picture that hung opposite. On the pretext of shifting in her chair she brought her hand to the waistband of her trousers, reassured by her gun there.

"I was smuggling it for my lover—the singer in Headzone."

Nisha watched in the picture's reflection as Devika threw up her hands at her own naive stupidity.

"So why didn't you tell the authorities that the stuff did not belong to you?"

"Headzone's management had contacts with a man named Munna. I expect you know him."

Oh, Nisha knew Munna all right. The rather few cops in Mumbai who wanted to see Munna behind bars were those not on his payroll.

"The management told me that they would ensure the police recorded the quantity as less than a kilo, in which case I'd serve less than six months. They also assured me they'd get Munna to have a chat with the police to suspend my sentence. I went along with it."

"But that's not how events played out, right?"

"Precisely," answered Devika. "The consignment was more than a kilo and I was given the maximum sentence. Headzone cut off all communication with me—apparently I left the band because of creative differences. I'd been tricked by them: Headzone, Munna, Nimboo Baba . . . they hung me out to dry."

"Nimboo Baba?" said Nisha. "What on earth does *he* have to do with it?"

"He works for—or with—Munna. He's Munna's money man." She chuckled at the alliteration.

"How much time did you get?" asked Nisha. She watched Devika carefully in the reflection.

"I was awarded the maximum sentence under the Act—ten years. A stupid mistake had cost me a decade of my life," said Devika softly.

"And that's why you're telling me this, is it?" said Nisha. "You want payback?"

"Maybe," replied Devika airily. "Maybe if you chose to act upon the information I've given you the outcome would be satisfactory for me, yes."

"Why now? Why not years ago?"

Devika fixed her with a look. "I expect you have heard the

rumors that Nalin D'Souza has a fondness for making wild bets."

Nisha spread her hands. Hadn't everyone?

"Well, those rumors are true," said Devika. "Nalin D'Souza owes Nimboo Baba millions. And I am in love with Nalin D'Souza. The downfall of Nimboo Baba would be my gift to him."

Nisha nodded. "One more thing," she said. "I have a name. I wonder if it might mean anything to you?"

"Yes?"

"Aditi Chopra."

Chapter 87

"SHE TURNED WHITE, boss, I swear," said Nisha excitedly, back in her car. "Denied all knowledge of Aditi Chopra. But it was written all over her face. She was lying, I swear it."

"Excellent," said Santosh. Rupesh had taken a seat on the other side of the desk. With his arms behind his head, he listened to Santosh's side of the conversation with interest. "What else did she have to say?"

"Very interesting stuff indeed," said Nisha. "The jail time was drugs-related, and mixed up in it all were Munna and Nimboo Baba."

"Right," said Santosh carefully. He looked across the desk at Rupesh, who smiled back.

Was that it? In the car, Nisha pulled a face. She'd been expecting a better reaction at the mention of Munna. Some kind of reaction at least. "*And* Nimboo Baba," she added, for emphasis.

"Right," said Santosh, who was thinking that the rumors were right, that Munna and Nimboo Baba were partners.

Across the desk, Rupesh was keeping his face blank. *Who else could Munna and Nimboo Baba count as a business partner?* Santosh wondered.

In her car, Nisha frowned. Then, glancing to her left, she saw the door to Yoga Sutra open and Fiona exit. By the look of her bag she was leaving for the night.

Next, the Yoga Sutra signage, a pastel yellow, blinked off. No doubt about it, Devika Gulati was shutting up shop early for the day.

"She's closing," she told Santosh.

"Early?"

"Oh yes."

"Perhaps we've spooked her. Wherever she goes, follow her."

"Right."

They ended the call.

"Interesting developments?" asked Rupesh.

Santosh shrugged, saved from having to explain himself by Mubeen who had just entered his office in a hurry.

"You have to see this," Mubeen exclaimed breathlessly.

"What?" asked Santosh.

"You remember we recovered saliva from the school principal's eyebrow?"

Santosh nodded. He glanced at Rupesh. "Yes."

"Well, humans have forty-six chromosomes. They come in twenty-three pairs in addition to some mitochondrial DNA," began Mubeen.

"Why are you telling me this?" asked Santosh impatiently.

"Because twenty-two pairs are irrelevant. It is only the twenty-third pair that threw up this remarkable result," gushed Mubeen, oblivious to Santosh's irritation.

"What result?"

"There is absolutely nothing in the mitochondrial DNA and

twenty-two chromosome pairs that can tell you whether a given sample of DNA came from a male or a female," babbled Mubeen. "The genetic difference between males and females lies in the last chromosome pair—the sex chromosomes. Women have two X chromosomes, while men have one X chromosome and one Y chromosome."

"And?" said Santosh, warming up to Mubeen's excitement.

"I tested the sample for the presence of Y chromosome genetic material. I did not find any."

"Tell me in simple language what that means," said Santosh, his face flushed with excitement.

"The DNA we found on Elina Xavier is female DNA. Your murderer is a woman."

"A woman?" repeated Rupesh. "The killer is a woman?"

"Devika Gulati," snapped Santosh. He clicked his fingers at Mubeen.

Rupesh had stood. "I'll call for backup at once," he said, and hurried out of the room, his phone to his ear.

Santosh watched him go then whirled, his hand at his forehead. A woman? But the killer was *anti*-women. He *hated* women. His mission was one of destruction of women—the destruction of strong, successful women: a doctor, a pop star, a film director—and not out of envy, oh no, everything about the ritual of the killings, the corruption of the Durga symbols, suggested that his was a mission to desecrate women.

And all this time it wasn't a he, but a *she* . . .

How? It didn't make sense.

He'd thought the killer was a man. He'd *assumed* the killer was a man. The figure caught on CCTV looked like a man, the MO was that of a man who had a deep-seated hatred for women, but what if . . . what if it *was* a woman?

Just now he'd assumed that Devika was covering for D'Souza.

But what if he were covering for her? What if she were killing on his orders? After all, he had good reason to kill Anjana Lal.

Or maybe there were two killers. *Strangers on a Train*-type stuff. One of the killers was Nalin D'Souza, the other was Devika Gulati.

"There's something else," Mubeen was saying, watching his boss carefully. "The DNA from the hair belonging to Nalin D'Souza tells us that he is this particular female's father."

Santosh froze. He glanced out into the main operations room where Rupesh stood at the far side, his back to the office as he made his call.

"The Attorney General is the killer's father?" he whispered to Mubeen.

"It would seem so, sir, yes."

Santosh hobbled over to the board. "Okay, let's think about this. What if Nalin D'Souza was Aditi's father, Lara Omprakash the mother? But Lara turned her over to the orphanage, where she was brutalized by Elina Xavier." Santosh was pointing to the magnet board. "That's motive for two of the murders."

"It would make the Attorney General a potential victim," said Rupesh from the doorway. Santosh grimaced, fearing the worst, but Rupesh was brushing past him to the magnet board, forgetting to strut for once, intrigued by what he was witnessing.

"It would, wouldn't it?" Santosh said, looking at his old friend, and for a moment it was as though the two of them had forgotten their differences.

"Mubeen," he said, without taking his eyes off the board, both he and Rupesh gazing intently at it now, "run the name Aditi Chopra through PrivateTracker."

Mubeen left them and for a few moments Santosh and Rupesh stood, each lost in thought.

"No," said Santosh, "I don't think so somehow—I don't think

D'Souza is a potential victim, not in the way we're thinking: the yellow garrote, the icons. It's women—women who are the targets."

"What about Mayank Patel, the security guy?"

"True," said Santosh. "But that was a killing of convenience. To hide his . . ." he corrected himself, "*her* tracks. There was no ritualistic element. And I don't think she'd allow the Attorney General to die in such a prosaic manner, not if our theory is correct. If we're right," he waved a hand at the magnet board with its emerging pattern, "and this has something to do with avenging the injustices of the past, then she'd have something special planned for the Attorney General. Something special that won't interrupt the pattern."

Something struck him, and gripping his cane, he hobbled to the other side of the desk, flipping up the lid of a laptop and hammering at the keyboard until he straightened with a triumphant noise.

"She bought the shoes," he said. "An 'A. Chopra' is on the list of fulfilled orders for the Oakley shoes."

Rupesh frowned, though his eyes shone. "Right. Well, I don't understand what you're talking about and we'll have words about that presently, but for the time being why don't you explain what you mean."

"I mean she was trying to set D'Souza up. The shoes, the hair. That's it," he exclaimed, and his cane was a drumbeat on the floor as he moved over to the magnet board and raised the stick to point at the names.

"Lara Omprakash was Aditi's mother. Let's say Lara gave her away to the orphanage, where she came into the orbit of Elina Xavier. But the orphanage burned and she was turned out on the street, only to be picked up by Ragini Sharma. Didn't Nisha say . . . ?"

Something struck him.

Something that turned his skin cold.

"Oh dear God," he said.

"*Sir.*" Mubeen had arrived at the door. "I have a match for Aditi Chopra on PrivateTracker."

"It's an arrest, isn't it?" said Santosh. He closed his eyes.

"Yes, sir."

"And the arresting officer," said Santosh, "it's Nisha Gandhe, isn't it?"

"Yes, sir."

She'd been sent the yellow garrote.

Nisha was the next victim.

PART THREE

Chapter 88

NISHA SAT IN the Honda, watching the front of Yoga Sutra. She could have sworn that there was a figure standing behind the window, looking out at her, made indistinct by the frosted glass of the frontage. It was little more than a shadow but even so—she couldn't shake the sense that while she was watching Devika, Devika was watching her.

"Come on now," said Nisha under her breath, "make your move."

Her phone rang and she answered it without taking her eyes off the shadow-figure standing on the other side of the window. It was Ajay.

"What can I do for you, Ajay?"

"Plenty, but not right now. There was something I should have told you."

The figure—it seemed to melt away from the window. Devika was on the move. Out of the front door? Nisha didn't think so. After all, the only car parked out here was hers. There had to be a back entrance. And what was the betting Devika was about to use it to give her the slip?

"What's that, Ajay?" she said. She was getting out of the car now, clicking it locked, reaching to the Glock at her waist and drawing it. She held it discreetly, close to her thigh, pleased to have the feel of it in her palm as she looked left and right along the near-deserted street, then trotted across the road, back toward Yoga Sutra. She tried the door.

"Right, well, it was something I should have mentioned before . . ." Ajay was saying, "maybe nothing important but I thought you'd like to know."

She cradled the phone between her cheek and neck, cupped a hand at the glass and tried to peer through the window, seeing nothing inside but the vague shapes of an empty reception area, an open door leading through to the studio. No movement. No sign of Devika.

No—no, she couldn't have lost her already.

"Actually, couldn't this wait, Ajay?" she said with a touch of irritation. She moved to the side of the building and glanced up a narrow alley that lay between the studio and a picturesque apartment block next door. She looked more carefully at the apartments. Probably had parking at the rear. Probably parking for Yoga Sutra, too.

"It's very quick," said Ajay.

"Okay, then fire away," she said, crabbing sideways down the alley, gun still held down at her leg, phone to her ear.

"It's that information you asked for about Lara."

"What about it?"

"The system lets you see the last person to access that information."

She cocked her head. "Yes?"

"Well, you wouldn't expect information like this to have

been accessed for a while."

"Maybe somebody checking up since her death, like we were?" she suggested, realizing she was speaking in a whisper now.

"Right. But as far as I can tell, I'm the only person to have looked at it since she died. I'm talking about *before* she died."

"How long before she died?"

"A month or so."

"And are you able to say who it was that accessed the information?"

There was the sound of a car engine from the far end of the alley and Nisha began to move more quickly now, cursing.

Can't lose her. Whatever I do, I can't lose her.

"Yes, it was Rupesh," said Ajay.

By now she had reached the rear of the building and peered carefully around the corner. The car was reversing from garages to her left, one of the apartment block's residents. The rear of Yoga Sutra, meanwhile, was silent. Two cars in the parking bays, a silver Mercedes and metallic-blue Audi, both exactly the kinds of cars you'd expect in an area like this. Exactly the kinds of cars you'd expect someone like Devika to be driving. Maybe she hadn't left.

There was a rear door, a glass-panelled back entrance, the kind that stars in dark sunglasses use when they wanted to be discreet. It was ajar.

"Thanks, Ajay," she said, even more quietly now. "That's really, really important. I owe you one."

"Why are we whispering?" said Ajay.

She grimaced. "The same reason I can't talk right now."

"Whatever you're doing, be careful," he said. There was no mistaking the genuine concern in his voice.

"I will be," she whispered, ending the call, resolving to tell

Santosh the news as soon as possible. Just as soon as she investigated this open door.

Coming closer now, she peered into the gap. Inside, the scented air of the yoga studio, shrouded in an after-hours darkness.

"Hello? Miss Gulati?" she said. "I wonder if I could just ask you a couple more questions."

There was no answer. But there was a movement from inside, a shuffling sound.

"Hello?"

Nothing. She raised her Glock. Stepped into the threshold of the door. "Hello? Is everything all right, Miss Gulati? Are you all right?"

She took another step inside, then another. Squinting in the half-light, she reached into the pocket of her jeans for a small flashlight, fumbling as she pulled it out so that it fell to the carpet. Raising her Glock slightly, not taking her eyes off the corridor ahead of her, she crouched, fingers reaching for the flashlight, not liking this. Not liking it at all.

Suddenly from behind her came the slam of a door, just as her fingers gripped the flashlight and she wheeled, raising the gun and the light at the same time.

She saw the shape looming. Something hit her before she could pull the trigger and she pitched back with a cry of pain, twisting too late as something came down over her mouth and nose. She inhaled chemicals. In her pocket, her phone buzzed.

Chapter 89

"NISHA WAS ENGAGED—NOW she's not answering," said Santosh impatiently. "Let's go."

"Santosh, we'll go in my Jeep," said Rupesh. "A siren might help us get there more quickly." Santosh flashed him a grateful look, waving for Mubeen to leave.

Mubeen was already pulling away by the time Santosh and Rupesh clambered into the Assistant Commissioner's Jeep and set off.

"Don't worry, Santosh," said Rupesh. "I called for backup. Nisha will be fine."

"Thank you," said Santosh. He clasped his cane and gazed out of the window, seeing but not seeing a riot of Mumbai color. Caught in the overspill from Colaba Causeway, the Jeep moved slowly at first, Rupesh leaning on the horn and every now and then thrusting his head out of the window to curse at cyclists and unwary pedestrians.

Santosh, meanwhile, was lost in thought. He was thinking

about Aditi Chopra, unwanted child of Lara Omprakash. *Had Aditi changed her name to Devika Gulati? Was she writing her biography in blood, each corpse a new chapter?*

And there was something else as well. Another question hanging around on the outskirts of his mind.

They had pulled away from the main throng now, were traveling faster, but not a route Santosh recognized. Not the way to Devika Gulati's studio.

He glanced at Rupesh. "Where are we going?"

The gun was in Rupesh's fist before Santosh had time to react, the barrel of it pointing across the seat at him. He grimaced. *Fool. What a fool*—so wrapped up in the Aditi Chopra lead that he hadn't questioned why Rupesh needed to leave the room to supposedly call for backup.

"This is something to do with Munna, isn't it?" said Santosh. "You're working for him now, aren't you?"

Rupesh gave a rueful smile. "Let's just say that this is an opportunity to mix business with the resolution of a little personal matter, Santosh."

"Where are we going?" asked Santosh.

"You'll find out—when we arrive," said Rupesh.

Chapter 90

THE RASP OF the vultures overhead. The dry flapping of their wings in the night sky. And the stench. The terrible, terrible stench of death—of corpses laid out to rot in the sun, dozens of bodies left as carrion for the maggots and the flies and the scavenging birds that constantly circled overhead.

This was where Rupesh had brought them. To the Tower of Silence on Malabar Hill, an oasis of green within the concrete hustle and bustle of Mumbai.

But a deserted one. The Tower of Silence was where the Parsis disposed of their dead—an individual's final act of charity, providing scavengers with food that would otherwise be destroyed. There, bodies were laid out to be shredded and eaten by the vultures that were a permanent feature of the sky above the tower.

With Santosh at gunpoint, he and Rupesh entered through an iron door on the east side—the only way in or out—and found themselves on the inside of a vast basin, a huge sunken ossuary pit in the middle.

A full moon illuminated bodies laid out on the stone, men in an outer ring, female corpses in the middle, and children in the innermost ring. Once the flesh had been pecked by vultures, and the bones bleached by the sun, the remnants would collect in the pit, where they would gradually disintegrate into fine powder.

"Go to the pit," said Rupesh.

Though he had one hand over his mouth, Santosh was still retching at the overpowering stench of rotted flesh and bird-shit. He turned and limped toward the edge. The moon cast the stone in a silvery glow. Tendrils of light reached into the pit where a mix of festering blood and tissue and human bones lay coagulating and decomposing.

Glancing to Rupesh, he saw the other man doing the same. Supposedly, the tower could only be entered by a special class of pallbearers, who would be asleep in their quarters. How had Rupesh gained entry? Perhaps, when you counted Munna and Nimboo Baba among your friends, anything was possible.

"Alas, the story must end here, my friend," said Rupesh. He reached into his back pocket with his left hand while his right continued to hold the Glock, pulling out something that he held up for Santosh to see. A pair of handcuffs. And in a voice from the heart of a nightmare said, "You killed them, you drunk bastard."

For a second, Santosh forgot the stink, the vultures, the corpses at their feet, and the gun pointing at him. He simply stared at Rupesh. It was almost as though every second had been stretched into an hour. He felt woozy. Rupesh's words echoed inside his mind as it went into flashback. *You killed them, you drunk bastard!*

And he had, hadn't he? He had killed them.

Chapter 91

THEY'D LEFT IMMEDIATELY after breakfast, Isha, and Pravir, happy and content. Thankfully there had been no discussion of Santosh's extended absence from home and they'd enjoyed a wonderful break at a resort recommended by . . .

Rupesh's sister.

Yes, Rupesh's sister. Santosh and Rupesh were the best of friends: Rupesh had been godfather to his son, even filling in for Santosh at school events.

They drove. The lush green hills were partially covered by monsoon clouds and the gentle spray of rain made the view even more magical. His son, entirely absorbed in his hand-held game, was seated in the rear seat of the car as Santosh drove, wondering why he had allowed himself to ignore the most important people in his life. He vowed that he would give more time to his wife and son, become more disciplined about his own habits and split his time more evenly between work and family. He needed to take care of himself too. Exercise, eat healthily, and cut down on the alcohol.

He cast looks at Isha, seated next to him. She seemed worried, almost as though she were trying to tell him something. When she noticed him staring at her, she smiled self-consciously. Her hands were in her lap, the fingers of her left hand fiddling with the wedding ring on her right.

"Papa, look at my score!" cried his son from the rear of the car. He crouched in the footwell and held the game through the space between their seats, urging his father to take a look.

And because the boy was excited. And because, even though it was just a silly game, Santosh wanted to be a good father and tell him well done, he took his eyes off the road to look at the game.

Just for a second. That's all it was. Enough to miss the bend.

"Watch out, Santosh!" screamed his wife, and he stamped on the brakes and wrenched at the wheel and a million thoughts crowded his head but none were enough to save them and the car spun into the thick trunks of the banyan at the crest of the turn, its horn stuck and blaring like a piercing scream.

Santosh did not know how he reached the hospital or who took him there. He had a vague recollection of dark corridors and of being wheeled on a gurney into the operating theater. He lost count of the days and nights that he was in the hospital. He also lost track of waking and dreaming, the two states mingling effortlessly to make his dreams seem eerily real and his reality a jumbled dream. The only recurrent theme was of a policeman—sometimes at his bedside, sometimes running alongside his gurney, sometimes towering over him—holding a pair of handcuffs and saying, "You killed them, you drunk bastard!"

Both dead. Him the only survivor. What he would have given for it to be the other way around.

Slowly, Santosh returned to the present. He had been staring without seeing, his gaze on the barrel of the gun, but now his eyes rose slowly to Rupesh.

"You were the cop who accused me of being drunk?" he said dreamily.

Rupesh shook his head as though dealing with a fool. "You never had time for them!" he sneered. "I was the one who was always there for them. Attending your son's school play, lending money to Isha when you disappeared for days, comforting her when your uncaring and selfish attitude was too much for her to bear. They became my life, and you killed them."

"You were having an affair with her?" asked Santosh quietly. He was in a state of shock. Later the news would hit home, and he'd wail with the pain of knowing Isha had been unfaithful. But right now there was nothing. Just numbness and shock.

"She was going to leave you," said Rupesh. "But before she could do it, you cut her life short."

"It wasn't my fault, Rupesh," said Santosh.

Or maybe it was.

"Papa, look at my score!"

Rupesh scoffed. "You were never there. And when you were, you were drunk. You killed them before they died."

"If you hated me so much then why did you visit me at the hospital?" asked Santosh.

"You were in a coma for days," replied Rupesh. "I came so I could ease my own grief by blaming you. I would stand by your bed and tell you that you had killed them. I used to hold out my handcuffs and imagine myself cuffing you."

"You killed them, you drunk bastard," said the cop, holding out a pair of handcuffs to Santosh.

"Isha was the finest woman I ever knew. You didn't deserve her. She made the biggest mistake of her life when she chose you over me."

Santosh's head was spinning. He had met Isha through Rupesh's sister. They had all become friends and would often go out to movies or for meals together. Santosh had never realized Rupesh had feelings for her.

"Look at you," spat Rupesh. "Look at you now. You're a lame drunk."

"The doctor says my limp is psychosomatic," said Santosh. Rupesh gave a short, contemptuous laugh but Santosh continued, "He says I don't need the cane, but I do. The pain in my leg is as real as the pain of their loss that I feel every single day, and none of the hatred you feel for me could ever be as strong as the hatred I feel for myself. You say I was responsible. Well, maybe I was, but not because I was drunk, Rupesh, you're wrong about that. But I made an error of judgment, that's right. I made an error of judgment and two people I loved died. If you want revenge, you're getting it, because if you kill me now I suffer now, but by living I suffer every day."

Rupesh gestured with the gun, backing Santosh further toward the edge of the pit. Overhead the vultures circled, cawing, dark shapes against a gray sky, around and around. Below them in the pit, the silence of death.

"I'm afraid I have a taste for vengeance, Santosh. You remember my sister, found dead at Andheri railway station," said Rupesh.

Santosh remembered with a twinge of shame. Too wrapped up in his own grief, he'd had no room to admit more. Hadn't contacted Rupesh; hadn't attended the funeral.

"Two men had taken turns raping and torturing her. Turned out they were both seventeen. They would have served three years in a remand home. *Just three years* for what they did to her. I couldn't let that happen."

"So you went to Munna?"

"I did," replied Rupesh.

"What did he want in return?" asked Santosh.

"Nothing," answered Rupesh. "He said he valued my friendship."

Santosh gave a short laugh. How many times had he heard that before?

"The warden was on Munna's payroll," continued Rupesh. "When the boys reached the remand home, they were picked up by Munna's men. They were taken to his weekend retreat on the outskirts of Mumbai where they were castrated in front of me. Munna had them thrown into his private lake—infested with crocodiles."

Santosh nodded sadly. "And now you're in deep with Munna?"

"We value each other's friendship."

"Then you know he has links with the Mujahideen? They could be planning an attack, Rupesh."

Rupesh nodded. "They are. Tomorrow night."

"*Tomorrow night*," Santosh gasped. "Rupesh, we can't allow this to happen. Please, why are we standing here when we should be out there?" He indicated across the city he loved and hated in equal measure, a city he'd once pledged to protect. And though he'd since left the Indian intelligence service, he had never rescinded that pledge, not in his heart. "We need to stop this, Rupesh," he urged, rapping the point of his cane on the stone for emphasis.

Rupesh snorted. "God, you're so arrogant. Why do you think I need your help? I'm quite capable of handling this myself, thanks for the kind offer. I can talk to Munna. I can talk to Nimboo Baba. They listen to me."

The cawing of the vultures. Bizarrely it reminded Santosh of trips to the zoo as a little boy. Huge birds with a five-foot wingspan. In the zoo you were protected by wire fencing but there was no fencing here.

Santosh shook his head. "No, Rupesh, they won't. You work for them, not the other way around."

"Don't concern yourself, Santosh. You'll be dead."

Santosh looked at him, breathing heavily, sure now that there was nothing left of the man he had once called a friend. "The garrote killings," he said. "You knew about those too, didn't you?"

Rupesh smiled ruefully. "Only that the killer enjoys the benefit of Nimboo Baba's affections. They are lovers, it seems."

"And because the killer enjoys the affections of Nimboo Baba, and thus Munna, she also enjoys the protection of the Mumbai police, is that it?" spat Santosh.

"To be honest I couldn't care less. It's Baba's lover's thing, her pet project."

Santosh shook his head. "And that's why you left the room to call for backup. You weren't calling for backup at all."

Rupesh gave a sideways smile. "In a manner of speaking, I was."

"You bastard. Nisha was there . . . *Women are dying*," said Santosh with disgust.

"It ends tonight. Your man Mubeen will find two bodies."

"*Two* bodies?" said Santosh.

"Gulati and your gorgeous assistant. That, I have to admit, is something of a loss to mankind."

"So Devika Gulati isn't the killer?" said Santosh quickly.

"Oh no," said Rupesh.

The vultures, although they'd been agitated by the new arrivals, were now swooping closer and closer, leathery wings beating the air above their heads, their shrieking cries becoming louder and louder.

And then one dipped. It soared over Santosh's head and he heard the rustle of air above him, flinched, hunched his shoulders, and saw as Rupesh went to ward off the vulture with his gun.

Santosh saw his chance. He drew his sword.

It was not the first time he had drawn the blade from the sheath of the cane. Most nights he worked the action. He often shook it close to his ear to listen for the telltale rattle common to cane-swords.

It was, however, the first time he had ever used the blade in anger.

But he was no swordsman. He carried the cane-sword because . . . Well, why not? He needed a cane, why not have it be a weapon as well? Who knows? It might come in handy on the off-chance he ever found himself staring down the barrel of a gun inside the Tower of Silence.

So he swung his blade wildly, grateful that at least it hit home.

Chapter 92

MUBEEN PARKED BEHIND Nisha's Honda, jogged to the window, and cupped his hands on the glass to stare inside. Empty. He glanced across the road at the yoga studio, seeing a dim light inside, then crossed the road and tried the front door. Locked.

Where the hell were Santosh and Rupesh?

He pressed his face against the frosted glass and could make out the reception area, a desk, framed photographs, like wall smudges in the half-light . . .

But wait a moment. Something wasn't right. As his eyes adjusted to the gloom he could see that a large statue of Buddha in reception lay belly-up on the floor. Yoga mats were in disarray, chairs overturned and, in fact, many of the photographs that should have hung on the wood-panelled wall were on the floor.

And through the door to the studio, covered with a white sheet, he could just see something that looked suspiciously like a body.

With a curse he stepped back from the glass, delving for his cell phone in his jeans pocket.

Santosh. No answer. *Shit.*

He dialed again. This time, he dialed for the cops.

Chapter 93

RUPESH YELLED IN pain and surprise. As he whipped his wounded hand away from the blade, his gun dropped to the stone and skidded close to the edge of the pit. Bleeding, Rupesh fell to his knees, clutching at his wrist. He was momentarily unable to believe the turn of events.

Santosh, meanwhile, was off balance. The force of the thrust had taken him onto his bad leg and he'd pitched forward, and for a moment the two men faced each other, kneeling as if enacting some bizarre greeting ritual—surrounded by rotting corpses.

"You fucker."

Rupesh was the first to recover. Hatred blazing in his eyes, he launched himself at Santosh, shoulder-charging him backwards before he had a chance to defend with the sword, then leaping away as Santosh swung from a sitting position.

The gun. Rupesh was going for the gun. With a shout of effort, pain lancing up his body, Santosh threw himself forward using the sword as a spear point and catching Rupesh on the calf. Rupesh screamed, fell, blood already gushing from the wound on his calf. He fell across the corpse of a child, half its face shredded by the beaks of vultures. He gave a cry of revulsion as he rolled away, then kicked out as Santosh pulled himself to his knees and swung once again with the blade.

Can't let him reach the gun, thought Santosh. *If he reaches the gun that's it.*

A cloud of disturbed flies billowed from a nearby corpse as Rupesh's heels slipped on putrefying matter. Throwing out a hand to lever himself up, he plunged it through the ribcage of an adjacent body, ripping it back out, stinking and dripping, with a scream of nausea.

Rupesh's flailing bought Santosh a precious half-second. Getting to his feet was too much of an effort, so he pitched forward from kneeling, swiping right to left with the blade and nearly catching Rupesh a third time.

Nearly.

Rupesh dragged himself to his feet. Blood poured from the wound at his wrist and his torn trousers flapped at the gash on his leg, but he left Santosh out of reach, marooned in a sea of rotting cadavers.

"*You fucker,*" Rupesh cursed again, but it was as though he were talking to himself now. With a Herculean effort he hobbled toward the gun and Santosh, stranded, watched him lurch away knowing he'd played his final card. Knowing he would die here and because of that Nisha and God knows how many bomb victims would die too. He had failed. He had failed them. Just as he had failed Isha and Pravir.

By now Rupesh had reached the gun and with a shout of triumph swept it up, and whirled to face Santosh . . .

And overbalanced. Lost his footing. Tumbled to the stone on the edge of the pit where his prone body seemed to teeter for a second and a look of absolute horror crossed his face as he realized what was about to happen.

And he fell. He fell screaming, landing with a sickening squelch in the rotted substance that lay in the bottom of the ossuary pits.

For a moment there was silence. The vultures had been scared off by the fight, but now it was as if they sensed the presence of a wounded animal in the tower and they began to caw, even more loudly than before, swooping into the pit to investigate.

Fingers scrabbling for the sheath of his sword, Santosh reassembled his cane again and used it to lever himself upwards, and moved carefully to the edge of the pit. In the cold, white light of the moon overhead he saw Rupesh below. He lay as though pressed into the ooze by an invisible hand, one broken leg at a hideously unnatural angle and the blood from his wounds gleaming darkly in the moonlight. A frightened, pleading look in his eyes.

The first, most intrepid of the vultures landed, its huge parchment wings obscuring the upper half of Rupesh for a moment as it pecked once, twice with its beak. Rupesh then began to shriek, and the bird took flight, a strip of his facial skin in its beak.

"No, no!" screamed Rupesh. His screams were wet, the most terrifying cries Santosh had ever heard. "Please, no . . ."

And he was still screaming as a second, and then a third vulture moved in, excited by the stink of fresh meat, and Santosh pulled himself away from the edge, the screams ringing in his ears as the vultures continued to feed.

Chapter 94

IT WAS TWO in the morning, and Yoga Sutra was a hive of police activity. Overall control of the crime scene had been given to Private, and Santosh and Jack stood over the body of Devika Gulati. She wore her loose kurta pajama practice clothes and her neck had the familiar yellow garrote tied around it.

There was no Nisha, which on the one hand was good news, because there was no second body. But on the other hand, it was bad news. It meant the killer had Nisha and she would die that night, the ninth victim.

And yet her death would be a footnote if the Mujahideen's attack went ahead.

"Oh God, Santosh, you look like shit," said Jack.

Santosh looked at him, his eyes tired and haunted behind his glasses. "You should have seen me before my shower," he said.

He'd been home to change. The bottle of Johnnie Walker had

called out to him and he'd looked at it, known it would blot out the screams of Rupesh and the image of Isha in his arms.

But instead he'd chosen Nisha. He'd chosen Mumbai.

"I've spoken to Commissioner Chavan," said Jack, his hands in his pockets. "The Rupesh business. They're going to recover his body and obviously they'll be launching a full investigation, but they've agreed to leave it twenty-four hours before they pull you in."

Santosh nodded, grateful, as Jack added, "For what it's worth, the Commissioner was not exactly blind to what Rupesh was doing. He told me as much over our round of golf. Truth be told, I arrived in Mumbai earlier at his specific request. I think you'll come out of it well. Meanwhile the Commissioner assures me we have the full cooperation of the cops to find Nisha. You know Nisha—to know her is to fall in love a little bit and all these guys," he gestured behind them at the cops moving in and out of the studio, "they all know her. Anything you want, Santosh, you shout."

"A trace on her cell phone?"

"Done. But no dice. You need a working battery in the phone and either Aditi's removed it or it's flat."

"And her RFID chip?"

Jack looked uncomfortable.

"What, Jack?"

"It's inoperative," said Jack quietly.

"And what does that mean?"

"It means Aditi's probably cut it out."

"Fuck"

There was a long pause as both men banished thoughts too terrible to contemplate.

"What about the other thing?" said Santosh in a lower voice. "Any news?"

Jack shook his head, spoke into his lapel. "Not yet. Old contacts at the Agency are working on it, but the problem is . . ."

"There isn't much to go on. An international target in Mumbai . . ."

"It could be any one of a hundred."

Santosh closed his eyes, wanting to open them and for it all to have been a nightmare. "Then we need to squeeze Munna. Nimboo Baba."

Jack looked pained. "They'll deny it, and we have nothing to connect them to it, apart from street gossip and the word of a bent cop who's currently passing through the digestive systems of several vultures on Malabar Hill."

"The killer," said Santosh thoughtfully, waving the tip of his cane at the corpse by their feet. "Aditi Chopra. She's the key to all this. If we can take her we can use her as leverage with Baba and Munna."

Jack clapped him on the shoulder. "Then find her, my friend. Find her."

Chapter 95

AND THEN, MUCH as it hurt him, much as he hated to be inside when he should have been out combing the streets for Nisha, Santosh went back to the Private HQ, recalled Mubeen and Hari too, then retired to his office—where he closed the door, picked up the phone, and dialed Nisha's home.

Sanjeev Gandhe became very silent when he realized his wife's boss was calling. "I'm afraid to inform you Nisha is currently missing, whereabouts unknown," Santosh told him.

He was some kind of stockbroker type, Santosh knew. "Oh God," he said in a small voice. "Is it something to do with the case she was working on, the strangler?"

"Mr. Gandhe, I'm afraid I'm not at liberty to say, but you can be reassured we are doing everything we can to find her."

He wished he were as confident as he hoped he sounded. But getting off the phone, he put his head in his hands as though to massage his brain into life and all he could see were vultures tearing at skin, Isha in the arms of Rupesh, Pravir wanting him to see his high score.

Think, dammit, think.

Devika's face had been whitened with talcum powder and in one hand she had been made to clutch a small drum, the sort of instrument used by street performers all over India. She'd been made to look like the eighth avatar of Durga—Mahagauri, who was always depicted with a fair complexion and holding a drum.

Which meant that the ninth would incorporate references to the discus, mace, conch, and lotus.

Great. They knew what to expect when they found Nisha's corpse. The trouble was the Durga reference had no bearing on the location of the crime. At their home, at their place of work—it was all the same to Aditi. The one difference being she was holding Nisha captive.

Aditi was Nimboo Baba's lover: "So where did the happy couple meet?" mused Santosh. "Where did you go to, Aditi? From the arms of Lara Omprakash into the clutches of Elina Xavier at the orphanage, and then . . . ?"

There was a knock at the door. Hari stood there—a reduced Hari, his shoulders stooped, his eyes averted, a shadow of the beefy, muscular guy he'd been.

"Hello, Hari," said Santosh, wishing that he could speak to him, wishing there was something he could say—something to ease the pain of his ordeal.

"I've got something, boss," Hari said, unable to meet Santosh's eye.

"Tell me."

"You asked me to check the name Aditi Chopra against clients represented by Anjana Lal when she was just a lawyer, not a judge."

Santosh looked at him. "Yes? And?"

"Anjana Lal represented her."

"Brilliant." Santosh hobbled excitedly over to the magnet board and his fingers moved names around, completing another section. "Look, the story continues: after leaving the orphanage Aditi fell into the clutches of Ragini Sharma, where we can assume she was forced into prostitution.

"She's busted by Nisha. Then represented by Anjana Lal, except Anjana Lal obviously fails her . . ." he moved names, "and she goes to prison, where . . . Does she meet Devika Gulati? Does she meet Munna? Hari, I need to know if those three shared jail time. Can you get that for me?"

"I think so, boss," said Hari from the door. He hadn't moved over the threshold.

"My bet is they shared jail time, but for some reason Devika Gulati fell foul of Aditi, whereas Munna did not. Perhaps it was Munna who introduced her to Nimboo Baba. They became lovers. What do you—"

He turned, but Hari had gone.

Chapter 96

THE CLOUDS IN her head drifted slowly away. The world gradually re-formed. And Nisha woke. Her jacket and sneakers had been taken, but otherwise she was clothed. White T-shirt and jeans.

She lay tied to an ancient, rusted four-poster bed, the kind of thing that looked as though it had been reclaimed from a dump site, her wrists and ankles secured to each corner using yellow scarves. She struggled. Then stopped and gasped as she saw what was attached to the posts by her hands and feet: a plastic frisbee was nailed by one hand, a rubber mallet with a rounded head hung near the other. On the posts near her feet were tied a conch and a lotus.

They were the four symbols—discus, mace, conch, and lotus—of the ninth and final form of Durga, Siddhidatri.

She felt a stinging on her upper back, the prickly sensation of surgical tape, and knew at once that her RFID chip had been removed. The bitch had taken it out while she was under.

Okay, okay, keep calm. They couldn't locate her using the RFID chip but they could trace her—

Laid out on the bed by her hip was her cell phone, the battery placed neatly on top.

Bitch.

Instead Nisha tried to figure out her location by taking note of her surroundings. Above her were ominously high ceilings criss-crossed by rafters of rusting metal. She seemed to be in a massive industrial space, the hard concrete floor on all sides of the bed stretching into infinity, meeting up with exposed brick walls containing vast boarded-up windows. Huge ducts and pipes ran overhead, giving the place a creepy feel. A single naked bulb hung on a wire from an ancient beam overhead, casting an eerie glow over the bed, itself incongruous in the warehouse-like space.

She fought back tears as she remembered her adoptive parents, her husband, and her daughter. She tried not to think about them, but couldn't help herself.

Four arms. A four-poster bed. A discus, a mace, a conch, and a lotus.

She'd been laid out here to die.

Chapter 97

COME ON. COME on.

The story of Aditi's life was forming on the board in front of him but still there were names left: Priyanka Talati, the doctor, the journalist.

"How did they piss you off, Aditi?" mumbled Santosh. "Why did they deserve to die?"

And what connected them?

Okay. Cell phone records showed that Dr. Jaiyen and Bhavna Choksi had spoken to each other. In fact, they'd spoken to each other several times on the day of Dr. Jaiyen's death. The next day, Bhavna Choksi was also killed.

"So was it something they were cooking up between them?" Santosh asked an empty room.

Dr. Jaiyen had been in Mumbai on a personal matter, according to her colleague in Thailand, Dr. Uwwano. Maybe she was mixing work with pleasure, granting an interview to the journalist at the same time.

"Boss?"

Hari startled him, skulking in the doorway.

"Sorry, Hari, come in."

"You were right, boss," he said. "The jail times coincide." Again his eyes swiveled to the floor, as though he could hardly bear to look at Santosh.

"Are you all right, Hari?" Santosh asked him.

A smile flicked on and off. "I'm fine, boss, fine."

"What you've been through—nobody should have had to suffer that. You need time to recover. Later, perhaps, try to rest."

"No," said Hari, so quickly and so sharply that Santosh almost flinched, "I'm not resting until we've caught the bitch."

"Good man," said Santosh. He went to clap Hari on the shoulder. He'd felt reassured when Jack had done it to him, that easy brotherly way Jack had. So *American*. And yet he, Santosh, couldn't bring himself to do it and instead sounded like a relic of empire: "Good man, good man. It's most appreciated."

The awkward moment passed, then Hari said, "The cooperation of the police is proving useful. We should have a picture of Aditi Chopra come through any second now."

Santosh felt his pulse quicken.

Chapter 98

"ARE YOU THERE?" she called.

"Aditi, isn't it? Aditi, I know it's you." She raised her head from the mattress, tried to squint into the gloom at the foot of the bed. Just beyond the reach of her eyesight was a figure who stood in the shadows, watching her.

"I was an orphan too," she called into the dark, trying to establish some kind of bond. "She abandoned you, didn't she, to the orphanage?"

Nisha had been doing some thinking in the hours since she'd recovered consciousness.

"Lara Omprakash, the film director. The world saw her as this gorgeous, talented director, glamorous boyfriends like my boss Jack Morgan. But we know the truth about Lara, don't we, Aditi? We know Lara for what she *really* was—gutless. A coward. She abandoned you, didn't she, Aditi? Or have I got it wrong? Perhaps you know something I don't. Perhaps Lara was simply trying to protect you. Was that what it was? Aditi?"

In reply, silence.

Nisha let her head fall back to the mattress in frustration. Then tried again. "Aditi, please, talk to me. I can help you. I know how you feel because I was an orphan too. I went to the Bombay City Orphanage. You were there, weren't you? Elina, she was a bitch, right? Corrupt, right? You know, a lot of the grievances you have, a lot of people are going to look upon those as being perfectly justified. You've been treated badly, Aditi. But one thing I need to know. You've got to tell me, Aditi. Why me? What did I do to hurt you, Aditi, and how can I put it right?"

There was no response. There was just a titter in the darkness and then the figure moved away.

Chapter 99

THE JOURNALIST AND the doctor had been talking. They were talking—but about what? What did the journalist want from the doctor?

Or what did the doctor wants from the journalist?

She had a story for her, perhaps. Something she had come to Mumbai to expose.

But what? Santosh paced his office, eyes going to the remaining three names on the magnet board.

Singer.

Doctor.

Journalist.

The doctor was from Thailand. The singer spent time in Thailand. The doctor traveled from Thailand to Mumbai. The killer was a woman—a woman who wore men's shoes, who looked like a man on the CCTV. Who clearly had the strength of a man . . .

Or were there two killers? Was that it?

A woman? Or a man?

And then it hit him. The mistake he had made—a question he had failed to ask.

He snatched up the lid of his laptop, retrieved a number, jabbed it into the phone, dialing incorrectly in his haste, hissing with frustration, having to dial again. He thought he knew the answers to his questions. He had to ask them anyway.

"Dr. Uwwano, please?"

Please let her be there. He glanced at his watch, realizing that he had no idea of the time, and it was morning, and Bangkok was an hour and a half ahead, so she should be at work.

"Mr. Wagh," she said, "to what do I owe the pleasure?"

She sounded guarded. He knew he'd have to proceed carefully. "It's . . . well, it's a bit embarrassing, I'm afraid. Call myself a detective, but when we spoke the other day, there was something rather important I wasn't quite sure of. You were telling me about the type of reconstructive work that Dr. Jaiyen was responsible for. Cosmetic surgery in the aftermath of a car crash, for example, and I'm afraid something you said hit a nerve and I rather cut you off."

"Yes," she said slightly impatiently. "What was it you weren't sure about?"

"The other applications for her work: what are they?"

"Well, Mr. Wagh, really any instance in which plastic surgery might be needed. I don't really know what you're—"

"Gender reassignment, Dr. Uwwano. Was Dr. Jaiyen responsible for gender reassignment?"

"Yes. She was one of the country's most skilled surgeons in that regard."

Oh God.

Santosh spoke slowly and clearly, keeping—or trying to keep—his emotions in check. "Dr. Uwwano, I have reason to believe that one of Dr. Jaiyen's patients is behind a series of murders in Mumbai. I have very good reason to believe this, Dr. Uwwano, you have to trust me. I believe this person has kidnapped one of my agents. The pattern of the murders so far indicates very strongly that this person will kill my agent within the next eight or nine hours unless I can track this person down. Dr. Uwwano, I appreciate that what I am asking you may go against certain principles you hold, but I beg you, can you help me?"

There was silence for a moment at the other end of the line.

"You can ask your question, Mr. Wagh. I can only hope that circumstances allow me to answer."

"Did Dr. Jaiyen perform gender reassignment surgery on a patient named Aditi Chopra?"

"You'll have to give me an hour or so to check that information."

Santosh took a deep breath, cast his eyes to the ceiling of his office. "If you could do that for me, Dr. Uwwano, I would be most grateful. You may be helping to save a young woman's life, and possibly many other lives too."

"I'll see what I can do, Mr. Wagh."

"Thank you, Dr. Uwwano," said Santosh. He very, very gently replaced the phone on its cradle, knowing he was this close—*this close*—to cracking the case.

As long as he was in time to save Nisha.

Chapter 100

AT LEAST IF she were to die here she would go knowing that she had put up a fight. When the chemical-soaked cloth had come over her mouth Nisha had known she was in trouble. But she had also known that in real life chloroform doesn't work the way it does in the movies—firstly, too much of it would kill her, and secondly, she had had minutes, not seconds, before it would work and she would be rendered unconscious.

She had yelled, twisted, pulled herself up from under her assailant, dabbing with her fingertips on the carpet in the hope of retrieving her gun but then giving up and darting toward the studio, her attacker in pursuit.

She had run into the body of Devika Gulati on the gym studio floor. A dim light had illuminated the yellow garrote around Devika's neck. Her tongue had poked slightly from between those perfect lips. Her eyes had bulged from her skull. Her death was a foul corruption of her beauty.

Nisha had fallen to her knees, feeling woozy now. She'd

prayed the dose of chloroform wasn't high enough to bring on an allergic reaction. She'd prayed she wouldn't meet the same fate as Devika there on the studio floor. A pair of jeans-clad legs and sneakers had appeared before her eyes. Sneakers like her own, she'd realized, her brain producing random thoughts now, as her body and mind shut down and darkness descended . . .

"What happened when you left the orphanage, Aditi?" she called out now.

The figure was there again, she was sure of it. She was being watched.

"I need to piss," she called.

At last her captor spoke.

"I used to piss myself at the orphanage, when Elina Xavier beat me."

It was a man.

"Come out where I can see you. Where is Aditi? What have you done to her?"

"Where is Aditi? I am Aditi. Dr. Jaiyen saw to that. But Dr. Jaiyen became greedy. Dr. Jaiyen wanted to blackmail me. So like the others, Dr. Jaiyen had to die."

"Come on then," Nisha growled at him, "show yourself. You're dying to show yourself. Show me who you are and why you hate me so much."

He stepped out of the shadows.

Chapter 101

"YES, ADITI CHOPRA came to us for gender reassignment."

Santosh fought to stay calm, control his breathing. "What name did he leave with?"

"She left with the same name with which she arrived, Mr. Wagh."

"Anything you tell me now—anything may help in saving people's lives. Do you remember her?"

"Oh yes. I remember her. She was visited by a man who arrived in a large black Mercedes, quite an entourage he had."

Nimboo. Her financier, no doubt.

"He talked about wanting to study hairdressing when he left," Dr. Uwwano was saying. "He wanted to work in Bollywood."

Santosh's mind was working, thinking, *He did*—he did work as a hairdresser. He worked as a hairdresser to the Attorney General, which is why he was able to collect samples of his hair and leave them at the crime scenes.

"One last thing, Dr. Uwwano. While I hate to risk casting

aspersions upon your colleague, I must ask—is it possible that Dr. Jaiyen could have been blackmailing Aditi?"

Uwwano's voice was frosty now. "Well, of course it's *possible* . . ."

"In your opinion, is it likely?"

"Dr. Jaiyen had a taste for what you might call the high life, and it doesn't come cheap. Perhaps if she had discovered what Aditi was doing, maybe."

Some kind of hairdresser to the stars, thought Santosh. A celebrity hairdresser. It would give him the access he needed. The film sets, to women's houses, a face they trusted. It would make sense that Bhavna had somehow got in the way while researching her article.

"Thank you, Dr. Uwwano, thank you. You don't know how helpful you've been," he said, and was about to end the call when she stopped him.

"Do you think Aditi is responsible for those murders, Mr. Wagh?"

"I'm very sorry to say, Dr. Uwwano, but yes."

She sighed, as though somehow not surprised. "There was something . . . *damaged* about her, even more so than . . . Well, many of our patients have what you might call 'issues.' But with Aditi, she was a beautiful girl. Now that I have reviewed her case file, I remember some of the nurses were commenting as though it was a waste of such a gorgeous creature, and of course we don't see it that way—but in any case there was something about her beauty, as though it had caused her great hurt in the past."

"I think you're right, Dr. Uwwano," agreed Santosh. "And I think that for Aditi having a sex change wasn't enough. You're right, her beauty had caused her great misery. In the end she took it out on all womankind."

He finished the call, knowing he had it now. He had all the pieces except for the last one.

"Hari, where's that mugshot?"

"Coming, boss," called Hari from the other room.

He hobbled through to Hari's desk just as the picture appeared on Hari's screen.

She had been right, Dr. Uwwano. Aditi had been beautiful. She had her mother's high cheekbones and her full mouth. She had her father's eyes.

"Look," he said, almost to himself, as he leaned forward, placed one hand on the screen at Aditi's brow, cutting off her hair, another one on the lower half of her face. Left just the eyes, the rise of the nose, and the mouth.

"Look who it is," he said.

Chapter 102

AAKASH STEPPED OUT of the shadows.

Nisha stared at him, hardly able to believe her eyes, and yet . . . it all made sense. Her head dropped back to the mattress with frustration, surprise, and, if she was honest with herself, even relief that although she was going to die she would at least die knowing the answers to her questions.

"You don't remember, do you?" he said.

"I remember you from the Shiva Spa, Aakash. You lied about having no celebrity clients, didn't you?"

He smiled, almost apologetically. "I'm afraid so. But I mean from before, when you fucked up my life?"

"'Before'? You were a woman, then?"

He pulled a face, as though smelling something bad. *"Don't* remind me. Yes, I was born wearing the wrong skin. Born a woman."

"Born Aditi Chopra?"

"Very good, yes. You would have got there in the end, wouldn't you? You know my famous mother, then?"

"And your famous father."

Aakash chuckled and jutted his chin slightly, preening in spite of it all. He was a good-looking guy, thought Nisha. He would have been a devastatingly attractive woman.

"Back then Nalin D'Souza was a big shot in a law firm who abandoned her the moment she got pregnant. You were right about her. She was gutless. She left me at the orphanage when I was eight."

"And she's the source of your Durga fascination?"

"Fascination?" scoffed Aakash. He curled a lip. "Hatred is the word I think we're looking for. Yes, Mother was a worshiper of Durga. 'Pray to Durga if you're ever in trouble, Aditi.' And you know what? I did. And you know what good it did me? Fuck all. It brought me to the orphanage, where I met Elina Xavier—the enforcer from hell, who'd cane me mercilessly, hold my head under water, make me piss my pants with fear. She'd fly into a rage and try to strangle me with her bare hands."

Strangulation, thought Nisha. That figured.

"Durga brought me the riots that burned me out of my home and took me into the clutches of Ragini Sharma. Durga brought me cops who raided the brothel. Durga brought me you, Nisha Gandhe."

And now she understood. "Oh God. I busted you?"

"Yes!" he said, with a flourish. "Enter Nisha Gandhe, stage left, fearlessly raiding the brothel and ensuring I was prosecuted for possession of narcotics, even though the drugs weren't mine."

"I was a junior officer," protested Nisha. "I was acting on the orders of my superiors."

Aakash gave a short, dry laugh. "If you're trying to say you haven't earned your place as the ninth Durga, dear Nisha, then I must respectfully disagree. I kept trying to explain to you that the drugs weren't mine, but you never listened."

He reached into his back pocket and withdrew a yellow scarf. She felt a whimper build in her throat but stifled it.

Don't give him the satisfaction.

Chapter 103

ALL AROUND THE car were spanking new structures—corporate towers shimmering with steel and glass facades. Albert Mills stood out like an eyesore, a desolate island of abandonment and neglect surrounded by a sea of prosperity.

This, though, was where a trace on Aakash's cell phone had led them.

Santosh turned in the passenger seat. Behind him was Jack, checking his Colt, and Hari, who stared out of the window with a vacant, cloudy expression. In his lap he held his Glock, thumb stroking the safety catch.

"I don't like the look of those guns," said Santosh. "We need to take him alive. Aakash is the leverage we need to find out information about the attack."

Jack nodded. "Hari?" prompted Santosh. Hari tore his gaze from the window and Santosh dreaded to think what thoughts had been plaguing him. Good God, what had they done to him?

"Yes, boss, understood," replied Hari, with a forced smile.

A token security guard at the gate sleepily prevented their car from driving through. Rather than arguing with him, Mubeen rolled down his window and silently handed over a five-hundred-rupee note to the man. His sleepy scowl was suddenly transformed into a toothless smile and he snapped to attention, offering his smartest salute to them.

"Does anyone stay or work from here?" asked Mubeen.

"No, sahib," replied the guard. "All the industrial sheds are absolutely empty. Only one single north-facing shed has been rented out to an upcoming beauty parlor, but no one uses this gate to get there. There is a rear entrance to the mill premises and the architects and designers come and go through that. Renovation work is yet to start."

"Tell us how to get there," said Mubeen.

They drove on. Santosh spoke into a walkie-talkie—speaking to an army of cops waiting half a mile away.

Chapter 104

"AND YOUR DEFENDER, that was Anjana Lal, wasn't it?" said Nisha.

Aakash cocked his head at her. "Have you thought of becoming a detective? You're really rather good at it."

"And in prison you met Devika Gulati?"

He pulled another face. "Yes. Evil sex-mad bitch that she was. She violated me repeatedly in the most disgusting and demeaning manner possible." He shuddered at the thought. "She was an angry woman—confused about her sexuality—and took out all her anger on me."

"How did you eventually get out of her clutches?"

"Munna. I discovered a plot to kill him, told him, and received his undying gratitude in return. When I was released he arranged for me to find refuge in one of Nimboo Baba's ashrams. For the first time in my life I was at peace."

"You became close to Nimboo Baba?"

"Well, yes, and Nimboo Baba is a very naughty boy. He is

what you'd call a pansexual, with a special liking for trans men." Aakash pushed up the sleeves of his jacket and pointed at himself. "That's me. So when I admitted to him that I hated women—they had tormented me for most of my life—and that I did not want to be female anymore, and I wanted to become a male, well, that sent him into a state of frothy longing. Nimboo Baba arranged for me to become a man—and in return I agreed to let him have his way with me."

"It was in Thailand you met Priyanka Talati, wasn't it? What did she do, Aakash? What did she do to inspire your hatred?"

He cast her a withering look. "Drunk one night, she tore at my clothes and discovered my secret. Her laughter cost her her life." He stopped. "Oh, that's it. We've reached the end. Every victim accounted for." He smiled at her. "Even you."

Standing by the side of the bed like an attentive nurse, he lifted her head and passed the scarf behind her neck, gathering the two ends by her throat. "I don't usually have the chance to savor my kills like this," he said in the tone of someone breaching a confidence. "God, some of them struggled. They really struggled." His eyes went misty for a moment. "Mother struggled the most, especially when she knew it was me." He let the ends of the scarf drop and with a hairdresser's gesture he reached to pull Nisha's hair free of it. "There," he said. "Much better."

"You don't have to do this," she said in a parched voice.

"I do," he said dreamily. "I have to, or I shall never have peace."

"You'll *never* have peace, Aakash. You're a troubled soul." She looked at him with beseeching eyes. "You can't soothe your soul with yet more pain."

His lips twitched slightly. "Well, Nisha, we shall see, shan't we?"

He began to tighten the garrote.

Chapter 105

DRAWING HIS COLT, Jack tiptoed up the stairs with Hari close behind him. As they approached the loft they heard two voices, one of them belonging to Nisha. At the top was a door inset with a dirty window. Raising himself up slightly he was able to peer through the dust and grime on the glass.

He saw a large warehouse space. A bed in its center. The whole scene like a film set, except there were no cameras, no guys in baseball caps hanging around, just Aakash leaning over the bed. And Nisha. Or what he could see of her at least.

And then Jack saw a flash of yellow in Aakash's hands. He saw Nisha's legs tauten at her bonds. The garroting had begun.

On the bed, Nisha felt the material tighten around her neck. She felt dizzy as her oxygen supply began to diminish. She was blacking out.

Jack tore open the door and took aim with the Colt. At the bed, Aakash turned just as Santosh barreled from the door behind Jack and knocked his gun arm. "No, Jack! We need him alive."

Jack cursed and threw himself forward, covering the yards to the bed as Aakash returned to his work, straining with the effort of tightening the garrote, no longer savoring the kill but wanting to finish it fast. Jack saw Nisha's hands and feet straining at her binding. He saw her eyes that seemed to be popping out of their sockets. In the final moment, Aakash swung with his fist but Jack caught him around the waist, using his forward impetus to take Aakash off balance. The two of them crashed to the boards of the warehouse floor.

The fight was over in a matter of seconds, Jack easily overpowering Aakash, grateful to hear Nisha cough and splutter—hurt but alive—as he planted a knee into Aakash's back, dragged his arms behind him, and secured his wrists with a plasticuff. As he picked up Aakash to drag him away from the bed, Aakash looked up at Nisha, still coughing and spluttering, with a grin.

"You were right," he said, "I never will find peace."

She turned her head away, and when Santosh sliced the first of her hands free with his sword, she covered her eyes and began to cry.

Jack glanced over. "Get him out of my sight," he told Hari. As Hari dragged Aakash away, Jack went to the bed, fishing his hip flask from his jacket pocket. He offered it to Nisha's parched lips—maybe not the best remedy for her thirst, but a remedy all the same.

What happened next, nobody was sure. Did Aakash goad Hari? Had Hari planned it all along? The first Santosh saw of it was when he glanced toward where Hari stood with his gun trained on Aakash, and realized that Hari wasn't simply holding Aakash captive—he was about to execute him.

Aakash knew it too. Kneeling on the ground with his hands cuffed behind his back, he looked up at Hari and he smiled, and it was as though the two men knew and shared each other's madness.

"*No!*" shouted Santosh. Mubeeen and Jack, both tending to Nisha, swung around. "*No, Hari, no!*"

But he was too late, and the sound of the bullet reverberated high up in the rafters of the old warehouse, scaring birds that were nesting up there. Aakash's body pitched sideways, half his skull torn away.

A moment later, another shot rang out as Hari put the gun into his own mouth and delivered himself from his suffering.

Chapter 106

SANTOSH AND MUBEEN sat in the Private India conference room. There was nothing to say. Shock, grief, and guilt hung over them.

Nisha was in hospital, sedated for shock. Alive, at least: the case hadn't been a complete disaster. No, wait—yes, it had. Santosh stared at memos on his desk, hardly seeing them: Bhosale, the driver of the vanity van, was to bring a wrongful confinement suit against the state; the government was asking the Attorney General to step down over allegations of mis-management of the Sir Jimmy Mehta Trust.

And these were good things. Tiny glimmers of light in the dark. Staring off into space, Santosh wondered if he was in shock. Dimly he heard the call of a drink, and knew he would answer it, and the drinker's voice inside told him that the case going wrong had an upside, and the upside was that it gave him an excuse to drink.

He should have seen it. He should have known. Hari should

never have been with them. Rest was what he had needed. Probably a shrink. And because Santosh had failed to see that, Hari was dead and Aakash, their last chance of reaching Munna and Nimboo Baba, was dead too.

"There's one last option open to us," Jack had said, taking off, and Santosh had thought he knew where Jack was going— to reach Munna before the news of Aakash's death. To play their last remaining card as though it were an ace when in fact it was a two.

Santosh wondered if, after his ordeal, Hari had been suffering from post-traumatic stress disorder, and whether Santosh himself was, too. He thought these things with a sense of detachment, totting up the trauma of the past forty-eight hours and wondering if a human being could possibly cope with it all.

Little knowing there was more to come.

Chapter 107

"HELLO, MUNNA."

Jack Morgan had been shown to Munna's usual booth at the Emerald dance bar, wondering why Munna's goons hadn't bothered to search him but grateful all the same. He'd have felt naked without his gun.

And in front of him sat Munna, Jabba-like, his shirt open to display the gold ropes at his sweat-glistening chest, shining with grease beneath the lights. In his lap was a very young and very strung-out girl wearing next to nothing. Lank, greasy hair, a vacant expression. She should have been at home counting teddy bears and staring longingly at posters of Bollywood pin-ups on her wall, not here.

Munna had been stroking pudgy fingers through her hair, but now he clicked his fingers. The bodyguard to his left used a remote control and the music in the booth dimmed, the bassy *thump-thump* coming through the walls.

"The famous Jack Morgan. Didn't I see you on the arm of Lara Omprakash the other day?"

He gestured at a television mounted in a high corner of the booth.

Jack nodded carefully, face blank, his heart hardening.

"A beautiful girl," added Munna slyly. "A shame what happened to her."

Jack thrust his hands into his pockets. "You'll be pleased to hear her killer's now in custody."

Munna looked at him sharply. "Is that so?"

"Sure," said Jack. "Aakash, formerly known as Aditi Chopra. An old friend of yours, I believe?"

Munna pursed his lips. "No friend of mine."

"No, that's right, a friend of Nimboo Baba's. Well, at least Aakash is singing. He's with the cops right now, telling them everything he knows about you and Nimboo Baba. And given that he's Nimboo Baba's lover, I'm guessing he has a lot of dirt. Enough to put you both back inside."

"Is that so?" said Munna. "And I suppose you're here to tell me this because of your great regard for me? You just want the best for me, is that right, Jack?"

Jack glanced from one expressionless bodyguard to the other, and then back at Munna. This was why they hadn't searched him. He was outnumbered, outgunned.

"No," said Jack, shaking his head, "quite the opposite, but what I want more than your downfall is to know the whereabouts of the bomb."

"Bomb?"

"Come on, Munna. The bomb planted by the Indian Mujahideen, aimed at an international target in Mumbai. You know where it is. I bet you could even abort it if you needed to."

"You credit me with far too much influence."

"Do I? Look, Munna. Let's get down to business. Let's you and me do a deal. You give up the bomb and I lose Aakash. I make him disappear. You let that bomb go off and I'll nail you. I'll nail you for everything, I'll place you with the bomb, and the whole fucking world will want to see you hang. Give up the bomb, Munna, it's a no-brainer."

Munna sighed. "Jack Morgan, Jack Morgan, you have such a reputation. I expected something more from you, something more sophisticated."

Jack felt his heart sink. That had been his last gambit. But he flashed Munna a smile, a Jack Morgan smile that said what he was really thinking, which was, *Fuck*. "I'm sorry to disappoint," he said.

"Life is full of disappointments," said Munna, as if saying "*c'est la vie*." "Because this—this is your great bluff? Fuck you, Morgan, I have more contacts at the Mumbai police than you give me credit for. Your boy Hari flipped out and put a bullet in Aakash. My troubles ended there. And as for your bomb? Fuck you, I'm admitting nothing. Now get out." A nod to his left, and the music was turned back up.

Jack swallowed, desperately trying to think.

An idea nagged at him. He let it nag, the beginnings of a dread realization beginning to form.

The gun at his hip. He felt it there.

You're just going to let me leave, with me knowing you're behind a bomb about to explode in Mumbai?

On Munna's face was an odd, uneasy expression. He reached for the drink in front of him and brought it to his lips, and Jack saw the gesture for what it was: an attempt to hide duplicity. He knew that in an ocean of wrongness there was something extra wrong here . . .

Jack felt himself go cold, and all of a sudden he knew—he

knew exactly why Munna wanted him to leave, and time slowed down. Music pounded, but for Jack it faded into the background. He was watching. His face stayed the same, but he was watching: he saw sweat glistening on Munna's forehead, Munna's chubby fingers stroking the hair of the girl at his side, the young strung-out girl. He saw the bodyguards, the telltale bulges in their tailored jackets, their watchful eyes, their itchy fingers.

Okay. The bodyguard who stood to the right of Munna was left-handed. He was wearing a gun beneath his right armpit, but he'd need to take a step away from Munna and the girl in order to draw and fire.

In a firefight, he would draw second. Mentally, Jack designated him Costello.

The music throbbed.

From the way he was sniffing, the guy standing to the left of Munna had recently snorted cocaine. Even so, he was right-handed. He could draw and fire across Munna and the girl with ease.

In a firefight he would draw first. Jack designated him Abbott.

And Munna? Well, Munna was sitting, so his draw would be impeded. What's more, Jack knew that Munna's sidearm was a gold-plated Desert Eagle, and gold-plated Desert Eagles were notoriously heavy and inaccurate. He'd have been better off carrying a wok.

In a firefight, Munna would draw a dismal third.

He had men stationed in the adjacent booths, through which you had to pass if you wanted to get in or out. No doubt the music was also loud in those booths, but they'd hear the shots and come running. Four more men, two on either side. He'd seen drinks, lots of drinks, and if one of the close protection was doing bumps it was safe to say those guys were coked up to the gunnels too.

So—seven altogether. Not great odds. But Jack had faced worse.

Actually, no. Maybe he hadn't faced worse.

"So what are you waiting for, the great Jack Morgan?" jeered Munna, inviting him to the door of the booth with a ring-adorned hand. "Get out of here. Go find your so-called bomb."

And you're trying to piss me off now, aren't you?

"I know where the bomb is," said Jack.

Munna raised his eyebrows, as though amused by a flight of fancy. "Oh? Do tell."

Chapter 108

THE BOY HAD run away when a mob attacked his family during the riots of 1992. Upon returning some hours later, he had found the charred remains of his father, mother, and two sisters.

A day later, members of an Islamic charity had found him lying alongside his family's remains. He had passed out from shock, hunger, and dehydration.

The head of the charity had been the principal of an Islamic seminary, and the boy had been placed in it along with countless other orphans. He had learned all aspects of the faith, as well as English, science, and mathematics. The result was that he could eventually gain admission to a medical college in Saharanpur. Saharanpur was also home to Darul Uloom Deoband, India's biggest and most influential center of Islamic learning.

During his second year of medical college, the boy had begun to pray five times each day at the mosque. One of the people he had prayed with had carried out some surveillance work for Pakistan's ISI in India. The man would later become head of the Indian Mujahideen.

The boy had gradually shunned his friends at college and had begun to spend most of his time lecturing on the perceived wrongs inflicted upon the Muslim community in places such as Afghanistan, Chechnya, and Kashmir.

The process of radicalization had begun.

His name was Abdul Zafar.

Chapter 109

"HEY," SAID MUBEEN at the door. "What are you doing?"

Dr. Zafar had been kneeling by a gurney in the storage room and, startled, he swung around. As he did so, Mubeen saw some kind of attachment to the gurneys. Wires. A stopwatch device.

And in an instant Mubeen knew where the Indian Mujahideen had planted their bomb. It was there in front of him, in the science lab of Private India.

Chapter 110

"AM I RIGHT?" asked Jack. "Is it at Private?"

"I really don't know what you're talking about," said Munna. As though bored.

"Sure I'm right. That's why you were so keen for me to leave. An 'international target in Mumbai'? It's Private, isn't it?"

Munna looked at him, apparently deciding that he might as well reveal all. "It's really rather clever," he said. "Your man Mubeen has helped set up the bomb himself. Tell me—after the various autopsies he's been performing, are there now a number of gurneys in his lab?"

Jack had no idea. Munna looked delighted. "No, of course not. I don't suppose the great Jack Morgan concerns himself with what goes on in the lab. Oh, by the way, you have until nine and it's currently three minutes to nine. I think you'd better make a call, don't you?"

"Sure," said Jack, reaching for his phone. "Good idea." With one hand he threw his cell phone at Costello, with the other he drew his gun on Abbott.

Abbott hadn't cleared leather when Jack's first bullet took out his eye, spraying lumpy brain matter on the red flock wallpaper behind. Dropping to one knee, Jack whipped around, felt the air above his head shudder as Costello loosed off a wild shot, and with a two-handed grip made his reply. Costello dropped, hands at his throat, blood spurting through his fingers.

Munna lurched forward in his seat and reached behind for the waistband of his trousers, but Jack sidestepped, leaned, and kicked him once in the jaw, then planted the same foot on his chest, temporarily stopping him from moving.

The doors. They swung open at the same time, front and back. Jack put a bullet through one, swiveled at the waist, took aim and fired at the second, where a goon had just arrived and died, a look of surprise on his face and a flower of blood at his chest. Dazed, Munna was struggling beneath Jack's foot, so Jack kicked him again. His Colt fired again, and another guard died.

Two guards left, but the booth was clear and they were staying out of sight for the time being, which gave Jack a second to regroup. He pulled Abbott's unfired Glock from his lifeless fingers, pumped a couple of bullets at the wood surround of the door, and was rewarded with a shriek of pain from the other side.

Then came a shot and he felt the searing pain almost as soon as he heard it—a pain in his thigh, and he dropped to his knee, yelling in agony.

Chapter 111

EVERYTHING FELL INTO place for Mubeen. He remembered the night when he had picked up the first two bodies from Cooper Hospital. He'd wondered then why he was retrieving them from there instead of JJ Hospital. Zafar must have ensured that Private India–related autopsies were assigned to him alone.

He'd insisted on being present during the autopsies.

The examination of Priyanka Talati. *"Do you mind if I leave the gurney here and have it picked up later?"* he had asked.

He'd been building up a store of gurneys in the lab.

And those gurneys would be packed with explosive.

Mubeen saw a digital readout that began counting down. With a shout, Dr. Abdul Zafar launched himself at Mubeen, a knife in his hand. Mubeen felt his shirt sliced open and warm blood course down his front. He grabbed at the knife hand and tried to wrench the weapon away from Zafar, but Zafar had the strength of a zealot and twisted until he was over Mubeen and pressing down with the knife, his lips pulled back over his teeth and beads of sweat popping on his forehead.

Chapter 112

MUNNA, WITH BLOOD pouring from his nose, still dazed, grinned. But Munna hadn't fired the shot.

It was the girl. Somehow she'd grabbed Munna's Desert Eagle from the waistband of his pants and used it to shoot Jack.

Jack kneeled with arms like a signpost, the Glock trained on the girl, the Colt on Munna, and his eyes going from one to the other, skittishly returning to the door of the booth. He had just seconds before the last gunman got his act together.

"Drop the gun," he told her in a faltering voice. The bullet had gone through, thank Christ for that. He'd be losing blood. It gushed down his leg, filling his shoe. He could actually feel it pouring out of him, and that wasn't a good sign.

"Drop the gun," he said, more loudly this time.

Conscious of one, maybe two bodyguards cowering on the other side of the booth door, waiting for the chance to take him out. Didn't want to shoot the girl, though. Not if he could help it.

"Shoot him," growled Munna through his teeth.

"Shut the fuck up," snarled Jack from the side of his mouth. "Just drop the gun, darling, or I'll have to shoot you. You hear me? I don't want to shoot you, but I'm going to shoot you unless you drop that gun—*right this fucking second.*"

"Shoot him." This helpful advice from Munna.

"I said, shut the fuck up," shouted Jack.

And then the last bodyguard made his move. He came bundling through the door, like a man determined to die, all twitchy eyes and bared teeth, firing indiscriminately, before he'd even had a chance to take aim.

His first shot went wide, smacked harmlessly into the wall. His second ripped off the girl's jaw and she fell in a welter of blood.

He didn't have the chance for a third. Jack fired twice and he spun off, fell face first to the table, dead before he hit the glass.

Jack looked at the dead girl, wondering how many more innocent people were going to die today, and decided none.

Nobody else died. Not if he had anything to do with it.

He advanced on Munna.

Chapter 113

MUBEEN TRIED TO pull away. Couldn't. He saw the bomb readout counting down. He saw Zafar's knife inches away from his chest, the tendons in their arms standing out as they both struggled.

And then Zafar jerked, as though electricity had been passed through him, and looked down to where a blood-dripping blade sprouted from his chest.

Santosh stepped over him, already pressing a hand to Mubeen's wound as he crouched on the blood-slicked tiles to peer at the base of the gurneys. He saw small stopwatch-like devices and looked at the timer.

They had two minutes. An injured man and a cripple in the lab.

Chapter 114

"ALONE AT LAST," Jack snarled at Munna. "Now, what's the protocol? Is there an abort code that can be issued remotely? A safe word? What?"

Munna blinked. "You're bleeding, Jack," he said, playing for time.

Jack glanced at his watch. Two minutes to nine.

"Yes. I'm bleeding and there's a bomb about to go off in my building. So you think I give a fuck right now? You think I won't start with your knees and move on to your dick until you tell me what I need to know to defuse that bomb?"

Munna flinched as the barrel of the gun pressed into his balls. "They issued me with an abort word to use in an emergency," he said quickly.

"Then use it."

Munna shook his head. "Uh-uh. They're not going to classify this as an emergency."

Jack dug the barrel of the Glock in harder. "What do you think?"

"I think I'm a dead man if I do it."

"You're a dead man if you don't."

He scooped up Munna's gold-plated cell phone from the floor and tossed it into the fat man's lap. "And don't even think of raising the alarm, Munna, because the next call I make is to Private and if there's no answer I'm leaving with your balls in a bag."

Munna dialed.

Chapter 115

TWENTY SECONDS LEFT.

"You shouldn't have waited," said Mubeen. "You could have made it out without me."

"No," said Santosh. He thought of Isha, of Pravir, of Rupesh and Hari. Tears filled his eyes. "No, Mubeen, there was never any question of leaving you."

Ten seconds left.

Chapter 116

"IT'S DONE," SAID Munna.

Jack dragged out his phone, dialed Private.

"I quit," said Santosh, when at last he answered, and the line went dead.

Epilogue

"THE LIMP?" SAID Jack. "Doc says it'll clear up and I'll be good as new. In the meantime I come with news of a clean bill of health for Mubeen and Nisha. We're practically a full team at Private India now."

"We?" said Santosh.

It was two weeks since the events of the foiled bomb plot. The Attorney General's disgrace dominated newspaper head-lines; Munna had apparently left the country in fear of the Mujahideen; and Nimboo Baba was said to be expecting a knock at the door any day now.

And Santosh Wagh?

Santosh Wagh had been listening to the little drinking voice, the one that called him to oblivion each day. He'd been sitting in his apartment listening to the voice, obeying the voice, defy-ing it some days, but most days toasting its health.

"There is no 'we,'" he told his visitor.

"You're right. Without Santosh Wagh there is no Private India," said Jack. "If you're really serious about quitting, the shutters come down. The whole operation ceases to be. You want that on your conscience?"

Slowly Santosh raised his eyes to look at his boss. "That's your tactic, is it? Emotional blackmail?"

With a sheepish smile, Jack shrugged. "I guess."

"Well, it hasn't worked."

"Private India needs you, Santosh."

"Nisha is a first-class investigator."

"She is. Oh, she is. But she's not Santosh Wagh."

Santosh squeezed his eyes shut. "I don't think I'm up to it. I think it'll kill me."

"Really," said Jack, "because you know what? I think *that*'ll kill you." He indicated the bottle of Johnnie Walker. "The investigation, it was tough, and nobody should have had to go through what you did. The thing at the Tower of Silence, I can't imagine what that must have been like for you . . ."

Santosh closed his eyes, took a deep breath, tried to banish those images.

". . . but there were times—and you've got to admit this, Santosh—there were times when you were on fire. There were times I swear I could see sparks coming off you. Now, be truthful, were you thinking about booze those times?"

Santosh shook his head.

"No. I swear I saw you forget to limp on occasion. You won't believe that Private India needs you, then how about this? You need Private India." Jack stood. "We need you back, Santosh. Do it for us. Do it for yourself. Don't get up. I'll see myself out."

When Jack had gone, Santosh took a deep breath, thought for some moments about what he'd said, then poured himself a generous shot of whisky. He placed the glass on the table in front of him, sat back in the couch.

He had a choice to make.

About the Authors

JAMES PATTERSON is one of the best-known and biggest-selling writers of all time. He is the author of some of the most popular series of the past decade – the Alex Cross, Women's Murder Club and Detective Michael Bennett novels – and he has written many other number one bestsellers including romance novels and stand-alone thrillers. He lives in Florida with his wife and son.

James is passionate about encouraging children to read. Inspired by his own son who was a reluctant reader, he also writes a range of books specifically for young readers. James is a founding partner of Booktrust's Children's Reading Fund in the UK. James Patterson has been the most borrowed author in UK libraries for the past seven years in a row.

Find out more at www.jamespatterson.co.uk

Become a fan of James Patterson on Facebook

ASHWIN SANGHI is counted among India's highest-selling English fiction authors. He has written three novels, all best-sellers – *The Rozabal Line, Chanakya's Chant* and *The Krishna Key*. Ashwin was included by *Forbes India* in their Celebrity 100 list. Educated at St. Xavier's College, Mumbai, and Yale University, Ashwin lives in India with his wife and son.

Ashwin can be reached via his website:
www.ashwinsanghi.com

Turn the page for an extract of the next thrilling instalment in the Private series

PRIVATE VEGAS

Coming January 2015

LORI KIMBALL HAD three rules for the Death Race home.

One—no brakes.

Two—no horn.

Three—beat her best time by ten seconds, every day.

She turned off her phone, stowed it in the glove box.

On your mark. Get set.

She slammed the visor into the upright position, shoved The Electric Flag's cover of Howling Wolf's "Killing Floor" into the CD drive, pressed the start button on the timer she wore on a cord hanging from her neck.

Go.

Lori stepped on the gas and her Infiniti EX crossover shot up the ramp and onto the 110 as if it could read her mind.

It was exactly ten miles from this entrance to the freeway to her home in Glendale. Her record was twelve minutes and ten seconds, and that record was made to be broken.

The road was dry, the sun was dull, traffic was moving.

Conditions were perfect. She was flying along the canyon floor, the sides of the roadway banked on both sides, forming a chute through the four consecutive Figueroa tunnels.

Lori rode the taillights of the maroon 2013 Audi in front of her, resisting the urge to mash the horn with the palm of her hand—then the Audi braked to show her he wasn't going to budge.

Her ten-year-old boy Justin did this when he didn't want to go to school. He. Just. Slowed. Down.

Lori didn't have to put up with this. She peeled out into the center lane, maneuvered an old Ford junker out of her way. As soon as she passed the Audi, she wrenched the wheel hard to the left and recaptured the fast lane.

This was *it*.

At this point three lanes headed north on the 110 and the lane on the far left exited and merged into the 5. Lori accelerated to seventy, flew past a champagne-colored '01 Caddy that was lounging at sixty to the right of her, and proceeded to tear up the fast lane.

As she drove, Lori amped up the decibels and the eleven-speaker Bose pounded out a blend of rock and urban blues. Lori was now in a state that was as close to soaring flight as she could get without actually leaving the ground.

Lori was six minutes into the race and had passed the halfway mark. She was gaining seconds on her best time, feeling the adrenaline burn out to the tips of her fingers, to the ends of her hair.

She was in the hot zone, cruising at a steady seventy-two, when a black BMW convertible edged into her lane as if he had a right to be there.

Lori wouldn't accept that.

No brakes. No horn.

She flashed her lights, then saw her opening, a sliver of empty space to her right. She jerked the wheel, careened into the middle lane, her car just missing the Beemer's left rear fender.

Oh, wow, the look on the driver's face.

"It's a *race*, dontcha get it," she screamed into the 360-degree monitor on the dash. She was lost in the ecstasy of the moment when the light dimmed and the back end of a gray panel van filled her windshield.

Where had that van come from? Where?

Lori stood on the brakes. The tires screeched as the Infiniti skidded violently from side to side, the safety package doing all it could to prevent the inevitable rear-end smash-up.

The brakes finally caught at the last moment—as the van pulled ahead.

Lori gripped the wheel with sweating hands, hardly believing that there had been no crash of steel against steel, no lunge against the shoulder straps, no shocking blunt force of an airbag explosion. She heard nothing but the wailing of The Electric Flag and the rasping sound of her own shaky breaths.

Lori snapped off the music and with car horns blaring around her she eased off the brakes, applied the gas. Sweat rolled down the side of her face and dripped from her nose.

Yes, she called it the Death Race home, but she didn't want to die. She had three kids. She loved her husband. And although her job was boring, at least she had a job.

What in God's name was wrong with her?

"I don't know," she said to herself. "I just don't know."

Lori took a deep, sobering breath and stared straight ahead. The Beemer slowed to her speed and the driver, his face contorted in fury, yelled silently at her through his closed window.

To her surprise, Lori started to cry.

THE TWO MEN sat in the satin-lined jewel box of a room warmed by flaming logs in the fireplace and the flickering light of the flat screen.

The older man had white hair, strong features, cat-like amber eyes. That was Gozan.

The younger man had dark hair and eyes so black they seemed to absorb light. He was very muscular, a man who took weight-lifting seriously. His name was Khezir.

They were visiting this paradise called Los Angeles. They were on holiday, their first visit to the West Coast, and had rented a bungalow at the Beverly Hills Hotel, palatial by any standard. This opulent three-bedroom cottage was as pretty as a seashell, set at the end of a coral-pink path and surrounded by luxuriant foliage, banana trees and palms.

It was unlike anything in their country, the landlocked mountainous triangle of rock called the Kingdom of Sumar.

Now, the two men held the experiences of this hedonistic

city like exotic fruit in the palms of their hands.

"I am giving you a new name," said Gozan Remari to the rounded, blond-haired woman with enormous breasts. "I name you 'Peaches.'"

There were no juicy women quite like Peaches in Sumar. There weren't many in Southern California where women with boy-like shapes were considered desirable and ones like Peaches were called "fat."

As if that was bad.

"I don't like you," Peaches said slowly. She was doing her best to speak through the numbing effect of the drugs she had consumed in the very expensive wine. "But . . ."

"But what, Peaches? You don't like me, but what? You are having a very good time?"

Gozan laughed. He was an educated man, had gone to school in London and Cambridge. He knew six languages and had founded a boutique merchant bank in the City of London while serving on numerous boards. But, as much as he knew, he was still mystified by the way women allowed themselves to be led and tricked.

Peaches was lying at his feet, "spreadeagled" as it was called here, bound by her wrists and ankles to table legs and an ottoman. She was naked except for dots of caviar on her nipples. Well, she had been very eager for wine and caviar a couple of hours ago. No use complaining now.

"I forget," she sighed.

Khezir had gone into the bedroom just beyond the living room, but had left the double doors open so that the two rooms merged into one. He lounged on the great canopied bed beside the younger woman who was the daughter of the first. This woman was even more sexy than her mother; beautifully fleshy, soft to the touch, with long blond hair.

Khezir ran his hand up her thigh, amazed at the way she quivered even though she could no longer speak.

He said to the young woman, "And I will call you . . . Mangoes. Yes. Do you like that name? So much better than what your pigs of parents called you. Adri-anne." He said it again with a high, affected voice. "Aaay-dreee-annnne. Sounds like the cry of a baby goat."

Khezir had cleansed many towns of people who reminded him of animals. Where he came from, life was short and cheap.

The girl moaned, "Pleease."

Khezir laughed. "You want more, please. Is that it, Mangoes?"

In the living room, the CD changer slipped a new recording into the player. The music was produced by a wind instrument called the kime. It sounded like an icy gale blowing through the clefts in a rock. The vocalist sang of an ocean he had never seen.

Gozan said, "Peaches, I would prefer that you like me, but as your Clark Gable said to that hysterical bitch in *Gone with the Wind*, 'Frankly, I don't give a shit.'"

He leaned over her, slapped her face, pinched her between her legs. Peaches yelped and tried to get away.

"It's very good, isn't it? Tell me how much you like it," said Gozan.

There was a loud pounding at the door.

"*Get lost!*" Gozan shouted. "You'll have to come back for the cart."

A man's voice boomed, "LAPD. Open the door. Now."

SPRINKLERS SHOT BROKEN jets of water over the lush gardens at the back of the Beverly Hills Hotel. Night was coming on. I was armed, waiting behind a clump of shrubbery a hundred feet from Bungalow Six when footsteps came up the path. Captain Luke Warren of the LAPD with a gang of six cops right behind him came toward me.

For once, I was glad to see the LAPD.

I had information that Gozan Remari and Khezir Mazul, two heinous cruds who were suspected of multiple rapes, but hadn't been charged, were behind door number six. But unless there was evidence of a crime in progress, I had no authority to break in.

I called out to the captain, presented my badge, handed him my card that read, *Jack Morgan, CEO, Private Investigations*.

Warren looked up at me, said, "I know who you are, Morgan. Friend of the Chief. The go-to guy for the one percent."

"I get around," I said.

Cops don't like private investigators. PIs don't play by the same rules as city employees and our clients, in particular, hire Private because of our top-gun expertise and our discretion.

Captain Warren was saying, "Okay, since you called this in. What's the story?"

"A friend of mine in the hotel business called me to say that these two were bounced out of the Constellation for assaulting a chambermaid. They checked in here two hours ago. I've got a couple of spider cams on the windows, but the drapes are closed. I've made out two male voices and one female over the music and the TV, but no calls for help."

"And your interest in this?"

I said, "I'm a concerned citizen."

Warren said, "Okay. Thanks for the tip. Now, I've got to ask you to step back and let us do our job."

I told him, of course, no problem.

And it *was* no problem.

I wasn't on assignment and I didn't want the credit. I was just glad to be there for the takedown.

Captain Warren sent two men around the bungalow to cover the back and garden exits, then he and I went up the steps and across the veranda to the front door with two detectives from the Beverly Hills PD. Warren knocked and announced.

We heard a shout through the front door, sounded like "Go away."

I said, "He said, 'Come in,' right?"

The captain smiled to show me that he liked my way of thinking. Then he swiped the lock with a card key, cocked his leg and kicked in the door.

It blew open, and we all got a good view of what utter depravity looks like.

THE LIVING ROOM was done up in silk and satin in the colors of peaches and cream. Logs flickered in the marble fireplace and atonal music oozed from the CD player. Empty glasses, liquor bottles and many articles of clothing littered the floor. A room-service cart had been tipped over, spilling food and broken china across the Persian carpet.

I served for five years as a pilot in the US Marine Corp. I've been trained to spot a glint of metal or a puff of smoke on the ground from ten thousand feet up. To be able to do that in the dark.

But I didn't need pilot's training to recognize the filth right in front of me.

The man called Gozan Remari sat in an armchair with the hauteur of a prince. He looked to be about fifty, gray-haired with gold-colored, cat-like eyes. Remari wore an expensive handmade jacket, an open pinstriped shirt, a heavy gold watch and nothing else—not even surprise or anger that cops were coming through the door.

A nude woman lay at his feet, bound with silk ties. Her arms and legs were spread and she was anchored hand and foot to a chair, a footstool, a table, as if she were a luna moth pinned to a board. I saw bluish handprints on her skin and food had been smeared on her body.

There was an arched entrance to my right that led to a bedroom. And there, in plain sight, was Khezir Mazul. He was naked, sitting up in bed, smoking a cigar. A young woman, also naked, was stretched face-up across his lap, her head thrown over the side of the bed. A thin line of blood arced across her throat and I saw a steak knife on the cream-colored satin blanket.

From where I stood in the doorway, I couldn't tell if the women were unconscious or dead.

Captain Warren yanked Gozan Remari to his feet and cuffed him behind his back. He said, "You're under arrest for assault. You have the right to remain silent, you piece of crap."

The younger dirtbag stood up, let the woman on his lap roll away from him, off the bed and onto the floor. Khezir Mazul was powerfully built, tattooed on most of his body with symbols I didn't recognize.

He entered the living room and said to Captain Warren in the most bored tones imaginable, "We've done nothing. Do you know the word 'con-shen-sul'? This is not any kind of assault. These women came here willingly with us. Ask them. They came here to party. As you say here, 'We aim to please.'"

Then, he laughed. *Laughed*.

I stepped over the room-service cart and went directly to the woman lying near me on the floor. Her breathing was shallow and her skin was cool. She was going into shock.

My hands shook as I untied her wrists and ankles.

I said, "Everything is going to be okay. What's your name? Can you tell me your name?"

Cops came through the back door, and one of them called for medical backup. Next, hotel management and two guests came in the front. Bungalow Six was becoming a circus.

I ripped a cashmere throw from the sofa and covered the woman's body. I helped her into a chair, put my jacket around her shoulders.

She opened her eyes and tears spilled down her cheeks. "My daughter," the woman said to me. "Where is she? Is she—?"

I heard the cop behind me say into the phone, "Two females; one in her forties, the other is late teens, maybe early twenties. She's bleeding from a knife wound to her neck. Both of them are breathing."

I said to the woman whose name I didn't know, "Your daughter is just over there, in the bedroom. She's going to be all right. Help is coming."

Clasping the blanket to her body, the woman turned to see her daughter being helped to her feet.

A siren wailed. The woman reached up and pressed her damp cheek to mine. She hugged me tight with her free arm.

"It's my fault. I screwed up," she said. "Thank you for helping us."

I DRAFTED BEHIND the ambulance as it sped the two assault victims through traffic on Santa Monica Boulevard toward Ocean Memorial Hospital. When the bus turned inland, I headed north until I reached Pacific Coast Highway, the stretch of road that follows the curve of the coastline and links Malibu to Santa Monica.

My Lamborghini can go from zero to ninety in ten seconds, but this car draws cops out of nowhere, even when it's quietly humming at a red light. So, I kept to the speed limit and within twenty minutes I was in sight of home.

My house is white stucco and glass, shielded from the road by a high wall that is overgrown with vines and inset with a tall wrought-iron gate.

I stopped the car, palmed the new biometric recognition plate and the gate slid open. I pulled the Lambo into my short, tight parking spot and braked next to the blue Jag.

As the gates rolled closed behind me, I got out, locked up

the car, checked for anything that didn't belong behind the wall and within the landscaping. Then, I went up the walk to the door.

I'd bought this place with Justine Smith about five years ago. Later, after we'd broken up for the third, impossibly painful time, I bought out Justine's share of the house. It was comfortable, convenient to my office, just right—until a year ago last May.

On that night, I came back home from a business trip abroad to find another former girlfriend, Colleen Molloy, dead in my bed, her skin still warm. She'd been shot multiple times at close range and the killer was a pro. The way he'd fixed it, all of the evidence pointed to me as the shooter.

I was charged with Colleen's murder, jailed, and after some extraordinary work by Private investigators, I was free—if you could call it that. I still opened my door every night to an expectation that something horrible had happened here while I was out.

I put my eye up to the iris-reader beside the front door, and when the lock clacked open, I went inside.

A woman's blue jacket and a sleek leather handbag were on a chair, and her fragrance scented the air as I walked through the main room. I followed the light coming through the house, crossed the tile floors in my gumshoes, then peered through the glass doors that opened out to the pool.

She was doing laps and didn't see me. That was fine.

The door glided open under my hand and I went out again into the warm night. I took a chaise and as the ocean roared at the beach below, I watched her swim.

Her lovely shape was up-lit by the pool lights. Her strong arms stroked confidently through the water and her flip turns had both grace and power.

I knew this woman so well.

I trusted her with everything. I cared about her safety and her happiness. I truly loved her.

But, I was unable to see my future with her—or anyone. And that was a problem for Justine. It was why we didn't live together. And why we'd made no long-term plans. But we had decided a couple of months ago that we were happy seeing each other casually. And, at least for now, it was working.

She reached the end of the pool and pulled herself up to the coping. Her skin glistened as light and shadow played over her taut body. She sat with her legs in the pool, leaned forward and wrung out her long, dark-brown hair.

"Hey," I said.

She started, said, "Jack."

Then, she grabbed a towel and wrapped herself in it, came over to the chaise and sat down beside me. She smiled.

"How long have you been sitting here?"

I put my hand behind her neck and brought her mouth to mine. I kissed her. Kissed her again. Released her and said, "I just got here. I've had a night you won't believe."

"I want to take a shower," Justine said. "Then tell me all about it."

THE HOT SPRAY beat down on me from six showerheads. Justine lightly placed her palms on my chest, tipped her hips against mine.

She said, "Someone needs a massage. I think that could be you."

"Okay."

Okay to whatever she wanted to do. It wasn't just my car that could go from zero to ninety in ten seconds. Justine had the same effect on me.

As she rubbed shower gel between her hands, sending up the scent of pine and ginseng, she looked me up and down. "I don't know whether to go from top to bottom or the other way around," she said.

"Dealer's choice," I said.

She was laughing, enjoying her power over me, when my cell phone rang. My fault for bringing it into the bathroom, but I was expecting a call from the head of our Budapest office who said he'd try to call me between flights.

Justine said, "Here's a joke. Don't take the call."

I looked through the shower doors to where my phone sat at the edge of the sink. The caller ID read *Capt. L. Warren.* It could only be about the rapists the cops had just arrested at the Beverly Hills Hotel.

"The joke's on me," I said to Justine. "But, I'll make it quick."

I caught the call on the third ring.

"Morgan. We've got problems with those pukes from Sumar," the captain said. "They have diplomatic immunity."

"You've *got* to be kidding."

He gave me the bad news in detail, that Gozan Remari and Khezir Mazul were both senior diplomats in Sumar's mission to the UN.

"They're on holiday in Hollywood," Warren told me. "I think we could ruin their good time, maybe get them recalled to the wasteland they came from, but the ladies won't cooperate. I'm at the hospital with them, now. They wouldn't let the docs test for sexual assault."

"That's not good," I said. I put up a finger up to let Justine know I would just be a minute.

"Mrs. Grove is very grateful to you, Morgan," the Captain was telling me. "I, uh, need a favor. I need you to talk to her."

"Sure. Put her on," I said.

Justine turned off the water. Pulled a towel off the rack.

"She's in a room with her daughter," Warren said. "Listen, if you step on the gas you could be here in fifteen minutes. Talk to them face-to-face."

I told Justine not to wait up for me.

By way of an answer, she screwed in her ear buds and took her iPod to the kitchen. She was intensely chopping onions when I left the house.

It was a twenty-minute drive to Ocean Memorial and it took

me another ten to find the captain. He escorted me to a beige room furnished with two beds and a recliner.

Belinda Grove was sitting in the recliner, wearing the expensive clothes I'd last seen strewn around Bungalow Six—a black knit dress, fitted jacket, black stiletto Jimmy Choos. She'd also brushed her hair and applied red lipstick. And although I'd never met her before today, now that she'd cleaned up, I recognized her from photos in the society pages.

This was Mrs. Alvin Grove, on the board of the Children's Museum, daughter of Palmer Tiptree of Tiptree Pharmaceuticals, and mother of two.

Now I understood. She would rather die than let anyone know what had happened to her daughter and herself.

MRS. GROVE STOOD when I came into the room, took my hands in hers, said, "Mr. Morgan, I want to thank you, again."

"My name is Jack. Of course, you're welcome, Mrs. Grove. How are you doing?"

"Call me Belinda. I'm ashamed that I was so easily tricked," she said. "We were having lunch in the Polo Lounge, my daughter and I, and we were talking about the Children's Museum. Those monsters were at the next table and overheard us. Gozan said he had many children and would be interested in making a donation to the museum.

"Jack. They were well dressed. Well heeled. They said they were diplomats. They were staying at the hotel. Gozan said he wanted to talk about making a sizable donation to the museum, but wanted to discuss it privately.

"I ignored any warning signs. We went to the bungalow. I said that we couldn't stay long, but a short chat would be all right. We are always looking for benefactors, Jack. They used Rohypnol or something damned close to it. It was in the champagne."

"Don't blame yourself. These are dangerous men."

"I hope never to see either one of them again, unless they're hanging by their balls over a bonfire. I don't think that Adrianna will be physically scarred, but emotionally . . . Emotionally, my daughter is in terrible shape."

"Terrible shape" was an understatement. Adrianna had been drugged, probably raped, maybe by both men, and Khezir Mazul had stroked her throat with a serrated blade. She would have a scar across her neck for as long as she lived.

I hated to think what would have happened to these women had I not been tipped off, if we hadn't shown up when we did.

I started to reason with Mrs. Grove, explain to her that if she made a complaint, Remari and Mazul might be deported.

She shook her head, warning me off.

"My daughter is a senior at Stanford. It would be tragic if she had to leave school. What happened today is something Adrianna and I will both learn from and at the same time try to forget. That's how one deals with horror, don't you think?"

I said, "I'd suggest some counseling . . ."

She ignored me and went on. "My responsibility now is only to Adrianna, and I'm going to make sure that she has whatever she needs in order to heal."

She stood up. "You take care, Jack. God bless. I mean that."

Belinda Grove left the beige room with her head down, passing Captain Warren who was on his way back in.

Luke Warren and I talked together for several minutes. There were no angles to work, no strings to pull. But, there are a few cases every year that I want to work *pro bono*, and I thought this might become one of them.

I told the captain to call me anytime, that I would work with him, free of charge. Happy to do it.

I thought if we caught them, I could convince Mazul and Remari to leave the country for good.

STAND-ALONE THRILLERS

Sail (*with Howard Roughan*) • Swimsuit (*with Maxine Paetro*) • Don't Blink (*with Howard Roughan*) • Postcard Killers (*with Liza Marklund*) • Toys (*with Neil McMahon*) • Now You See Her (*with Michael Ledwidge*) • Kill Me If You Can (*with Marshall Karp*) • Guilty Wives (*with David Ellis*) • Zoo (*with Michael Ledwidge*) • Second Honeymoon (*with Howard Roughan*) • Mistress (*with David Ellis*) • Invisible (*with David Ellis*)

NON-FICTION

Torn Apart (*with Hal and Cory Friedman*) • The Murder of King Tut (*with Martin Dugard*)

ROMANCE

Sundays at Tiffany's (*with Gabrielle Charbonnet*) • The Christmas Wedding (*with Richard DiLallo*) • First Love (*with Emily Raymond*)

FAMILY OF PAGE-TURNERS

MIDDLE SCHOOL BOOKS

Middle School: The Worst Years of My Life (*with Chris Tebbetts*) • Middle School: Get Me Out of Here! (*with Chris Tebbetts*) • Middle School: My Brother Is a Big, Fat Liar (*with Lisa Papademetriou*) • Middle School: How I Survived Bullies, Broccoli, and Snake Hill (*with Chris Tebbetts*) • Middle School: Ultimate Showdown (*with Julia Bergen*) • Middle School: Save Rafe! (*with Chris Tebbetts, to be published October 2014*)

I FUNNY SERIES

I Funny (*with Chris Grabenstein*) • I Even Funnier (*with Chris Grabenstein*)

TREASURE HUNTERS SERIES

Treasure Hunters (*with Chris Grabenstein*) •
Treasure Hunters: Danger Down the Nile (*with Chris Grabenstein, to be published September 2014*)

HOMEROOM DIARIES

Homeroom Diaries (*with Lisa Papademetriou*)

MAXIMUM RIDE SERIES

The Angel Experiment • School's Out Forever •
Saving the World and Other Extreme Sports • The Final Warning •
Max • Fang • Angel • Nevermore

CONFESSIONS SERIES

Confessions of a Murder Suspect (*with Maxine Paetro*) • Confessions: The Private School Murders (*with Maxine Paetro*) • Confessions: The Paris Mysteries (*with Maxine Paetro, to be published October 2014*)

WITCH & WIZARD SERIES

Witch & Wizard (*with Gabrielle Charbonnet*) • The Gift (*with Ned Rust*) • The Fire (*with Jill Dembowski*) • The Kiss (*with Jill Dembowski*) • The Lost (*with Emily Raymond, to be published November 2014*)

DANIEL X SERIES

The Dangerous Days of Daniel X (*with Michael Ledwidge*) •
Watch the Skies (*with Ned Rust*) • Demons and Druids (*with Adam Sadler*) • Game Over (*with Ned Rust*) • Armageddon (*with Chris Grabenstein*)

GRAPHIC NOVELS

Daniel X: Alien Hunter (*with Leopoldo Gout*) • Maximum Ride: Manga Vols. 1–7 (*with NaRae Lee*)

For more information about James Patterson's novels, visit
www.jamespatterson.co.uk

Or become a fan on Facebook